WHAT'S A GHOUL TO DO?

A GHOST HUNTER MYSTERY

What's a
Ghoul to Do?

Victoria Laurie

THORNDIKE
C H I V E R S

LIBRARY OF CONGRESS CATALOGING-IN-PUBLICATION DATA

Laurie, Victoria.
    What's a ghoul to do? : a ghost hunter mystery / by Victoria Laurie.
      p. cm. — (Thorndike press large print mystery)
    ISBN-13: 978-0-7862-9639-2 (hardcover : alk. paper)
    ISBN-10: 0-7862-9639-9 (hardcover : alk. paper)
    1. Large type books. I. Title. II. Title: What is a ghoul to do.
  PS3612.A94423W48 2007
  813'.6—dc22
                                                     2007012429

BRITISH LIBRARY CATALOGUING-IN-PUBLICATION DATA AVAILABLE

Published in 2007 in the U.S. by arrangement with NAL Signet,
a member of Penguin Group (USA) Inc.

Published in 2007 in the U.K. by arrangement with NAL Signet,
a division of Penguin Group (USA) Inc.

U.K. Hardcover: 978 1 405 64174 6 (Chivers Large Print)
U.K. Softcover: 978 1 405 64175 3 (Camden Large Print)

Printed in the United States of America on permanent paper
10 9 8 7 6 5 4 3 2 1

This book is lovingly dedicated to two
women of profound beauty and
intellect:

Adell Chase, my southern bell of truth
and the wisest woman on earth;
and
Karen Ditmars, a bella in her own right
and the coolest woman on the planet.

ACKNOWLEDGMENTS

Here's a news flash — writers are selfish people. Truth is, creative types like me are driven by one impulse — to make up a world in which we get to control everything and everyone. We decide who enters and who exits, what the weather will be, who will hook up with whom, who will win and who will lose. It makes us feel powerful and, in all honesty, has relatively little to do with thinking about what will make anyone else happy.

Which is why, at the end of pounding out three-hundred-plus pages, we are often surprised by how many of our friends, colleagues, fans, and family have generously helped us perfect our creations. And I suppose that's what tempers us a bit, to know that while we may love to play God, we still need some angels to help us get it right. It's these angels that I'd like to humbly thank right now:

First and foremost, my incredible editor, Molly Boyle, who takes my overly wordy, addicted-to-adjectives manuscripts and turns them into what I *meant* to write. Molly, you're so good at what you do that you have not just impressed me — you've blown me away. I'm unbelievably grateful for all your patience (didn't know you'd need so much of that with me, did you?), your hard work, and your fantastic instincts. You and I shall make one helluva team, girlfriend — thank you, thank you, thank you!

Next, my astounding and amazing agent, Jim McCarthy. What can I say that I haven't said before? (No, seriously, help me out here, cuz every time I mention you, I gush and gush and I'm runnin' out of gushy things to say!) LOL . . . Truly, Jim, I think you must be some sort of cosmic gift from the Big Guy upstairs who either took great pity on me or got me mixed up with some other far more deserving schmuck when he sent you my way. And just to be clear . . . if there was a screwup? I'm *not* giving you back . . . ever! So plan on stickin' around, sugar; we gots a looooong way to go just yet.

Adell Chase and Karen Ditmars, to whom this book is dedicated: Ladies, I've been so lucky in my life. Everywhere I go, I meet the best of humanity, and a few of them, like you, I am blessed to call friends. You two leave me breathless with your wisdom, your courage, and your will to be strong, independent, smart, and capable women. When I grow up, I swear I want to be just like you two!

My sister Sandy Upham and my brother and sister-in-law Jon and Naoko Upham — you guys have no idea how much I love you and how very much your support means to me. I'm so proud of you three fantastic human beings that I'm lucky enough to be related to. Huge hugs and kisses comin' your way!

Also, a relative newcomer to my troupe of favorite people on earth, Michael Torres, aka The Boy. Thank you so much for the incredible way you inspire me, cheer me on, and never have an unkind word. You're such a beautiful man, M.T., both inside and out, and I'm beyond thrilled that you've come into my life. That morning phone call to cheer me on when I'm in my writing slump is such a gift; please know that I appreciate and adore you for that and so much more.

Dr. Stephen Pap, who gave me the inspiration for Dr. Delicious, thank you first and foremost for fixing my hand — which is all healed now, thank God — and also for being so generous with your boyhood stories and background. I told you that you'd make a great character — I wasn't wrong.

And last but certainly not least, please let me thank all my incredible friends who have never wavered in their support, love, and encouragement: Kristy Schiller, Nora Brosseau, Silas Hudson, Laurie Comnes, Pipa Terry, Betty Stocking, Jaa Nawtaisong, and Leanne Tierney. You guys rock, and I'm so grateful. ☺

CHAPTER 1

"Good morning, Miss Holliday," the real estate agent cheerfully greeted me outside 84 Dartmouth Street.

"Hi, there. You must be Cassandra," I said, shaking her hand. "Please call me M.J."

"You're younger and prettier than I thought you'd be," she commented as she nervously twisted the pearls at her neck.

"Thank you," I said, then quickly got down to business. "I know we talked a little on the phone, but what can you tell me about this house?"

Cassandra paled slightly and looked up at the three-story brownstone, a turn-of-the-century gem that was right at home in Boston's opulent Back Bay neighborhood. "I've had the listing for almost a year, which, as you can imagine, is unheard-of here in the Back Bay. Brownstones like this one sell around here in a matter of weeks, not months."

"Sticker shock?" I asked.

"No, nothing like that. At one million it's an absolute steal! And we've had a lot of interest in it, despite its history. But every time we get close to making a deal, the buyer backs out. They all say the same thing: The place just has bad energy."

"You said someone was killed inside?"

Cassandra nodded. "Yes, the daughter of the current owners was raped and murdered a little over a year ago."

"That's awful," I said, looking back toward the brownstone. "Did they catch the killer?"

"He was shot by police as he tried to make a getaway out the back. Unfortunately, they arrived too late to save the girl."

"So, really, two people died in the house."

"Yes, I suppose so," she said.

"And what's been happening since then?"

"Well," she said, her hand going back to twist the pearls, "every time I show the house I get the feeling I'm being watched. And more than that, sometimes I feel like I'm being followed. People come in and don't seem to want to stay. Most folks just take a tour of one or two rooms; then they leave like they're being chased out."

"I see," I said, but I had a feeling there was more. "Is that all?"

"No," she said after a moment. "The other

day I was showing the house to this couple who really seemed to be okay with the history of the place. They considered it a good trade-off for such a bargain. But just as we were getting ready to leave, we all heard a woman's scream from one of the bedrooms upstairs. I thought someone had come in while I was showing the couple around, so I ran up there and looked all over but no one was there. Then, just as I was coming back downstairs, I felt . . ." She paused.

"What?"

"I felt someone *touch* me."

"Like a hand on your shoulder or something?"

"No," she whispered, her eyes large and frightened. "Like someone touched me *inappropriately.*"

"Ah," I said with a nod. Now I knew who the aggressor was. "Okay, if you'll unlock the door I'll get to work."

"Can you really help us, M.J.?"

"That's what I do, Cassandra," I said. "I'm a ghostbuster. Give me a few hours and let me see what I can do."

Cassandra followed me up the six steps to the front door and unlocked it for me. "You'll be all right in there by yourself?" she asked, her face suddenly worried.

"I'll be fine," I said confidently. I'd faced

scarier stuff than this before. Pausing as the door swung shut behind me, I moved into the foyer and looked around, setting my duffel bag down in the corner by the staircase. I wanted to get the lay of things before reaching into my bag of tricks.

I let my eyes travel around the room, getting a feel for the brownstone's configuration. The front foyer had several doorways leading to the rest of the house. To my right a corridor led to the kitchen. The living room was directly in front of me, and off to my left was what looked like a study. From my back pocket I pulled out my electrostatic meter, a small gadget that measures variances in electrostatic energy. I held my arm out and waved it in a circle around the foyer, noting the thick, luxurious carpet, high ceilings, crown molding, and expensive wall covering. The digs were definitely opulent, and even without furniture you could tell this place oozed money. And, according to my electrostatic meter, the place oozed something else, too.

With an eye on the needle bouncing back and forth across the gauge, I moved ahead through the foyer and into the living room. The needle gave a jolt as I edged over to the French doors that swung out onto the terrace. The needle bounced again. I put the little gadget in the back pocket of my jeans and closed my eyes for a moment and got myself centered.

Before I was a ghostbuster, I was a professional medium, which has proven to be the most beneficial skill for my success rate as a top-notch buster. In other words, I can sense energies that both have crossed over to the other side successfully, and those that have become stuck, or "grounded," as we like to call it. In 84 Dartmouth I had immediately picked up the energies of two grounded spirits, one female and one male. I decided to focus on the female first.

Moving away from the French doors, I followed the small tug in my solar plexus, heading through the hallway and up the stairs. As I closed in on the female energy, something slightly disturbing happened. I felt the male energy, which was thick with ill will, begin to follow me. "Back off a little, pal," I said quietly to him. "I'll deal with you in a moment."

The male energy didn't want to listen, but continued to shadow me up to the second floor, where I paused on the landing before continuing up to the third floor. There, at the end of the hallway, I saw a dark shadow dart into one of the bedrooms. "It's okay," I said to the shadow. "I'm not going to hurt you." I walked down the hall and into the bedroom, and noticed an immediate dip in temperature. I crossed my arms and shivered slightly, feeling the icy coolness penetrate my clothing and my skin, seeping into my bones. I'd never gotten used to the deep chill that comes with rubbing up against spectral activity, but I pushed my discomfort aside and focused hard on the task at hand. "What's your name, sweetheart?" I asked the empty bedroom softly.

There was no response, but I could feel the fear emanating from the woman's spirit. I sensed her in the corner of the room, and sure enough, my mind's eye flashed an image of a young woman in her early twenties, crouched and cowering by the window. I moved over to that area and felt the temperature dip even lower. I knelt down and closed my eyes to concentrate. I said aloud, "I'm here to help you. He can't hurt you anymore, honey. And I'll make sure he doesn't get away with what he's done. Please talk to me. Tell me your name."

With relief I felt the name Carolyn float into my mind. I smiled sadly. The poor thing — not only had she been raped and killed by the beast behind me, but now she was stuck in a confusing state of limbo. *Where are my parents?* she asked me desperately.

"They're safe, but they're very worried about you, Carolyn. They've asked me to help you. Will you allow me to?"

I opened my eyes and stared at the blank space in front of me. I couldn't see Carolyn, but I could definitely feel and hear her. She didn't answer me right away, so I continued to try to win her over. "I promise to keep you safe, but you've got to trust me. I will guide you home, but I can't do that if you're unwilling. Will you trust me?"

He promised!

"He promised what, honey?" I knew she was talking about her attacker.

He promised not to hurt me if I cooperated!

I sighed heavily. The rat bastard. I was going to enjoy dealing with him. "I know, my friend, I know," I said gravely. "He lied. But that's in the past. He cannot hurt you again. I absolutely forbid it."

Where are my parents? This plea was even more urgent in my head than the first time she'd asked me. Carolyn was coming close to panicking, and if she did I'd lose contact with her. She would no doubt seek the comfort of the limbo plane that hovered just beyond the one we existed on. This was where lost spirits typically hung out, coming into our reality only when they were strong enough to deal with what had happened to them.

"Carolyn, you must listen to me," I said sternly, hoping the command would snap her out of her desire to run. "You have to stay with me. I can get you out of here, but only if you do exactly as I say. I will guide you to safety, but we need to be quick —"

He's here! she interrupted me. *Hide! We've got to hide!*

"Damn it," I muttered as I turned around. Sure enough, an ominous dark shadow hung in the doorway, floating back and forth in the opening. If I didn't do something quickly, I'd lose Carolyn. "Stay right here, Carolyn," I said as I stood up. "I'm going to get rid of him if you hide right here until I return. I promise I'll help you find your way. Will you wait for me?"

A feeling that I can only describe as a nod touched my mind. "Good girl," I said, walking toward the black shape. As I got close I could see my breath as I exhaled, and my teeth wanted to chatter. I resisted the urge to shiver and walked purposefully at the black shape.

I stopped when the shadow disappeared in front of me. To my right came a loud thumping noise. I snapped my head to where the noise had come from, but only the wall stared back at me. "So that's how we're going to play it, huh?" I whispered, then gathered my anger and shouted, "Listen, you miserable slug of human compost! You coward! You evil, vile excuse for a man! I think you're afraid of me, and I'll bet you dollars to doughnuts that you won't follow me if I leave this room, because you don't have the guts!" With that I dashed out of the room, and immediately felt the dark male energy give chase.

I tore down the hallway and grabbed the banister, turning the corner to jump down several stairs in one leap. The dark energy behind me seemed to thrum with excitement as my adrenaline surged. I could feel him trying to gather his strength. In a moment he would try something dirty, and I made sure to keep one hand on the railing for balance. It was a good thing I did, because in the next moment I felt a hard thud in the center of my back, and a microsecond later a strong tug on my right breast. "You son of a bitch!" I swore at him as I shook it off and continued down the stairs. "I'll get you for that!" I said as I reached the first floor and dashed to my duffel bag. I scanned the living room, looking for what I knew had to be there, and feeling the slow, prickly sensation of something snaking around my neck.

I scowled and moved forward into the living room, searching the walls intently. "Eureka," I said after a moment. "Gotcha, you rat bastard!" I moved closer to study the small black hole that I'd spotted in the atmosphere just above the wall. The hole was nothing more than a small one-foot-by-one-foot section of air right next to the wall that to the naked eye looked vaporous and was tinted a light gray. I could sense the energy behind me shift from hungry to nervous. "You didn't think I knew about this little doorway of yours, did you?" I said over my shoulder as I set the duffel down and squatted to pull out my drill. "Let's see how much of a bully you are after we close up this bad boy, shall we?"

I dug out three spikes made of magnetized metal, and a hammer to help drive them home. The force behind me thudded into my back with all his might, and I pitched forward as my head hit the wall. "You ass!" I said, turning to face him. In front of me I saw the dark shadow again, and in my mind's eye conjured a face that was mean and full of rage.

Stop! he shouted at me.

I laughed and held my drill up to him. "Time to shut the portal," I said, and turned back to the wall. My drill was battery operated, which prevented the likes of him from screwing around too much with it, and allowed me to begin the drilling.

No! he screamed again, and to my right there was an incredibly loud bang!

I laughed at his futile efforts, and after I'd completed three holes I turned around. "Not so tough now, are you?"

The black shadow hovered in front of me, and I could sense that his attention was quite focused on the three spikes at my feet. "This is your little gateway, isn't it?" I said, pointing to the area where I'd drilled the holes. "Well, let me tell you something, pal. I'm not going to stand for it. You have ten seconds to make a choice. If you stay here I will help you cross over to the other side, where you'll have to face what you've done and be held accountable. Or you can head through here now, and be locked in down there until you're ready to face your own demons and go home on your own."

The energy in front of me wavered for a moment, and for a split second I thought I'd convinced him to let me help him. But I was sorely disappointed when the miserable scum grabbed my boob *again!* I growled low in my throat and whirled around, snatching the magnetic stakes and inserting the first into the hole. Behind me there was an audible male scream as I lifted my hand with the hammer, preparing to drive it home on the head of the spike. "Do-or-die time, buddy!" I yelled, and brought the hammer down. A split second before I made contact with the spike I felt the ghost behind me dash into the portal I was preparing to close. "Coward!" I roared at him as his energy dissipated into the wall.

I finished pounding in that stake, then moved on to the other two. After I'd finished I stood back a little, eyeing my handiwork. The wall was a mess, with plaster and bits of drywall on the floor, but at least the portal was gone, never to return — that is, as long as the stakes were in place.

I tucked the drill and hammer into my duffel, then quickly went back upstairs. To my immense relief I could sense that Carolyn was still hovering in the corner. "Hey, there, girl," I said gently as I eased into the room. "I'm sure you heard everything. He's gone, Carolyn. The man who hurt you is gone for good."

I'm afraid, I felt her say.

"I know you are, but trust me: I can help you with that. First, show me what happened."

I don't want to. . . .

"I know, I know. But sweetheart, I need to

see it. We both need to see it. Take me to the end of it, if the beginning and the middle were too painful. Take me to that time right before you found yourself confused and lost."

There was a pulling sensation to my right, and I looked over to the far corner of the room. I saw a struggle taking place. Carolyn was naked and bleeding from her nose. Her attacker was standing over her and had her gripped by the throat. She was clawing at him, her eyes wild with terror. My own insides tightened as I watched the scene unfold. This was the worst part of the job. Seeing what really happened to innocent people in those final terrifying moments was an awful thing to experience.

"That's good, Carolyn," I said, hating that I was putting her through this, but knowing it was absolutely necessary. "Now go a little bit further, honey. Go beyond that moment where you're fighting for your breath."

The scene changed, and I saw Carolyn's murderer drop her limp body on the floor. His head then snapped up as I heard the faint sound of a siren. In the next instant the killer dashed out of the room, leaving Carolyn lying where she was.

"Good, honey," I said when his image had left the room. "That's terrific. Now, I need you to focus on your body for a moment. Can you see that?"

I need to get up! she said. *I need to run away!*

"But you can't, can you?" I said. "You can't, Carolyn, because you're not breathing. See?" I said, pointing to the lifeless image of her. "Your body has died, my friend. It's time for you to accept that."

I had a sudden, almost overwhelming sensation of deep sadness in my chest, and I knew that Carolyn had finally registered that she was dead.

I said, "Carolyn, listen to me. Even though your body has stopped functioning, your soul needs to move forward. I can help you do that, but you'll need to do exactly as I say. Pay close attention to my words and follow my directions and I'll get you out of here, okay?"

With relief, I felt that mental nod come into my mind. "Good girl. Now, above you I want you to sense a great bright light coming down from the heavens, through the ceiling, and descending onto your head. Can you sense this, Carolyn?"

There was a pause, and then, *Yes.*

"Wonderful! You're doing great!" I praised. "Now, as this light envelops you, I want you to feel its warmth, its goodness, its purity, and its love. Can you feel all of those things, Carolyn?"

Another pause, then an excited, *Yes!*

"Awesome! Now, in front of you there should be a path. It may look a bit like a tunnel; sometimes it's different depending on the person. Can you see this path?"

I can.

"Great. I need you to be very brave and take a step onto it. It leads to more of the light, more of that love that you're sensing right now. It's a good path to follow, and while you're on it you will never be hurt again."

I held my breath, waiting for Carolyn to make that next oh, so critical move. If she blanched, I'd have to come back and try to coax her over another time. If she went for it, she'd find her way to the other side without worry. Finally I sensed something like acceptance from her, and right before I felt her move forward, I clearly heard her say, *Tell my parents I love them. Tell them I'll look after Midnight and I'll be all right now.*

I smiled brightly. "I promise I'll get the message to them, girl. You take care — okay?" But she was already gone. In the next instant I became aware of the silence. I opened my eyes and looked around. The room was empty; there was no energy in it besides myself. As I sent out my intuitive feelers, the room felt warm and clean and happy. I smiled and stood up, and, glancing at my watch, I realized I needed to get a move on. My next client was meeting me at my office in about a half hour.

I made my way back down the stairs, retrieved my duffel, and headed out the door. Cassandra's car was parked in front of the brownstone. I met her at the bottom of the steps and she said, "Well? How'd it go?"

"Ghost is clear!" I sang. I loved that line.

"You got rid of it?" she asked me, peering anxiously up the stairs.

"Yep. And there are a few things I need to tell you before I take off."

"Go ahead," she said as she fished around in her purse and pulled out her checkbook.

"Carolyn has a message that needs to be delivered to her parents. She says that she'll look after Midnight, and that she's going to be all right now."

Cassandra gasped. "Oh, my," she said.

"That message makes sense to you?"

"Well, yes. Midnight was the Kettlemans' cat. I know that because I have a few cats of my own, and Mrs. Kettleman was very fond of her pet. Last week when I called to tell her that we had an offer on the house, she

26

sounded so sad. When I asked her why she said that they had to put Midnight to sleep that morning; the poor thing had kidney failure."

"Good, then the Kettlemans will know that the message truly came from their daughter."

Cassandra scribbled in her checkbook while I went on with my directions. "Also, there are three spikes pounded into the living room wall —

"There are three *what* driven into *where?*" Cassandra squealed. *Oops.* I may have forgotten to disclose that sometimes I needed to make a few handy adjustments to the architecture.

"It was completely necessary, Cassandra. It was either pound in a few stakes or have this house hang on the market for another few years."

"But why?" she asked me.

I inhaled and tried to explain. "The man who murdered Carolyn was as nasty in death as he was in life. Energies like him often create a portal or doorway to a lower plane of existence where they can become stronger and more deviant. The only way to combat them is to shut their access back to this plane, and that means closing the portal."

"Okay," said Cassandra. "I think I'm following you."

"The way to close them is by using magnets that create a barrier, because they screw up the electromagnetic energy of the portal. The stakes I used are highly magnetic, which should keep that nasty man from ever bothering anyone again."

"But how am I supposed to explain stakes driven into a wall to prospective buyers?" Cassandra asked me.

"You hire a handyman to come over and patch over the stakes. They're driven far enough into the wall that, with a little spackle and some paint, no one will ever know."

Cassandra looked relieved. "Well, I can handle that," she said with a chuckle. "Is there anything else?"

"Nope. That about does it. The house is clean and clear and shouldn't give you any more trouble, but just in case, here's my card," I said, extending it to her. "And if you know of anyone who can benefit from our services, I'd appreciate it if you'd pass it along."

"Of course," she said, taking my card and giving me a broad smile. "Thank you, M.J., I'll get a handyman over here right away."

I took my leave of Cassandra and jogged

to my car, checking my watch again. I was cutting it really close.

A few feet away from my auto, I hit the button on the key chain to release the locks. The car gave a toot of the horn, and from inside I heard a perfect mimic of the noise. "I'm comin', Doc," I said as I peered through the glass. My African Gray parrot sat perched on the steering wheel, bobbing his head in excitement as I reached for the handle. Sliding into the seat I asked, "What's up, Doc?"

"Doc's cuckoo for Coco Puffs!" he answered back, flipping his red tail and bobbing his head.

"You're cuckoo all right," I said, giving him a pat on the head as I started the engine.

At the age of twelve I'd received Doc as a Christmas present from my rather eccentric grandmother, Pearl. She'd given me the six-month-old bird only three months after I'd lost my mother to cancer. It'd been her very clever way of coaxing some life back into me, as I'd refused to speak a word since the death of my mother.

Grandma Pearl had offered me the noisy bird that day, and even now her words still rang in my ears. "Mary Jane," she said as I opened the cage and extracted the parrot, my eyes wide with wonder, "this is a unique type of parrot that bonds for life with only one person, so you must take special care to treat him with respect and friendship. He will learn to talk soon, so you'll need to work on his vocabulary, and make sure the words you teach him are acceptable for polite society, because once an African Gray learns a word, they never forget it."

She'd said that last bit with a wink, knowing full well that I was the sort of kid who would not limit my pet's vocabulary if I could get away with it.

I'd named my bird after an old relative of mine, the infamous Dr. John Henry Holliday, who had survived the gunfight at the OK Corral, and called Wyatt Earp his best friend. Doc Holliday was my great-great-granduncle, and I liked to think that I'd inherited all my rebellious genes from him.

That had been an important year for me, as not only had I lost my mother and gained Doc, I'd met Gilley Gillespie, my best friend and business partner. On the first day of school I'd been wandering around on the playground when I'd noticed a little boy was playing with two G.I. Joe figures. Something about the way he was making them interact fascinated me. I'd stared at him as he played with the dolls, and the moment he'd crashed them together and mimicked kissing noises I knew I had to meet him.

We'd been best friends within five minutes, and it had been Gilley who had convinced me to flee my high school graduation party and the Georgia backwater where we'd grown up for the bright lights of Boston, where he had a full scholarship to MIT and I'd had far fewer prospects.

We'd shared a tiny apartment on Cambridge Street, and while Gilley went to school majoring in computer science, I'd waitressed and worked odd jobs. Then one fateful night Gilley had come home and announced, "I got you a gig."

"What kind of gig?" I'd said.

"There's this girl in my HTML study group. Her father just died, and she can't concentrate. We have finals in three days, and I need her to help me through this exam. I told her you could make sure her dad was okay. She's coming over in an hour."

Ever since I was a very little girl I'd been able to communicate with people who were no longer living. In the beginning I'd called them spookers, as most of them were slightly spooky to a little tyke like me, but a few I recognized, like my grandfather and my aunt Carol. Gilley knew about my talent, and had never even batted an eye when I'd make general comments to him like, "I was sitting on the subway today and this woman's dead husband told me he'd suspected all along she was really a lesbian. Now he knows for sure."

And as irritated as I was at Gilley for setting me up like that, when the girl arrived I knew I had to help her. I connected her to her father, both her grandparents, and a friend who'd died in a car accident. As the very grateful girl got up to leave, she asked me how much I charged.

Now, I'm not dense, but for whatever reason it had never even occurred to me to charge money for this, so I think I charged her some paltry sum, like twenty dollars. And after her session I'd had six more phone calls, all from people excited to hear from their deceased relatives.

The rest was history — I'd had a booming practice going by the time Gilley graduated, and he'd graciously taken over managing my appointments while doing some computer hacking on the side. Our business changed forever after we'd gotten an unusual request from a woman who was afraid to stay in her own home. A former roommate had hanged himself there, and since then things had been weird.

It was my first bust, and the high I got from it made me quit the medium business and dive headfirst into ghostbusting, which I've been doing ever since.

My cell rang, shaking me out of my musings. "Holliday," I said as I moved Doc from the steering wheel to my shoulder.

"*Where* are you?" Gilley demanded.

"I'm on my way, Gil. Take a chill pill."

"M.J.," he began — Gilley's big on lectures. "You have an appointment in, like . . . twenty minutes!"

"And I'm a mere fifteen away, my friend. Besides, you should be proud of me. I've already collected on the Kettleman case."

"The one in the Back Bay?"

"Yep. And before you remind me that you were right, let me just congratulate you on your business acumen."

"Told you so," he said, sounding smug. It had been Gilley's idea to start advertising to the real estate community. He'd been actively soliciting brokers for a few weeks now.

"You just can't resist saying it, can you?" I answered with a chuckle.

"It's my nature; what can I say? So about this next case. I have the scoop on this Dr. Sable."

"Cyberspying again?"

"If the information exists, I might as well look at it. Anyhoo, this guy is worth big — and I do mean *big* — bucks. Dr. Steven Sable is the son of Andrew Jackson Sable. . . ."

"That tycoon who offed himself?" I asked, remembering the news article I'd read a few weeks ago.

"That's the one," Gilley sang. "And he has major connections. M.J., if we pull this one off, we could be sitting pretty. We could become a fad for rich people all over New England. You know, folks at cocktail parties could ask one another if their home has been busted or not. We could be the next big thing!"

I rolled my eyes and stifled the laugh that wanted to burble up from my throat. Gilley was always predicting our imminent success. "Sure, sure. So what else can you tell me about him?"

"Oh, nothing interesting . . ." Gilley said quickly. I knew he was hiding something.

"Gil," I said, my voice dropping an octave, " 'fess up. What'd he do?"

"Nothing horrible," Gilley said. "He's just had a little trouble with the IRS recently."

"Tax evasion?"

"Nothing proven yet. I mean, no indictments have come down . . . so far."

I groaned. "I don't want to take work from a criminal, Gil."

"M.J., he's innocent until proven guilty. Let's just hear him out, okay?"

"Fine," I said, sighing at the traffic. I was stuck behind a shiny black Aston Martin, a car that had the ability to go from zero to sixty in, like, three heartbeats, but the guy driving this one was plodding along doing ten under the posted speed limit. "Crap," I said into the cell phone.

"What's the matter?" Gilley asked.

"I'm stuck behind the Batmobile, and I can't move around this guy." I noticed with irritation that the driver had his head cocked to one side, talking on his cell phone. "Man, I hate people who talk on their phones and drive at the same time."

"Good point. Let me let you go," Gil said.

"Uh . . . right. See you in fifteen," I said, and hung up. Groaning, I waited for a hole in traffic that would allow me to scoot around the moron, but things just weren't going my way today. My eyes kept inching back and forth to the clock on the dash. "Come on, dude," I muttered. "Just move over a little so I can get around you."

After four more blocks, an opportunity came up for me to shoot past the Aston. As I stomped on the gas, I rolled down my window and yelled, "Get off the friggin' phone!"

The man in the car next to me glanced over, and his blank expression seemed to ask, *What?*

I gave him a quick snarl while Doc squawked, "Get off the friggin' phone! I'm cuckoo for Cocoa Puffs!"

We arrived with barely a minute to spare, and I wasted no time as I burst through the door. "You're going to give me a heart attack one of these days," said a man about my height, with thick brown wavy hair, a strong jaw, and a Roman nose, as he pointed to a clock and handed me a folder.

"I know, Gil, I know," I said, hurrying into my office. Just as I had put Doc on his perch I heard the front door of our suite open and Gilley announce jovially, "Good morning! You must be Dr. Sable. So nice to meet you."

Discreetly I shut my door and tossed my jacket on the coatrack in the corner, sat down behind my desk, and pulled open the file. A picture of a handsome man who looked to be in his mid- to late fifties stared back at me, and I scowled as I read the headline of the article: *Wealthy Family Heir Questioned for Tax Evasion.* "Great," I said with a heavy sigh.

Before I'd had a chance to read through the file, my door opened and in hustled Gilley with a look of absolute glee on his face. "Ohmigod! M.J., this guy is gorgeous!"

"The doctor?" I asked, taken aback, because Gilley's tastes never ventured north of his own age.

"Yes, he's beautiful, delicious . . . he's *Dr. Delicious!*"

"Dr. Delicious! Dr. Delicious!" Doc called from his perch.

"Great," I said, looking over at my parrot. "That's all I need."

"Anyway, he's filling out the paperwork, and I'll send him right in. Remember, be polite, M.J. We could use this job."

"Yeah, yeah . . ." I said, waving him away.

I skimmed the rest of the article and moved on to another one that documented Andrew Sable's death. The article was heavy on Andrew's background as a shipping tycoon and light on details of his demise. The official cause was listed as suicide, and no further investigation was planned. I switched my attention over to the other side of the folder, where Gilley had jotted his notes from the telephone call he'd received from Dr. Sable three days earlier.

Sable was interested in talking to the ghost

of Andrew, which he was convinced was currently haunting the family's hunting lodge in upstate Massachusetts. I finished scanning the notes as my door opened again and in stepped Gilley. With a huge smile and a grand sweep of his hand he announced, "M. J. Holliday, this is Dr. Steven Sable."

I stood up and came around my desk as a very tall, broad-shouldered man with black hair and ebony eyes moved through the doorway. He held little resemblance to the man in the article, as this was clearly someone much younger and more ethnic-looking. "Hello, Dr. Sable," I said, extending my hand to shake his. "I'm sorry, but I thought you were older," I said, shooting a look at Gilley.

Gilley glanced at the file on my desk and quickly explained. "This is Dr. Steven Sable, the Second."

"Ah," I said, nodding my head and gesturing for him to sit down.

Taking his seat, Dr. Sable said, "Thank you for seeing me, Miss Holliday." His deep baritone was laced with an accent I couldn't quite place.

Gilley excused himself, giving me a wink as he shut the door, and I resisted the urge to roll my eyes, since I could clearly see his feet in front of the crack at the bottom of the door. My partner thought nothing of eavesdropping.

"Please call me M.J., Dr. Sable," I offered.

"Then please call me Steven," he said easily, with a hint of a smile that further accentuated his good looks.

Uh-oh, I thought. *The last thing I need is a client this attractive. . . .* "So, tell me what brings you here?" I said, getting right to the point.

"I may need your assistance. My grandfather has passed away, and I would like to employ you to talk with him and find out the truth of what happened the day he died."

As I listened to Steven talk, I couldn't help but focus on the sound of his voice mixed with that unusual accent. It seemed to be a cross between Latin and European, and the sound was silky, as if he were melting a bite of chocolate on the back of his tongue. And there was also a measured cadence to his speech, as if he were thinking of the words in his native language first, then doing the translation before speaking. "I'm sorry for your loss. I had heard your grandfather's death was ruled a suicide."

"Incorrectly," Steven said, his features tensing.

"I see," I said, studying him. "And why do you suspect he didn't commit suicide?"

"His . . . how do you say it, this woman who cleans the residence?"

"His housekeeper?"

"Yes, that's it. She said my grandfather asked for oatmeal the morning he died."

Now I figure, given the stuff I do for a living, that I've seen and heard it all. But I'll have to admit when Steven made that statement it was really hard not to look surprised. "Come again?" I asked when he offered no further explanation.

"The night before his death my grandfather telephoned me and said that he'd been to his physician, who suggested his cholesterol level was elevator."

"Elevator?" I asked, working hard to hide my smirk. "I think you mean elevat*ed*."

Steven waved his hand. "Yes, yes. It was elevated. As I was saying, my grandfather didn't like to take pills, so he asked if I had any advice for him. I told him to begin with his diet, and try oatmeal instead of his usual bacon and eggs."

"Uh-huh . . ." I said, trying to connect the dots. "So because he took your advice and had oatmeal for breakfast you think he wasn't suicidal."

"Correct," Steven said, nodding gravely.

"My grandfather was not depressed. He enjoyed his life and was in excellent health. He wasn't in pain, and his mental state was very good. So you can see there was no reason for him to turn to suicide."

"How exactly did your grandfather die?" I asked. The article I'd read had been light on the grim details.

"It is my belief that he was forced off the roof of his hunting lodge."

"Long way down?" I asked, picturing a log cabin in the woods somewhere.

"Three floors."

"Ouch," I said, wincing. "Are you sure he didn't just fall out a window or something?"

"The windows on the third story are all . . . how do you say, pushed back?"

"Recessed," I offered.

"Yes, recessed above the roof of the second floor, which comes out over the west side of the lodge. My grandfather's slipper was found on the roof."

I nodded. "Which means he would have had to climb through the window and lower himself onto the roof, then walk several feet to the edge."

"Correct," Steven said.

"So who would gain from your grand-father's passing?"

"It would be easier to tell you who

wouldn't," Steven replied with a frown.

"And Gilley tells me that you've witnessed your grandfather's ghost walking the lodge's property?"

"Yes, last weekend. I inherited the lodge from my grandfather, and I decided to spend the weekend there. I arrived late at night and went straight to bed. In the middle of the night I heard my grandfather's voice. He called to me."

"Could have been a dream," I commented. I didn't really think it was a dream, but decided it might be wise to play devil's advocate and see just how serious this young doctor was.

"It was not a dream. I was awake. And then, when I went to the hallway where I heard his voice, he whispered my name in my ear, and I felt his touch on my back, but when I turned around he was not there."

"What'd you do?"

Steven smiled sheepishly. "I must admit, I gathered my things and quickly left. It frightened me a great deal."

I inhaled a breath and sat up straight. Leaning in over my desk to rest my elbows on the blotter, I said, "Okay, Steven. Gilley and I will give this a go. We'll need directions to the lodge and a key to get in. And I know Gilley has already talked to you about how difficult it can be to communicate with ghosts, so if I make contact there's no guarantee that your grandfather will tell us what happened to him."

"I understand," Steven said. "Which is why I am coming with you."

"Excuse me?" I asked, cocking my head.

"Did I say something incorrectly?" he asked me.

"No, you said that last bit fine; it's just that we don't allow clients to accompany us when we do our thing."

"Why not?"

I blinked at him a few times. The truth was, other than thinking they would get in the way, I hadn't really thought up a good reason why not. "Because, with all due respect, you'll likely get in the way. Gilley and I work alone."

Steven gave me a look that said he wasn't buying it. After a moment he said, "M.J., I am believing you that you and your partner can work my case alone, but I am still . . . how would you say . . . with concern over all this thing you do."

"You're skeptical about our abilities," I clarified.

"Yes, septical. I am a septic."

I pulled my lips into a grimace so that I wouldn't sputter a giggle at Steven's use —

or abuse — of the English language. "I see," I said after a moment, trying to think of a way to convince him there was no frickin' way I'd allow him along.

Steven continued, "So, if I employ you, it will be with the . . . eh, term?"

"Condition."

"Yes, condition that I will be involved in this . . . er . . . bust, as you say on your Web site."

I raised an eyebrow and replied firmly, "Sorry, Doc, Gilley and I work alone."

"Doc is cuckoo for Cocoa Puffs!" my parrot announced from his perch.

Steven turned in his chair to look at my parrot. "Funny bird," he said.

"He's not talking about you," I was quick to explain, mentally slapping myself for using Doc's name to address Steven.

"Dr. Delicious! Dr. Delicious!" Doc sang, fluttering his wings and sidestepping along his perch.

Steven chuckled. "Very vocal."

"Get off the friggin' phone!" Doc yelled, bobbing his head.

At that Steven looked sharply at me and asked, "What kind of car do you drive?"

"A Volvo," I answered tentatively.

"What color?"

"Silver, why?"

"This morning when I was coming to here, a woman in a silver car shouted at me to get off my cell phone, then . . . how do you say . . . she zigzag in front of me?"

I gulped. "Cut you off," I said.

"Yes, cut me off."

"Doc's cuckoo for Cocoa Puffs!"

I felt my face flush. "Ha, ha. Yeah, sorry about that," I said, mortified. "I was running a little late for this appointment and obviously I didn't realize it was you. . . ."

"I was on the phone with the hospital. One of my patients was in distress."

"Again, I'm really sorry about that," I said, kicking myself under my desk. "I get grouchy when I'm late for an appointment."

"Pop goes the weasel!" Doc chirped. I made a mental note to remember to move that perch out by Gilley's desk, really, *really* soon.

"If you are preventing me from coming along, Miss Holliday, then I see no need to talk any more," Steven said formally, his voice suddenly tight.

I stared at him unblinkingly for a few moments, irritated that he was trying to back me into a corner. Finally I extended my hand across the desk and said crisply, "It was a pleasure meeting you, Dr. Sable. Thank you for coming in, and good luck finding someone to help you with your case."

CHAPTER 2

After Sable left and I'd ducked out on Gilley and the tantrum he was about to throw at the loss of a major client, I decided the thing I needed was a good cup o' joe. This brought me to Starbucks, which was a mere block away, and from there I crossed the street to my favorite hangout — Mama Dell's.

Now, Mama Dell's is also a coffee shop, at least in theory. The place is always packed, but the allure is definitely not the java. The patrons don't really know why Mama's secret brew tastes like tar, but the fact that absolutely no one is willing to tell Mama about it makes for one of the best inside jokes in Arlington.

Mama Dell is from South Carolina and has a delightful Southern accent that brings out my own. She came to Boston thirty-odd years ago on a full scholarship to Harvard, majoring in biotechnology, and met her soul mate, a tall, kind man known only as the Captain.

Together the two worked on some biophysics project that resulted in a patent and a huge chunk of money. They took their bundle of cash and invested it in a coffee shop. The interior of Mama Dell's is inviting, with plenty of overstuffed love seats and comfy chairs arranged in cozy little groupings where packs of pedestrians can mingle and hang out.

On a shelf by the door are rows of original — and often hilarious — coffee mugs gathered from all over the United States and a few foreign countries. Regulars come in, discreetly pour their Starbucks coffee into their favorite mug, head to the counter for a pastry, and lounge the day or evening away.

I'd first met Dell and the Captain two years ago — they were one of my very first clients, and they'd called on me to rid the place of a hyperactive poltergeist who insisted on smashing all the original coffee mugs to pieces. It had taken me almost a week, but I'd finally cornered the ghost of a British soldier who'd been trapped since the Revolutionary War, and sent him on his surly way.

In a town full of New England accents, I found a little taste of home whenever I was around Dell, and I had quickly become a regular.

I breezed through the door, tucking my Starbucks coffee under my coat, and I looked for my mug on the wall, frowning when I couldn't find it.

"Morning, M.J.!" Mama Dell sang when she saw me.

"Hey, there, Dell," I said, still scanning the shelves for the Halloween mug with a black cat painted on the cup and a handle shaped like a ghost. "Have you seen my mug?"

"I've got it in the dishwasher; someone was in earlier and used it. It should be out in a moment. Why don't you go have a seat and I'll bring it over when it's clean. You take it black, right?" she asked.

Damn. I'd forgotten the extra empty cup I usually ordered at Starbucks just in case Dell managed to fill my cup with her black, syrupy brew before I had a chance to dump my own coffee in. "Yep. Great. Black. I'll be over there," I said, pointing to my usual table and the familiar face I saw sitting there.

Dell hurried into the back while I made my way over to the blond woman seated at our table by the fireplace. "Mornin', M.J.," she said as I approached.

"Hey, Teeko, good to see you," I replied to my best girlfriend. Teeko is not actually her name, mind you. It's a combination of her initials, K.O., plus a T on the front because the woman is a total knockout. Karen O'Neal is five feet, six inches of utter gorgeousness, with long legs, blond hair, and very blue eyes. There is also an air of supreme confidence about her, but without a hint of condescension.

Today she was dressed in her usual style — fabulous — wearing knee-high suede boots, silk gaucho pants, and a beautiful low-cut embroidered silk blouse that showed off the "ladies" something fierce. "Geez, Karen," I said as I sat down. "Trying to put someone's eye out with those things?"

Teeko laughed and moved her laptop over to make room for me. "What's wrong with allowing the girls a little air and sunlight?" she asked. At that moment a gentleman walking by our table tripped over a chair and spilled coffee all over himself.

"You're a hazard," I whispered with a grin as we watched him mop his shirt with his napkin. "You should come with road flares and some traffic cones."

"So has Mama Dell told you yet?" she asked me, changing the subject.

"Told me what?" I asked.

"About the guy?"

"What guy?"

"The guy she wants to set you up with."

"Noooo," I said with a groan. "Teeko, you have got to help me out here. The last guy she set me up with chewed with his mouth open, and that was the most attractive thing about him."

Teeko giggled. "It couldn't have been that bad," she said.

"He had hair plugs!" I added, grabbing her arm as I saw Mama making a beeline toward me, Halloween mug in hand.

"Well, I've seen this one, M.J., and all I can say is yummy."

"You're killing me," I said under my breath as Mama reached our table.

"Here you go, M.J. Black. Just like you like it."

My cup from Starbucks was carefully hidden under my coat, and as I looked at Mama it became clear she was waiting for me to sip the coffee to make sure it was to my liking. Teeko hid a grin as I smiled gamely and raised the mug to my mouth. Making a loud slurpy noise I sipped just a tiny bit. It was god-awful. "Mmmmm!" I said, choking it down. "Perfect. Thanks, Dell."

Mama rocked on the balls of her feet, a

big grin on her face. "It's my special recipe," she said.

"Delicious," I said, and coughed, then quickly cleared my throat, muttering, "Damn allergies." Teeko stifled a giggle.

"I'm so glad you're here!" Mama said with a little hand clap. "Karen and I just met the most wonderful man and —"

"I'm busy tonight," I said quickly.

"You are?" Teeko said, looking at me with big innocent eyes. I'd have to kill her later.

"Yes," I said, giving her the evil eye. "I have a ghostbuster thing."

"Can't you get out of it?" Teeko asked. Yep, she was definitely mincemeat.

"Nope."

"Is this that big job you've been working on?" Teeko asked me. *Ahhh.* Finally, some help!

"Yep. Sure is."

"The one Gilley's been talking about?" I wasn't sure where she was going here, but I liked the direction.

"Uh-huh. The very one," I said, nodding my head vigorously.

"Oh, well, in that case, Mama," she said, turning to Dell, "you can call our man and tell him M.J. would be happy to meet him on Saturday, because Gilley expressly told me that your night off from this big case

52

was Saturday." *Crap.* Teeko was back on my shit list.

"Perfect!" Dell said with a snap of her fingers. "I'll go call him right now. M.J., you are going to love this one! And you know I'm rarely wrong about these things!" she added as she bustled off.

Now, it was true that Mama had a certain reputation to uphold. After all, she was the premier matchmaker in the metro Boston area. And she really did seem to have a knack for bringing the right couples together. It was also true that her track record was somewhere in the ninetieth percentile . . . but when it came to me, that woman could no more find me someone suitable than she could brew a good cup of coffee.

As Mama hurried away I turned on Teeko. "What are you doing to me?" I asked her sharply.

"You need to do something other than work, work, work . . ."

"I *like* work," I said.

". . . and sit alone in that condo of yours letting the best years of your life drift by, afraid of putting yourself out there because you might get rejected."

I scowled at her. "It's not that easy, Teek," I said. She gave me a look that said, *Oh, please,* so I elaborated. "First of all, I really do like my work. And I'm in the middle of trying to build this business and do not need the distraction of a relationship right now."

"So you work," Teeko said with a shrug. "Plenty of busy singles get together and make it happen. Going out with someone doesn't mean you become joined at the hip, for God's sake, M.J."

Again, I scowled at her. "Granted. But along with my very busy schedule, it's just not easy for me."

"It's not easy for anybody, my friend, and yet people *do* pair up."

"*Normal* people pair up, not people like me."

"People like you? What do you mean by that?"

I swirled the black liquid around in my mug for a minute before answering her. "Teeko, most men do not want to date a woman who can talk to dead people. They think it's freaky, weird, hell, even that guy with the plugs couldn't wait for the night to end. I'm just tired of seeing that look in their eyes, is all."

"What look, specifically?"

"That I'm cuckoo for Cocoa Puffs," I said borrowing a quote from my parrot.

Karen threw her head back and gave a hearty laugh. "M. J. Holliday," she said, shaking her head back and forth. "I've never known you to be afraid of anything. You're the bravest woman I know, in fact."

I rolled my eyes and stared at the wall. This entire conversation was really making me uncomfortable. Teeko continued. "You walk into places spookier than the Amityville Horror, and deal with stuff twice as freaky, but going out on a little date has you clucking like a chicken."

"It's not that I'm scared," I said defensively. "I just don't feel like dealing with it."

"What you need to find is a *real* man. Someone who's not intimidated," Teeko mused. "And I swear, this guy that Dell and I met today, he just might be able to give you a run for your money."

"He's probably a commitment-phobe," I groused. Sometimes I can really be a ray of sunshine.

Teeko laughed again. "He's *not* a commitment phobe, and trust me, I am an expert at spotting those."

"How is John these days, by the way?" I asked her, referring to her beau of three years, John Dodge.

Teeko's smile wavered. "Actually," she said, turning her attention to her own cup of coffee, "he proposed the night before last."

That got me. John was a *very* wealthy real estate tycoon, and had recently been voted one of Boston's most eligible bachelors. It had always been my firm belief that John liked his bachelorhood, and he never seemed the type to get down on bended knee and do the right thing by Karen, so this news was quite a surprise. "He what?" I asked.

"I gave him the marry-me-or-I'm-gone ultimatum, and he proposed."

"You're engaged?" I said, ready to throw my arms around her in a giant hug.

"No."

"No?"

"I said no."

"Did I miss something?"

"M.J.," she said, turning to me. "I realized the moment I gave him the speech about taking the plunge or I'm out of here that it was the wrong way to get what I wanted. What I want . . . what I've always wanted . . . is for it to be John's idea. For him to love me so much that he was willing to make the commitment all on his own."

"So what happened?" I asked, reaching out to squeeze her arm.

"I left him."

"You didn't!" I said.

"Yes. We're done," she said as I noticed the smallest quiver to her bottom lip before she cleared her throat and shook her head a little, trying to hold it together.

I sat there, stunned. Teeko had been dating John so long that I didn't think they'd ever split up. Truthfully, I'd always thought that if the end ever came, it would be John's idea. The fact that Karen had had the courage to walk away from something she'd wanted so much — and a man she'd absolutely adored — floored me. "I am so sorry," was all I could say.

Teeko smiled sadly at me and reached over to squeeze my hand. "Don't be," she whispered. "I'm fine."

I cocked a skeptical eyebrow at her.

"Seriously," she said, and the smile brightened just a bit.

"So now what?" I asked her.

"Now I let Mama fix me up with whomever she wants," she said, indicating the paperwork she'd been working on when I walked up.

I noticed that it was one of Mama's profile sheets, where single applicants, like gullible me, filled out an extensive questionnaire. "You're really just going to throw yourself out there?" I asked.

"You betcha," Teeko said with a smile. "You can't let life pass you by, M.J. You've got to become an active player in creating your own future. You, more than anyone, should understand that."

She had me there. How many grounded spirits had I come across who were simply stuck because they refused to move forward, while all around them the living marched on with their lives as the spirits just resentfully watched?

With a sigh I said, "When you're right, you're right, Teeko. Okay, I'll go on this date, but tell me about the guy. Is he normal?"

Karen smiled brightly at me. "Oh, he's so *not* normal you're sure to fall for him." She laughed.

I cocked my head at her. "He's weird?"

"No. Most definitely not weird. He's fabulous, and completely not what you would pick for yourself."

I scowled at her. "So why would you think he's a good match for me?"

"Because your track record proves that you just can't pick 'em, M.J."

She had me there. "What does he look like?"

"Nope," she said, holding up her hand and shaking her head. "You will get no details from me. You'll just have to approach this with an open mind."

"That has never been my strong suit," I admitted.

"Which is exactly why you'll need to adopt it as your new attitude. Now, I've got to go. Call me Sunday and let me know how it went." And with that she got up, gave me a peck on the cheek, and headed over to Mama's to turn in her profile. I watched the fire in the fireplace for a while, thinking about all she'd said and struggling with how right she was.

Gilley had been saying the same thing to me for years, and after a while he'd given up, knowing I was just too damn stubborn to change. "It's all set," I heard off to my left.

I looked up and saw Mama back at my table, her excitement bubbling over as she bounced again on the balls of her feet. "What's all set?" I asked.

"Tomorrow night. He's going to meet you at Tango's at six thirty sharp."

Ah. The blind date. Maybe I could milk Mama for details. "So tell me about this fabulous man," I said, putting on my most inviting smile.

"Oh, no," Mama said with a chuckle. "Teeko told me not to tell you anything.

She doesn't even want me to tell you his name, because she knows you'll just have Gilley cyberspy on him and find lots of excuses to get out of going."

Crap. Foiled again. "Okay, so how will I know him?" I asked, trying to hide the impatience in my voice.

"He'll be wearing black," Dell said.

"That narrows it down."

"I told him you'd be wearing the same."

"Ah," I said, giving her a look. "Funeral theme. This should be *buckets* of fun!"

"Try to have a good time," Mama said, a plea in her voice.

I pulled in the sarcasm and reached for her hand, "Okay, Mama. Sorry. I'll do my best."

"I have a good feeling about this one, M.J.," she said.

I failed to remind her that she'd had a good feeling about the other five duds she'd fixed me up with and simply nodded. "Okay, Mama. I'll be there, in black, at six thirty."

Mama seemed to relax and leaned in to give me a hug. "That's my girl," she said.

"Awww. A Hallmark moment," I heard behind her, and I looked up to see that Gilley had arrived. "What'd I miss?" he asked as he plopped down in the seat Teeko had been sitting in.

"I've set M.J. up on a date," Mama said, releasing me.

"And she *let* you?" Gilley said, giving me a wink.

"She had very little choice in the matter. Karen and I double-teamed her."

"Ooooh. You play rough," Gilley said. "When's the blessed event?"

"Tomorrow night. Gilley, would you make sure she's dressed and ready?" Mama said.

"What's the attire?" Gilley asked.

"I'm sitting right here, you know," I groused.

Mama ignored me. "Black. I know she'll go for pants and a baggy sweater, but maybe you can get her into something a little more va-va?"

"Leave it to me, Mama. I'll even add some voom, no charge."

"I'm leaving," I said, getting up from the table.

"You're not going anywhere, M.J. We need to talk," Gilley said sternly.

Mama glanced at him, then back at me, and said, "I'd better get back to the counter and help the Captain. The lunch rush should start any second." And with that she was gone.

Reluctantly, I sat back down and looked at my business partner. I could tell Gilley was miffed. I knew I'd played it wrong when I'd announced to him that we wouldn't be taking the Sable case and bolted for the nearest exit. "What's on your mind, Gil?"

"Don't be coy, M.J. We had a solid lead with Dr. Sable. What the hell happened?"

I took a covert sip of my now-cold Starbucks coffee and shrugged my shoulders. "We couldn't reach an agreement."

"Was it over price? Because we could still cut him a deal."

"No, it wasn't price."

Gilley waited me out, and I did my best to fill the pregnant silence by stirring my coffee. "I'm waiting," Gilley said after a few moments.

I sighed and met his eyes. "He wanted to be a part of the bust."

Gilley gave me a puzzled look. *"And?"*

"And nothing," I said, looking back at the fire. "I didn't want him to get in our way, so I turned him down."

Gilley took several seconds to sputter incoherently, before raising his voice a few octaves. "You *cannot* be serious!"

I scowled at him, "Pretty sure I am, Gil."

"M.J.," he began, his voice low and irritated. "Do you realize we haven't had a really good paycheck in several weeks?"

"I just got paid on the Kettleman job

today," I interjected.

"Which barely catches us up to current!" Gilley screeched. Seeing several eyes look in our direction, he cleared his voice and tried again. "We cannot keep doing this," he said to me. "I got into this partnership with you because I thought it had potential, and from day one you have set limits that have restricted our income. I have a mortgage to pay, and so do you!" he chastised.

"I'm fully aware of my financial obligations," I snapped back.

"Then why, M.J.? Why would you turn down such a good and profitable job?"

I frowned as I searched for a reason Gilley would accept. "Because," was all I could come up with.

"Because *why?*" Gilley pressed.

"Because we work alone, Gil! The minute we invite our clients along on a bust is the moment we lose control."

Gilley shook his head back and forth. I could tell he was struggling with his patience. "You can't have it both ways, my friend," he finally said.

"I'm sorry?" I asked.

"You cannot do what you do and expect that there is only one way you're going to get the job done. If we turn down everyone but the ones who fit specific criteria, then we'll go bankrupt."

"I didn't realize we were doing so poorly," I snapped.

"That's because I do the books. You won't allow me to book readings anymore, which quite frankly was keeping us solidly in the black. M.J., you've got to be willing to compromise. Running your own business is tough enough, and may I remind you that we live in one of the most expensive cities in the country?"

I didn't reply, but simply glared at him. Apparently today was Lecture M.J. Day.

Gilley ignored the glare and continued. "Now, I want you to think about what I've said. And you think hard, because if you want me to continue in this partnership then you're going to have to be willing to make some allowances for our clients."

"So it's come to that?" I asked, shocked that Gilley was playing hardball.

"It's come to that," Gil said, and stood up. "I'm headed to a meeting with another group of Realtors. Doc's been fed and watered. I'll call you later and we can discuss options for your date on Saturday, and by options I mean get your MasterCard out, because there is nothing even remotely suitable hanging in that closet of yours."

"Gil —" I started, wanting to say something that would make things all right between us.

"Go home and think about what I've said," Gil said, cutting me off. And with a quick kiss on the top of my head he was off.

I sat there in Mama Dell's for a little while, wondering why the whole world wanted to pick on me, then decided to shake myself out of my funk by taking a walk. With a wave to Mama Dell, I headed out the door and began to walk the few blocks that make up Arlington Center.

I gazed without looking into storefronts made up of quaint boutiques and gift shops as my thoughts looped around the conversations I'd had that morning. First with Dr. Sable, then with Teeko, and finally with Gilley. I think I was most upset by Gilley's ultimatum — not that I could blame him.

It also sucked that I knew he was right on the money. If Gil left, I'd be totally screwed — the man even balanced my checkbook. What was I going to do without him?

As my thoughts continued to swirl I looked up at the storefront I was passing and stopped short. There, in the window, was a gorgeous black cocktail dress. I snickered to myself, because it was so obvious the universe had set me up, then took a big breath and walked inside. I was met by a pleasantly plump young woman who couldn't have been a day over nineteen.

"Hi!" she said enthusiastically.

"Good afternoon," I replied.

"Need some help?"

"I saw that dress in the window," I said, pointing behind me. "Can I try it on?"

"Sure! What are you, about a size four?"

"About that," I said, thanking myself for my daily run and a healthy metabolism.

"The dress runs small, so I'll bring you a six just in case."

Gee, just when I was riding a sizing high. "Great. Where do I go . . . ?" I asked, turning my head around the small boutique.

"Right over there," she said, pointing to a curtained room off to my left.

Three minutes later I was staring at myself in the mirror and thinking that I must definitely be crazy. The dress was way too short. Okay, so it was also way too low. This was a dress Teeko would wear in a heartbeat, but did it really suit me? Just then there was a knock on the outside of the dressing room. "How's it going in there?"

"Uh . . ." I said as I scowled at the mirror.

Without warning the curtain was pulled aside and the salesclerk poked her head in. "Ohmigod! You are totally smokin' in that dress!" she squealed.

I winced at the pitch in her voice. "You don't think it's too short?"

"No way, you have great legs."

"Too low?"

"For you or a nun?" she asked. Ah, a clever nineteen-year-old.

"I'm serious," I said, hiking up the neckline.

"So am I," she said, stepping forward to gently tug the neckline back down. "Honest, you look amazing. Did you know you could be Sandra Bullocks's sister?"

I get that all the time, and while I love Sandy and think she's a brilliant actress, after so many years of being remembered as the chick who looks just like her, I was wishing my face were a little less familiar. "So I've been told," I said, turning around to view my rear. "Does my butt look big?"

"No," she said with a giggle. "And even if it did, guys are into big butts. You've *so* gotta buy this dress!"

"Gilley would be proud," I said quietly as I turned back and tried to square my shoulders so it would appear I was someone confident enough to wear this type of thing every day.

"Who?"

"No one." I sighed. "Okay, I'll take it, but just in case, what's your return policy?"

■ ■ ■ ■

Later that night, while Gilley cooked dinner at my place, I modeled the dress for him. I thought his eyes were going to pop out of his head. "Dial nine-one-one!" he shouted.

"What?" I asked, alarmed.

"Emergency?" he said, putting an imaginary phone to his ear. "Come quick! We've got a woman *on fire* over here!"

"I knew it," I said, heading back into the bedroom. "I'm returning it in the morning."

I heard quick footsteps behind me, and just as I was about to turn around I heard a snipping sound.

"Hey!" I yelled, whirling around to catch Gilley, scissors in one hand and sales tag in the other. "Gil, what are you doing?"

"You return that dress and I will personally spank you," he said with a grin.

"It's not me!" I complained, reaching for the zipper. "I don't even know why I bought it."

"Because for the first time in forever you had a clear thought?" Gilley said. "M.J., you have been a little old lady since you were six. Isn't it time you kicked your heels up and have a little fun already?"

"Okay," I said from my bedroom as I pulled the dress over the top of my head and shrugged back into my sweats. "So riddle me this: What if I meet this guy and I hate him? Then I will have just spent a fortune on a dress I'm never going to wear again."

There was an audible sigh from the hallway. "Don't you get that it's not about this one date?" Gil asked me.

"What do you mean?" I said, coming out of the bedroom.

"That dress is about you getting out of your comfort zone, which is what I've been trying to tell you to do for . . . like, ever."

"Ah," I said, pouring myself a glass of wine. "So why is it so important I come out of said comfort zone? I mean, I happen to like my zone."

"Why?"

"Why what?"

"Why do you like to play it so safe all the time?"

I thought about that for a long, long moment. Finally I said, "Because it keeps things simple. All these years I've been happy hanging out with you and putting my energy into our business."

"Not buying it, M.J.," Gil said to me. "What I think is that you've been so afraid to reveal the real you — the one that, sure, talks to dead people — that you've locked yourself away from any chance of love. Your approach since high school, has been, 'I'm going to get rejected anyway, so why try?' "

"And if you'll remember high school, it was no picnic for either of us."

Gil beamed at me. "The thing is, sweetie, that we're no longer *in* high school. Grownups are usually a lot more open to and tolerant of folks like us."

I smiled at him. "Folks like us?"

"Quirky," he said, walking over to the stove to stir the plum sauce he was cooking.

"How did I end up such a mess, Gil?" I asked him.

"Well, it wasn't for lack of me trying to get you to do something different."

I looked at him just as Doc squawked, "Dr. Delicious!"

"I've been thinking about what you said to me this morning," I said thoughtfully.

"I can tell," he said, pointing to my bedroom, where I'd left the dress. "You've been soul-searching."

I smiled. "I guess I have. Anyway, I think you're right. Maybe I have been a little too rigid. Any chance you can call Dr. Sable and ask him for another interview?"

"I left him a voice mail this afternoon,"

Gilley said with a grin as he pulled a pork roast from the oven. "And by the way — tomorrow we are going shoe shopping, because you cannot wear Birkenstocks with that dress."

The next evening I decided to walk the four blocks to Tango's, an Argentinean steakhouse that was a particular favorite of mine. By the time I was a block and a half into it I really wished I'd driven my car, because my feet were killing me in the three-inch heels Gilley had forced me to buy. And the skintight wowser of a dress kept riding up every time I took more than four steps.

By the time I reached the front of Tango's I had decided to splurge on a cab home. Walking into the restaurant I shook my head, allowing the many curls Gilley had put in my hair tonight to fluff out a little more, and unbuttoned my coat. I was met by the host, who gave me one look and put his hand to his heart, "*Señorita!* You are breathtaking! May I give you a table in the window to attract all the men in town to-night?"

I giggled and gave my hair another flip. "Hello, Estevan. I'm actually meeting some-one here, so I'll sit wherever you've put

71

him," I said, nonchalantly scanning the restaurant.

"And who are you meeting?" Estevan asked.

"Uh . . ." I said, suddenly realizing I didn't even know my date's name. "You know, that's a good question. I'm on one of Mama Dell's dinners. Is there a single gentleman here waiting on someone from Mama's?"

"Why, yes, there is!" Estevan said, looking at his seating chart. "I just escorted a man to a table a few minutes ago, and he is waiting on his perfect match from Mama Dell's."

I was already annoyed. "I'm not so sure we're a perfect match," I said quickly. "Actually, this is our first date."

"I see," Estevan said as he took my coat. "Well, after he sees how beautiful you look tonight he may consider you such, no?"

"Let's hope not," I said as my stomach bunched. I hated men who moved too quickly.

"Right this way," Estevan said as he led me toward a dark section. As we approached a table I clenched my teeth to hide my disappointment. The man seated at the table had a receding hairline, large ears, and fishy-looking lips. His torso was thin, along with his shoulders, and his eyes had a nervous cast to them. He was dressed in a brilliant green suede jacket, white turtleneck, and black pants. It suited him — he'd make a good turtle.

As we approached he looked at me and his mouth hung open. I forced a plastic smile to my lips while inwardly vowing to boycott Mama Dell's forever. Estevan stopped in front of the table and said, "*Señor,* your guest has arrived."

"Whoa," Turtle said, looking up at me.

Still smiling tightly, I stuck out my hand and said, "Hello, I'm M.J. I'm pleased to meet you."

"Whoa," Turtle said again.

Estevan pulled out my chair and I sat down, wondering how I was going to get through the evening with Chatty Cathy here. "I love your jacket," I tried.

"Whoa."

I nodded my head. "Yeah, you said that a few times now," I said as I snapped my napkin and smoothed it onto my lap.

Turtle gulped audibly.

I held in a sigh and went for small talk. "I was expecting someone in black. I mean, Mama Dell said that you would be dressed in black."

Turtle ogled me silently, his eyes crawling from my chest up to about my neck, then back again. I eyed the bread basket and thought about tossing a roll at his pointy head to get his attention back to my face. "Anyway," I said, dipping my chin to try to meet his gaze, "like I said, my name is M.J."

Turtle gave my eyes a quick glance, then headed south again to rest on my décolletage.

"And you are?" I said through gritted teeth. I was two seconds away from pulling back my chair and running for it.

"Too overcome by your beauty to speak," a deep baritone said over my left shoulder.

I turned in my chair to see Steven Sable grinning at me. I also noticed he was wearing black pants, a black silk shirt, and a black blazer. Gil and my bird were right: He was most definitely delicious. "Hello," I said, looking back and forth between Turtle and Steven.

"Are you here to meet the man from Mama Dell's?" he asked me, the mischievous grin never leaving his features.

"*You're* my date?" I asked, standing quickly, a huge sense of relief flooding through me as I realized I didn't have to spend one more second with Whoa Turtle.

"Yes," Steven said. "And I believe this is his," he added, indicating a woman behind him with a blond pageboy and a dark green blouse.

Turtle looked from me to the blonde and said to Steven, "That's okay; I like this girl better."

The blonde looked insulted, so I wasted no time. Grabbing the woman by the arm before she had a chance to run, I said, "Ha! He is *such* a funny guy! Boy, are you going to have a good time tonight or what? Now sit yourself right down here, honey — see that? I've already warmed it up for you. Okay, you two make some magic together, and remember, the wine here is fabulous! I suggest a bottle . . . each." And with that I grabbed Steven's hand and pulled him back over to Estevan.

"*Señorita,* I am most sorry. I did not realize Mama sent me two couples for dinner tonight."

"That's fine, Estevan, don't worry about it. But now we'll need a table, preferably as far away from them as you can get."

"*Sí, sí.* Come, I will put you in the window so that passersby can see what beautiful people frequent my restaurant."

A minute later Steven and I were sitting pretty at a table by the large picture window. Estevan had bustled off to get us a complimentary bottle of wine, and I realized then

75

that I was struggling with what to say next. We sat there for a few moments looking at our menus and taking small peeks at each other. I don't know why I hadn't noticed it this afternoon, but Steven had marvelous features: strong jaw, full lips, fabulous eyelashes. Taking him all in visually, I couldn't help but wonder why this rich, good-looking doctor would need a match-maker to fix him up. He seemed the type to be dripping with women, a girl in every port, so to speak. Catching me looking at him thoughtfully he asked, "You wish to ask me something?"

"No," I said, my eyes darting back to my menu. "Well . . . yes," I said a second later.

"I'm listening," he said, still gazing at his own menu.

"It's just that of all the people I would expect to need Mama Dell's services, you are definitely not one of them."

"Why would you say that?" he asked me as he closed his menu and set it down in front of him.

"Have you *seen* you?" I asked, waving a hand at him.

"Every morning in the bathroom mirror," he said matter-of-factly.

"You know what I mean," I said. "Don't girls just throw themselves at guys like you?"

"Guys like me?"

"Yeah. You know, rich, handsome doctor types?"

Steven chuckled and swept a hand through his black hair. "So your impression of me is that I am . . . how do you Americans say . . . not getting any?"

I blinked at him a few times. Was that my impression? "No," I said as I closed my own menu. "It's just that I would think that you would look at this type of thing as a waste of time when you could just as easily —"

"M.J., I can assure you that I am not having trouble gaining the attention of the women," he said, the deep rumble of his voice reverberating off the windowpane next to us.

"Confident, are we?" I said.

"No. I am just stating the truth of things."

"Then why go to a matchmaker?"

He chuckled softly as he leaned in over the table toward me, holding my gaze with his black eyes. "I did not go to a matchmaker. After leaving your office I stopped for an espresso. While I was at this shop for coffee, I met the charming patron known as Mama Dell. She began talking with me and told me that she knew of a beautiful woman I must meet, and she offered to arrange this for me. At first I was cautious, but she persuaded me with her . . . eh . . . Southern hospital."

"Hospital*ity*," I said, smirking a bit. I had to admit that I found Steven's abuse of the English language quite charming.

"Yes, yes," Steven said, waving his hand. "Shall we order?" he asked as our waiter appeared at our table.

By the time we'd given our order and had our glasses filled with wine, I'd managed to get a little grip on my attraction to the man in front of me, and I did that by reminding myself that if I didn't bring Sable's business back, Gilley would have a giant cow. Sadly, that meant I couldn't very well mix business with pleasure. What happened after Steven's case was solved, however . . . well, I'd just have to leave that up to fate.

"As it happens," I began in my most professional voice, "I had my business partner try to reach you after you left our office."

"Yes, I received his voice mail," Steven said coolly.

"I've had a chance to discuss your terms with him, and I believe we can reach an agreement that will be mutually beneficial to all parties."

"I see," Steven said as he picked up the basket of bread and offered it to me. After I declined, he pulled out a piece and began buttering it. "You're willing to allow me to come along?"

"Yes," I said, studying Steven closely. I didn't know what it was with this guy, but I was having a heck of a time getting a good read on him. "That is, in part, yes."

"In part?" he asked, meeting my eyes again.

"I'm not a private investigator. I'm a ghostbuster. And even though I hate that particular connotation, it does specify what I actually do. I help those poor souls who are stuck between this world and the one beyond to move forward, to bust out of their prison, so to speak, and go to where they belong. If, in doing that, the truth of your grandfather's demise comes out, well, then, that's just gravy. I cannot guarantee that what I discover will be satisfactory to you."

Steven studied me for a while, chewing his bread and looking thoughtful. "So tell me this: How am I to know that you are not lying?"

I frowned at the question. "Excuse me?"

"As you indicated, I am quite wealthy. And in this time of sorrow, most vulnerable. How do I know what you say is true?"

Now, I get this question all the time, but the way Steven said it, with just a hint of condescension, pissed me off. "How do your patients know when they come to see you that you're for real?" I snapped, crossing my arms and sitting back in my chair.

"Because I have diplomas and certificates which prove that I went to school, graduated, and passed the medical boards in both Germany and this country. Did you go to school for this? Do you have diplomas I can see?"

"Yes, I went to school, but not for this. They don't teach what I do in college, Steven." I didn't bother telling him I'd spent only two years in a community college. Best not to elaborate here.

"You see my dilemma, then," he said, wiping the corners of his mouth with his napkin. "I will need some kind of" — he paused, searching for the word — "proof before I agree to hire you."

"You know, it's amazing to me that you doctors get stereotyped as egomaniacs. Truly, you're one of the humble ones," I snapped. My temper was flaring. I didn't care if this man was delicious. Currently he was one of those appetizers that looked good on a buffet until you tried a tiny bite; then you wanted to stuff it into a cocktail napkin before the hostess could see you.

"Humility has nothing to do with this,"

Steven said. "In my country, women like you are scorned. They are the Gypsies that prey on tourists and use their magic tricks to deceive the foolish. No one in my standing would ever *think* to hire someone like you. And I am only considering this because I am without hope. So, you wish me to hire you? Then I will need to see some proof of your abilities before I do so." He finished by leaning back in his chair. The suspicious look he gave me said that he would be watching me carefully, waiting to catch me in any sleight of hand.

I snapped my mouth shut, realizing that it had been hanging open slightly as I soaked in that Steven was associating me with petty thieves. "First of all," I began, my voice dangerously low, "I am no Gypsy. I am a *legitimate* businesswoman with a unique talent that very few people possess. Second, and most important, what you're not getting," I said, stabbing a finger at him, "is that you don't make the rules, Doc. I do."

With that I got to my feet and threw my napkin on the table. I was about to turn on my heel when the insult of being referred to as a possible charlatan got the better of me. Hesitating a moment to turn my internal intuitive switch to the on position, I snapped, "You want proof? Fine, here's your damn proof. Someone named Miguel says to tell you he was stupid to have gone swimming in that river when the current was too strong. He says it's not your fault that you didn't jump in after him. He says you did the right thing running for help instead, because if you had tried to save him on your own, you would have drowned too.

"And someone named Rita is laughing about something to do with an object that had religious value, and she's pointing to you and what you did with it. It's something she would have been very upset about when she was here, but now she sees the humor and thinks it was very funny."

I finished my little demo with a flourish as I reached down and grabbed my purse. Glancing back up as I turned to leave I got a huge measure of satisfaction from the look of complete and utter shock on Steven's face. "Still want to see my diploma?" I demanded. When he didn't answer, I said, "Didn't think so," and stormed out of the restaurant.

CHAPTER 3

It was chilly outside, and the wind had picked up. The air was thick with moisture, and the clouds overhead were an ominous gray. I struggled quickly into my coat, pulling the belt tight around my waist and turning up the collar. I could only hope I'd make it home before the first raindrops. Taking a step forward, my very spiky heel caught in a crack in the sidewalk, and as I tried to twist it loose the heel came off. "Son of a . . . !" I hissed as I stopped to pick up the heel. "Why me?" I asked plaintively as I shoved it into my coat pocket and looked around for a cab. There were none to be found. "Rassa-frassa-rassa . . . !" I groused, and began limping quickly down the street up three inches, down three inches, up three inches, down three inches. To make matters worse, the up and down of my walk was making my dress ride up even more than it had before. I must've looked like a freak bobbing up and down, pulling at my dress.

I got about a hundred yards when out of the corner of my eye I saw a car keeping pace with me. I stole a quick glance and noticed a shiny black Aston Martin crawling along beside me. I snapped my head back to the sidewalk and concentrated on my up-down walk, discreetly pulling on my dress and feeling my cheeks grow hot at the spectacle I had created.

"M.J.!" I heard Steven call from inside his car.

"Go away!" I said, and kept walking.

"Can I offer you a ride?" he asked.

"Go. Away," I repeated, my jaw clenched and my brows lowered.

To my horror I heard Steven chuckle. "It's about to start raining, you know."

The very moment he finished this sentence, the sky above us lit up with a bright light, and the crack of thunder caused me to jump a foot. I looked from him to the sky and snarled, but kept limping.

"You're going to get wet in a moment," he coaxed, still following along beside me. "Why don't you let me take you home?"

I gave him one of the dirtiest looks I could muster. "If you care about seeing tomorrow, Sable, I would suggest you put that car in gear and move along." And then the sky opened up and water came pouring down. I shrieked and pulled the collar of my coat up as high as it would go, while looking for an awning that I could duck under.

Just as I spotted one a block away, the rain stopped hitting me in the face and I noticed someone standing to my right. I looked up to see Steven holding an umbrella overhead and wearing a wide grin on his face. "Come, let me take you home."

I looked from him to his car parked right next to us, then to the awning *way* down the street. I was cold, wet, and three blocks from home, not to mention that there was a blister on my foot the size of Texas.

"Fine," I said, giving in. Steven opened the passenger-side door for me and waited until I was settled in before he shut the door and went around to the driver's side. I noticed with a teensy bit of relief that the seats in the Aston were heated.

When Steven was seated, I said, "I live a few blocks from here. Just keep heading in this direction and make a left at that brick building by the fire station."

Steven clicked his seat belt and said, "Buckle up." He then waited until I groaned and fastened my seat belt. A moment later we were zipping down the street at a good clip, and I almost relaxed until we passed my condo.

"Hey!" I yelled, pointing behind me as we flew past. "That was my stop!"

"Yes, you said that earlier."

"You were supposed to stop!" I yelled at him.

"I decided to do something better."

"*Better?* What could be *better* than taking me home?"

"Taking you to my place."

"*What?!*"

"Taking you to my house to cook you dinner and apologize for my behavior in the restaurant."

I was speechless. I just looked at him for a long moment with my eyes wide and my mouth open, thinking about the several different responses that I could lob at him, but nothing felt really appropriate. I settled for, "Oh."

Fifteen minutes later we entered a part of Boston with the kind of real estate that came with price tags so high that if you had to ask, "How much?" you most definitely couldn't afford to live there. We stopped in front of an elegant brownstone lit up like a Christmas tree. Every single light in the house seemed to be on, and a few of the windows had the curtains pulled back to reveal snapshots of the lovely interior.

"Here we are," he said easily, then looked at my feet. "Hey, one of your heels came off," Steven said.

"Nothing gets by you, does it?" I dead-panned as I got out of the car. While I held the umbrella, Steven unlocked the front door and held it open for me while I did the up-down thing into his house.

As I entered the foyer, my breath caught. The front entry was gorgeous. It became apparent that Steven had marvelous taste as I glanced around at the white marble floor, golden yellow walls, and elaborate molding. A beautiful vase was artfully displayed on a podium, and a carpeted stairway with an iron railing led to the second floor. "Like what you see?" Steven asked me, a confident smirk turning up the corners of his mouth.

"It'll do," I said, putting what I hoped was a breezy look on my face. "But I'd watch your electric bill. Looks like you have every light in the place switched on."

Steven took my coat, hanging it in the closet before shrugging out of his. "My home was broken into recently, and the police said that extra lighting was a good detriment."

I smiled. "You mean *deterrent*."

"Yes, yes," Steven said with another wave of his hand. "My English is not so good as it once was. Now, how about dinner?"

"Ah, yes, you promised me some eats," I said. "I only hope you can cook as well as you can decorate."

Steven smiled wolfishly at me. "Oh, I can cook, all right," he said, and took my hand as he led me out of the front foyer.

I hobbled through a corridor and around a corner to the kitchen that would put most restaurants to shame. There were walnut-colored cabinets, stainless-steel appliances, a huge gas-powered stove and warming oven, and countertops covered in brown-and-black marbled granite. "Sit," Steven said, pointing to an island where I noticed two stools artfully situated at one end. "I can apologize and cook at the same time."

Taking my seat and removing my shoes I asked, "What's your specialty? Grilled cheese on white bread?"

"I am cooking you shrimp scampi over angel hair pasta with a white wine sauce."

"Ah," I said, raising an eyebrow. "Well, if you're out of white bread and cheese, I suppose that's an okay alternative."

"As I said, I must apologize for my rude behavior at the restaurant," he said as he pulled down a bottle of wine from a built-in wine rack above the sink. "All my life I've been a man of science. My mother tried to give me a sense of faith as well, but I've always thought that if you can't . . . ehm . . . like with a ruler?"

"Measure," I supplied.

"Yes, if you can't measure this thing then it could not exist. All of my education and training says that what you do cannot be done. And yet, you can do it."

"It's a gift," I said smugly as Steven placed a glass of wine in front of me.

He looked at me for a long moment, and I could tell the man of science was battling hard with the man of faith. "Tell me about what you said at Tango's. How did you do that?"

"It's just something I was born with," I said. "It's my firm belief that life continues after we die, but what becomes difficult is communication. So there are people like me who have a heightened sense of aware-ness, not unlike someone with a musical ear in a world full of people who are tone-deaf."

"You can hear these dead people?"

"Absolutely. But the communication isn't always crystal-clear. It's sometimes very muffled, and even on a good day I'm lucky to catch about every third or fourth word."

"What do they tell you?"

"Their names, how they died, who they're related to, stuff like that. It's pretty basic."

"How does this help you bust the ghost?" Steven asked as he tossed some shrimp into a frying pan.

I smiled. "Ghostbusting is a little different. For years I dealt only with connecting living people with their deceased relatives, or people who *knew* they were dead. But most ghosts don't realize that their physical bodies have died, and they float between our world and a place that's misty and confusing. Gil and I help these . . . what we call earthbound spirits face the fact that their physical bodies have stopped, and once they've accepted that they're no longer living, they move on to where they belong quite nicely."

"And where do they belong?"

"You might think of it as heaven, but I like the term the other side better."

Steven was silent for many minutes as he finished cooking our meal. Finally he slid a healthy portion of aromatic shrimp and pasta onto a plate and handed this to me. "Eat," he said, and came around to join me at the counter.

I tried the dish; it was delicious. "So you can cook," I said.

"I can do other things, too," Steven said. "Maybe one day I will show you."

I felt my face flush, and I took a large sip

of wine, then got back to the topic at hand. "As I was saying, Gil and I help these confused spirits cross over to the next plane, but sometimes we encounter an energy that is deviant in nature, and that makes the ghostbusting a little trickier."

"How?"

"These are people who were really bad in life, and for obvious reasons they don't want to head upstairs to face the Big Guy. Instead, they create a doorway to a lower plane, and travel back and forth between our plane and this lower one. When I come across them I offer them two choices: Head upstairs and meet your maker, or get locked into your portal forever."

"This is sounding dangerous," Steven said.

"It can be a little dicey at times," I admitted, thinking back to yesterday morning. "But as long as you keep a level head, you can usually come out on top." Twirling the pasta on my fork I asked him, "Tell me about Miguel and Rita."

Steven took a long sip of wine before he answered me. "We were ten years old when Miguel drowned in the river near my home in Argentina. We had been playing what you Americans call soccer on the banks of the river when the ball went into the water. It had rained the day before and we didn't realize the . . . what is the word for fast water?"

"I think you mean current."

"Yes, that's the word. We didn't realize the current was so strong. Miguel went in after the ball and disappeared under the water. I ran for help, but when we got back to the bank he was gone. His body was found later that night about a mile down the river. I always felt . . . er . . . with guilt?"

"Responsible," I said.

"Yes, that. Responsible," he finished quietly.

In my head I felt something like a vigorous head-shake no. "He says you're not to blame, Steven. He is insisting that it wasn't your fault, and there was nothing you could have done differently. You would have drowned too."

He nodded and gave a small shrug, then swirled the wine in his glass, taking a moment before he spoke again. "Rita was my mother's aunt. She was a nice enough woman but very . . . strong with the rules?"

"Strict."

"Yes, strict and religious. She lived with us and looked after me while my mother worked, which I hated because Rita insisted we spend long hours praying in front of a large statue of the Madonna."

"How old were you?"

"Five," he said. "One day Rita was called to a neighbor's house and I was left alone to pray in front of the statue. In my little-boy mind I thought that if I could hide the Madonna then I would not have to pray so much, so I got a rope and made a . . . er . . . like with a loop?"

"Noose?" I said.

"Yes, noose, and I tied it around the statue's neck and tried to pull it up to the floor above." My eyes widened. Oh, God, had he really *hanged* the Virgin Mary?

"I pulled and I pulled, but my arms grew very tired, so I tied the rope around a . . ." He paused and pointed to a column in the living room adjacent to the kitchen.

"You tied it around a column," I said, and felt a giggle in the back of my throat as I visualized Steven as a five-year-old thinking he could hoist a statue of the Virgin Mary out of view.

"Well," Steven said, "that was when Rita returned. All she saw was the Blessed Virgin swinging by her neck back and forth. She ran screaming from the house."

I began to laugh. "What did your mother say?" I asked.

"She told Rita to stop with all the pray-ing. It didn't seem to be working."

We both laughed, and then I switched topics. "I'm assuming you moved here to settle your grandfather's affairs and claim your inheritance?"

"That and I was made a very good offer from Boston University medical school. I have always liked America. I only wish I had chosen to come here while my grandfather was still alive."

"You thought you had more time," I said, feeling the wave of guilt coming off of him.

"Yes. But it was not to be. Thus, I have made a promise that I will find out what really happened the day my grandfather died."

"That must have been a shock," I said. "You get here and you go to the lodge and you see your grandfather's ghost."

Steven nodded. "That is how I knew something very bad had happened to him. His spirit was not at rest. I owe it to him to help him . . . how did you put it? To help him cross over."

I smiled. "We'll get him there; not to worry. Where is this hunting lodge?"

"West of here, very close to the New York border in a small town called Uphamshire."

"Why were the police so quick to rule it a suicide?" I wondered out loud.

"There was a note found on the table in the bedroom where he fell."

I cocked my head slightly. "He left a suicide note?"

"Either he did, or someone else trying to make it look like a suicide."

"What did the note say?"

"It was typed and it had two lines: 'Don't blame yourself. This is what I must do to make things right.' "

"Cryptic," I said.

"What is this word?" Steven asked.

"Cryptic. It means mysterious. The line about making things right suggests he felt guilty about something."

"This is the line that I struggle with too. What could my grandfather have done?"

"That's a good question, and one that we'll need to ask him when we find his ghost. By the way, who found him?"

"His . . . what was that word you used this morning? . . . ah, yes, housekeeper, Maria. She came back from the market and found him on the ground."

"Did she have anything to gain by his death?"

Steven shook his head. "Just a very small fund which my grandfather had set aside for her old age. Maria had been with my grandfather for almost thirty years."

"Was there anyone else in the house when he died?"

"No. Willis, who was the keeper of the grounds for many years, was at his cabin, which my grandfather recently had built for him and which is somewhere near the main house, but he said he did not see or hear anything unusual that day."

"Have you decided whether you're going to hire us?" I asked.

"I would like to, but again, I must insert I come along."

"Insert?"

"Yes. You know, to . . . demand."

I hid a smile. "You mean insist."

"That too," Steven said, standing. "We will leave tomorrow. I have already told the hospital that I will be taking some time off this week to tend to my grandfather's affairs."

"Fine — I agree, and we can start tomorrow. But we'll need to establish some ground rules first."

"Good idea," Steven said, then grinned as he eyed me and said, "Rule number one: You must wear that dress at all times."

I laughed and felt my cheeks grow hot. "Nice try. No, ground rule number one is that you must stay out of my way. I need to focus, and I can't have you distracting me by getting in the middle of what I'm doing."

"Agreed," he said. "What's next?"

"Ground rule number two is that you will let me be the judge of when to cross your grandfather over to the other side."

Steven gave me a puzzled expression. "Meaning?"

"Meaning that if your grandfather is truly the one you heard at the lodge, and he is stuck, then my main obligation is to give him some relief. It's no fun for them, Steven. Grounded spirits are often frustrated, scared, and on the verge of panic. I give you my word that I will attempt to find out if he was alone when he died or if someone else was involved, and the details leading up to his death, but I won't do that if it means delaying giving him some peace. And even if he does remember what happened the day he died, he may not be willing to share those details with me. Again, I'll do my best, but I'm not in this to solve what you believe to be his murder as much as I am to help him get to where he belongs."

I saw conflict in Steven's features, and I knew he was struggling with that decision. "Fine," he said after a long pause. "Anything else?"

"No, Gilley will be in touch with you in the morning to work out the rest of the details." I glanced at the clock above the stove. "It's getting late, and we have a long day ahead of us. I should get home."

Steven walked me to the hallway and helped me into my coat, then held the door for me. As I stepped outside I noticed two things: First, it had stopped raining, and second, the bushes next to me gave a terrific shrug and then a shadowy figure flew out of the end of the row and fled down the street. I was so startled that I jumped straight into Steven, who fell backward to land with a thud on the marble floor with me right on top of him. "There are other ways to let me know you would like to hop my bones," he said playfully.

I shook my head, both at what had just happened and his comment. "It's *jump* your bones, and a man just ran out of your bushes!"

Steven's eyes widened and he got up quickly, helping me to my feet as well. "We will do this jumping later; now I must call the police."

Before I had a chance to respond he'd gone back into the kitchen to dial 911. The police arrived in a record-breaking three minutes, and I told them what I'd seen, but couldn't give a description other than that a dark shadow at the end of the bushes had darted out and run down the street. They promised to patrol the area and report back to Steven if they found anyone suspicious in the neighborhood.

After they'd gone, Steven set the house alarm and again motioned me out the door. The police were good to their word, as we saw them making their way down the street with their spotlight on and combing the darker shadows.

When we got into his car I asked, "Didn't you say your house had been broken into recently?"

"Yes. About two weeks ago I got a call from the police, who were summoned to my house by the alarm. They found a broken window, but it didn't appear as if the thief had made it inside before being scared away by the alarm."

"Do you think that was him coming back to try again?"

"Let's hope not."

"Might be good to have a house sitter stay at your place while we're upstate," I suggested.

"Yes." Steven nodded. "I will have one of the interns stay there until we come back."

We drove the rest of the way mostly in silence back toward Arlington Center, and I pointed to my condo when we drew close.

"I'm just up there."

Steven pulled into my driveway and parked in front of the side door of the building. I turned to wish him good night when his hands cupped my face and he planted a glorious kiss on my lips. His lips were smooth and warm against mine, and the kiss started out light and soft but deepened quickly as his tongue found mine. I felt dizzy. It had been a *long* time since I'd been kissed so passionately. Steven pulled away and looked at me "What was that?" I whispered.

"Mother Dell wanted a full report about our date, and good dates always end with a kiss."

"So, you're just being thorough?"

"I'm a thorough guy," he said, and kissed me again, this time with a small moan.

Damn. I love men who moan when they kiss you. It is the sexiest sound in the world. And then he was pulling away and sitting back in his seat with a satisfied smile on his face. "Next time, maybe we can jump the bones," he said.

I shook my head a little to clear it. "Just so you know, I have a rule about mixing business with pleasure."

"Ah," Steven replied with a roll of his eyes. "More ground rules."

"I'm a by-the-book kind of girl."

"Yeah? Well, that makes one of us," Steven said as he got out of the car and held the door open for me as I exited.

He walked me to the door and I inserted my key and opened it, then felt an arm snake around my waist and pull me back into his broad chest. A moment later we were kissing again, and I realized I'd just thrown the rule book out the window.

CHAPTER 4

Gilley was sitting on the couch when I entered my condo. "I was wondering when you'd come home," he said, pointedly tapping his watch.

"It's only eleven. What? You were thinking I'd be back by eight?"

"Well, after I got out of Mama Dell who your date was with, I figured you'd be back about the time the wine was served."

I gave him a look and crossed my arms. "I can be diplomatic, you know."

Gilley snorted and pulled his legs up onto the cushion. Patting the space next to him he said, "Come, sit, and tell me everything!"

I walked over to him and sat down with a sigh. "There's not a lot to tell," I began.

"Is that why your lips are all red and swollen?" he asked me, cocking an eyebrow.

I rubbed them subconsciously. "It's cold outside. They must be chapped."

"*Really?*" he said.

I widened my eyes innocently and changed the subject. "Anyway, Steven and I worked out an agreement. We've been hired to work on his grandfather's hunting lodge."

"Good girl!" Gilley said, clapping his hands. "When do we start?"

"Tomorrow."

"What? Are you kidding me?"

"What's the big deal?"

"The *big deal*, M.J., is that my night-vision camera is still in the shop. And I think my spectrometer is on the fritz and needs a tune-up. The only things that are working with any sort of regularity are the thermometer and the monitors in the van."

"Why can't you just go to the repair shop in the morning and see if they can hurry it up? Steven has some things to wrap up at the hospital, so we won't be leaving until late afternoon."

"Fine," Gilley said moodily. "Give me the deposit check so we have some cash and I'll get it out of hock."

Oops. "Uh . . . yeah, about that deposit check . . ."

Gilley narrowed his eyes. "Please tell me you got a deposit check."

"I got a deposit check."

"Really?" he asked, his voice sounding hopeful.

"No, Gil. I didn't. I forgot, and I'm sorry."

My partner glared at me. "Maybe if you had your head on business rather than on playing tongue tag I'd have a check right now."

"I'll call him in the morning and have him cut one right away, okay?" I said, exasperated.

"Good for you. Now, how was dinner?"

"It was good."

"What'd you eat?"

"Shrimp scampi over angel hair pasta."

"Was there wine?"

"Yes, a really good chardonnay."

"Did he like your dress?"

"The way he checked out my cleavage suggested he did."

"Was there dessert?"

"Nope. We talked business and I came straight home."

"How was the kiss?"

"Really good, he's got great li— Hey!"

"Gotcha!" Gilley laughed.

"I'm going to bed," I said, getting to my feet.

"Good idea," Gilley said, standing up himself. "If we're going on this little excursion I might as well get in some nightlife."

"You're going out? *Now?*"

Gil gave me a winning smile. "A boy's

gotta have his fun, sugar."

"Fine. But I'm going to be in your kitchen expecting you to be ready to roll at nine a.m."

"Oh, please," Gil said with a flip of his hand. "You'll be in my kitchen expecting coffee and cinnamon rolls."

"Well, as long as you're baking," I said, smiling, then headed to my bedroom as Gil walked toward the door. Remembering something, I paused and turned back to Gilley. "Listen, can you do me a favor in the morning?"

"What's that?"

"Can you do your computer hacking thing and dig up any dirt you can find on Steven and his father? The one person he hasn't mentioned to me is his dad, and how he fits into all of this. See if you can find out anything about their relationship for me."

"Father and son don't get along?"

"I'm not sure. The fact that he failed to mention him at any point in our conversation suggests it, and Andrew had to leave the bulk of his estate to someone. It might be that he left more to grandson than to son. Can you also do some digging about how much the old man left to each of them?"

"Anything else?"

"Yeah, if you can hack into the Back Bay's police department, I need the scoop on a break-in at Steven's place. He mentioned that there was an attempted burglary there recently, and tonight I saw someone in his bushes."

"Someone in the bushes? Did you call the police?"

"Yes. Might want to check out the results of that too. It's just too much of a coincidence that he's had two incidents in such a short period of time."

"So, I'm supposed to get the equipment ready, pack the van, and do all this research?" Gilley asked me as his hands went to his hips.

"Yeah. Right. Way too much on your plate. Let me take care of the equipment and the bank. We can both pack the van, and that should leave you enough time to find out what you need."

"Deal. See you in the morning," he said, and breezed out the door.

When he was gone I peeked under the canvas that covered Doc's cage. The bird was perched with his eyes closed, his breathing slow and steady. "Night, Doc," I whispered, and blew him a kiss. He opened one gray eye, then closed it again and went back to sleep.

Walking down the hall to my bedroom, I ran a finger over my lips. They felt warm and a little swollen. I allowed the teeniest of smiles for myself, and trotted off to bed.

The next morning promptly at nine I was in Gilley's kitchen, mug in hand and ready to eat some rolls. I found Gilley already up too, dressed in a white terry-cloth robe with hair damp from the shower. And even though I knew he'd had only a few hours' sleep, he honestly looked no worse for the wear.

"Have fun last night?"

"No, I had Bradley last night," Gilley said, giving me a wink.

"Isn't he that real estate broker you've been working for leads?"

"The very one," Gilley said happily.

"Well, gee, Stella. I'm glad you got your groove back, not that you ever lost it in the first place," I said with a grin.

Gilley came over to where I was standing and poured me a cup of coffee while he gave my hip a playful bump with his. "One last fling before we ship out," he said.

"Uh-huh. Say, I've got to ask you something," I said. "And you're not going to like it."

"Sounds serious," Gilley said as he peeked

into the oven to check on the rolls.

"No, it's not. It's just that I may need you to help me inside the house when we do this bust rather than staying in the van."

It was a little-known fact that Gilley was terrified of ghosts. He was totally open to the idea of having me venture into spectrally inhabited places, but he'd be the last one to set foot in a haunted house until the ghost was clear. Lately he'd been begging off the smaller jobs and going with me only on the bigger busts, where his role was to drive me to the location and monitor my progress from the comfort and safety of the van. Gil had three monitors set up inside so that he could watch the feed from my night-vision camera and record the readings from my spectrometer and thermometer, but it was my firm belief that he turned off the video feed and only looked for spikes in temperature and electromagnetic energy.

We never spoke about it in public, so as not to embarrass him, but Gilley was clearly terrified of things that might go bump in the night. "You must be joking," Gil said, his voice tinged with a little panic.

"No, buddy, I'm afraid not. I need you to run interference with Steven so that he doesn't get in my way. My impression of him is that he's the curious type, and that he'll want to ask me all kinds of questions, so if you think it's okay for him to come along, then I'll need you to babysit him."

"Why can't he stay in the van with me?" Gilley asked, and I noticed an even sharper rise in his voice.

"You can try that, but my guess is that he'll want to be where the action is, and he won't like sitting in a van watching monitors all night."

"But . . . but . . . but . . ." Gilley stammered. I almost felt sorry for him, especially when I knew how scary some of my expeditions could be.

"No buts, Gil. I need you. End of story."

Gilley moved over to the small table in his kitchen and, sitting down with a thump, he gave me a rather pained expression. "But what if a ghost attacks me?" he asked.

I suppressed the urge to laugh. "Gil," I said softly. "No ghost is going to attack you. It's just Steven's grandfather, after all. I'll protect you." Gilley didn't look convinced, so I offered, "Listen, if Steven gets scared and wants out, you can leave too, okay?"

"You promise?"

"I promise." Just then there was a ding and Gilley jumped up from the chair. "That's our breakfast. M.J., while I get the rolls would you mind getting my slippers?

My feet are freezing."

I looked at Gil's bare feet. "Sure," I said as I headed into his bedroom. Once there I stopped short. There was a snoring sound coming from under the covers. Tiptoeing over to Gil's bed I took a closer look and saw the top of a messy strawberry-blond head. Shaking my head, I grabbed the slippers and left the room. When I had traded Gil's slippers for a steaming-hot breakfast roll, I asked, "Is that the famous Bradley in there?"

Gil looked puzzled, then asked incredulously, "Is he still *here?*"

"Yep. Snoring up a storm." I giggled as I popped a bite of bun into my mouth.

Gilley sighed wearily. "Honestly," he said. "I mean, it was bad enough that he wanted to stay and cuddle last night, but I thought for sure I'd woken him with all the banging around I did before getting into the shower. You'd think he'd have the decency to wake up and leave, already."

"Aww," I said, laughing at him. "A gay man's love. Is there a sweeter, more romantic kind?"

Gil heaved a sigh and said, "You know what I think it's time for?"

Knowing where this was going, I said, "You *wouldn't.*"

"I think it's time for a fire drill," Gil said, and with that he walked determinedly into his bedroom as I followed, trying to stop him, but it was too late. He reached the head of the bed and shouted, "Ohmigod! Fire! Fire!"

Bradley sat bolt upright from the covers, his eyes wide and panicky as he looked around the room. "Wha . . . ?" he managed.

"Fire!" Gilley hollered, waving his arms wildly above his head. "My God, man! Run for your life!"

Bradley threw the covers to the side and leaped out of bed, buck naked as he darted first one way, then the other in a clear search for his clothes. Gilley, meanwhile had moved over to the foot of the bed and was tossing a shirt and pants at Bradley. "Here!" he said, hurling a pair of shoes at the poor man. "Now get out before the smoke gets too thick!" For emphasis he added a few loud coughs.

Bradley caught clothes, and rushed to shove his skinny legs into the pants, hopping around on one foot as he tried to edge toward the door. "What about you?" he asked as he finally got his pants up.

"We're right behind you!" Gil said, grabbing my hand and moving quickly toward the door. Bradley dashed ahead of us, rushing through the condo until he stopped cold in the living room and looked this way and that, as it appeared he was looking for something.

"Move, man!" Gilley shouted, waving him toward the door.

"My keys!" Bradley said frantically. "I can't find my friggin' keys!"

Gilley rolled his eyes and scooted over to the kitchen counter. "Here!" he said with another loud cough as he tossed the keys across the room. "Now run before we all *fry* to a crisp!"

Bradley nodded and plunged toward the door that Gilley held open for him, still hugging his shirt and shoes to his chest. I couldn't help but feel sorry for him. That is, until he paused a moment in the doorway and looked wide-eyed at Gilley to ask, "So you'll call me?"

Gilley stood smugly with his hand on the door handle and all sense of panic gone as he replied, "Of course," and shut the door in Bradley's face.

"That was terrible," I said to him, trying really hard to look serious.

"Welcome to the gay man's one-night stand," he said, stuffing a cinnamon bun into his mouth.

After giving Gilley a short lecture about

his deplorable behavior, I went back to my place to pack enough clothes for a couple of days, get Doc ready for travel, and organize the equipment to load into the van.

Although Bill Murray and his gang needed lots of bells and whistles when they went on a call, true ghostbusting really requires only a couple of gadgets. Night-vision video cameras are neat little devices, but wicked expensive. We'd purchased ours on eBay, and the thing never really worked right. Digital cameras were an absolute must, as most spectral beings love saying, "Cheese!"

In fact, Gilley and I had quite a collection of interesting photographs. We had pictures of orbital lights in all colors, dark shadows, and even one or two transparent portraits where the facial features of the ghost in question show up remarkably well.

For proper ghost hunting one should also have several digital thermometers, voice-activated recorders, laser trip wires, and a good deck of playing cards — though these are used more to cure boredom, as ghost-busting can be a long, dull job at times.

After loading the van I called Steven to confirm our departure time and to slip in the fact that I needed a check to cover expenses. He told me he had to go out and run some errands, but that he'd leave an envelope with my name hidden under the welcome matt and I could pick it up anytime.

I'll admit that I was a little disappointed I wouldn't run into him that morning, then quickly shook that thought from my head and tried to focus on my lips — I mean my job. Yeah . . . my job.

I hit the ATM once I'd retrieved Steven's check and then raced across town to Reese's Camera and Video, where I retrieved our night-vision camera. "Hey, M.J.," Joe, the manager, said.

"How ya been?" I asked him as he placed the video camera on the counter.

"Good now that it's starting to warm up. I thought May would never get here. You and Gilley on another job?"

"Yeah, got one upstate, and I'm going to need this baby. Is she fixed?" I asked, indicating the camera.

"Sort of," he said skeptically.

"That doesn't sound fixed, Joe."

"Hey, it's not my fault, M.J. I think maybe one of them spooks got into your camera or something, because sometimes this thing works great and other times it don't. I've taken it apart and put it back together, and there ain't a thing wrong with it that I can see."

I scowled. "How often does it work right?"

"About every other time I turn it on," Joe said.

"In other words, it's only got a fifty-fifty chance of working?"

"I could sell you another one," he suggested.

"How much?" I asked, crossing my fingers that there was some kind of terrific sale on night-vision video cameras.

"For you? A grand."

"A grand? Are you crazy? I got this one on eBay for half that!"

"And it works half the time, so there you go."

I handed Joe a check for the repair and said, "Thanks, Joe, but I'll take my chances with this one for a little longer."

"We got payment plans, you know," he suggested.

I nodded and picked up my camera. "I'll keep that in mind."

Next I headed to the pet store to pick up some bird food for Doc, then made my way back to my place to see if Gilley had gotten back from the office, where he was doing the research on Steven and following up on a few business leads.

Gil had taken my car while I took the van, and as I pulled into my condo complex I noticed he'd parked it in my slot. Good, he was home. I stopped inside and found him just coming out of his condo with a folder in his hand and his backpack slung over one shoulder. "Hey," he said when he saw me. "I was just about to call you on your cell. You ready to hit the road?"

"We have to wait for Steven," I said, moving down the hall to my own door.

"Did you get the camera from Reese's?" he asked.

"Yes, and it's still not fixed," I groused.

"We really need a new one," Gilley said.

"Then start playing the lotto, Gil, because that's the only way we're going to be able to afford one."

"One of the trip wires is on the fritz too," he added.

"What?" I said, turning to him as we entered my condo.

"And two of the digital thermometers aren't reading accurately."

"How is it that all of our equipment is failing at the same time?" I asked.

"You know how it is with this electronic stuff, M.J.," Gilley said. "They're very sensitive, and when you use them the way we do . . . well, they're not going to last."

Gilley was referring to the fact that many of the poltergeists we encountered screwed around with our equipment. Electricity is one thing that ghosts can control fairly easily, and that means that anything with a circuit board is fair game. "So, how do we operate if we can't even afford the basics?" I asked.

"You could do some readings . . ." Gilley suggested.

I groaned. "Gil, I am so burned out on that stuff. It's emotionally draining, and I don't have the patience for people who refuse to let guilt or anger or bitterness go." Many of the last readings I'd done had been with people who weren't interested in hearing from a specific deceased family member, and often that was the strongest energy coming through. I'd grown tired of trying to convince the living to please forgive the dead and move on. Dead people never hold on to resentment — only the living do that — and it pissed me off that a spirit could work so hard to try to communicate with someone who was deaf to the message.

"I know, M.J., but it is a means to an end. Will you at least consider it?"

"Fine," I said, and handed him Doc's cage while I grabbed my suitcase. "Come on; let's wait for Steven in the van."

Steven arrived less than ten minutes later. He looked freshly showered, dressed in jeans and a white button-down shirt with the cuffs rolled up to mid-wrist. In other words, he looked good enough to eat. "Good afternoon, M.J.," he said to me. "Gilley, good to see you again."

Gilley actually giggled before catching himself. "Steven, good to see you as well."

I cut Gilley a look and noticed that his face was bright red. The boy had a crush. How cute. "So where are we headed?" I asked Steven.

"We'll take the pike west to I-Ninety; then we'll want to take Route Twenty to Route Seven, and finally over to Route Forty-one. You got my directions this morning with the check?"

"I got them," I said, patting the folder under my arm.

"Good. It sounds more difficult than it is. Just pay attention to the signs once you get onto Route Seven toward Uphamshire and you will find it."

"How long will it take us to get there?" I asked.

"Not long — three and a half hours unless you slow me down," he said with a wink.

"Not to worry," I said, narrowing my eyes and turning the key in the ignition. "I've seen you drive. Gilley and I will wait for you at the lodge." And with that I stepped on the gas.

"That wasn't very nice, M.J.," Gilley said.

"Hey, he started it," I snapped. "Besides, while he's off dragging his heels you can tell me what you dug up about his relationship with his father."

"It ain't pretty," Gilley said.

"How bad could it be?"

"Think disownment, and you'd be close," Gilley said as he opened his folder and began to read his notes. "Steven Andrew Jackson Sable — our Steven's father — was slapped with a paternity suit from an Argentinean woman named Rosa Sardonia in nineteen eighty-one. She claimed that she had been his mistress for ten years, and that he fathered her child. Senior denied the claim and fought the suit, refusing to give up his blood for a test, even going so far as to skip the country for a while when it looked like the judge was going to order him to give it up."

"I can't believe he would be such a jerk about it," I said.

"Did I happen to mention that Steven Senior has been married for thirty-five years to a Corrin Wharton?"

"*The* Corrin Wharton of Michael Wharton's Miracle Mile?" I was referring to a woman who was the daughter and sometime spokeswoman of a massive collection of automotive dealerships owned by Michael Wharton, who was himself a New England legend.

"Yep. I found a reference that says she's worth about a half a billion dollars."

I whistled low. "The plot thickens."

"Indeed. And one of the gossip columns I read suggested that Mrs. Wharton-Sable had done a tidy little job of protecting her assets when she married, with a prenup. If Steven Senior divorces her, he gets only a million or so."

"Hence he fled to Europe when things got dicey. She never filed based on all the gossip?"

"No. The same gossip columnist suggested there was a short separation, after which Steven Senior has been kept on a *very* short leash."

"How did the paternity suit end?" I asked, anxious for Gil to finish.

"Ah, yes. I came across a small article which reported that Andrew Sable was not too pleased with his son's behavior and did something dramatic about it."

"What?"

"He offered up his own blood sample, knowing the results would at least show

Steven and Andrew were related if Steven Senior was the father."

"You're kidding," I said, a little shocked that Andrew would go over his son's head like that.

"Nope. And soon afterward a settlement was reached with the mother, Rosa, but it was paid for by Andrew."

"Andrew must have been one hell of a guy," I said.

"Yep," Gilley agreed. "Anyhoo, Rosa wins a sizable chunk of money, and she does the smart thing: She sends Steven to boarding school in Germany, the name of which I couldn't possibly pronounce."

"Germany?"

"Yeah. I looked up the school's curriculum. It's amazing. It's like college for ten-year-olds, and only the smartest kids graduate."

"I'm assuming that means our Steven is a brainiac," I said.

"And then some. He graduates summa cum laude, wins a full scholarship to a top German college with another name I can't pronounce, then goes on to medical school. Again, he's at the top of his class. He interns at some hospital in Berlin and specializes in cardiology. A few years later he and two other doctors invent some sort of gadget that allows surgeons to operate on a beating heart."

My eyes widened. "If they can operate on a beating heart, then they wouldn't need bypass, would they?"

"Bingo. As far as I can tell this gadget hasn't been approved for use in the United States yet, but Boston University has been itching to get Steven here for the past year or so, so that when it is approved they can reap the rewards of having cardiologists from all over the globe come here to learn how to use it."

"The man will be set for life," I said with a little envy. "And how old is he?" I asked, not wanting to sound too interested.

"Thirty-four," Gilley said with a smirk.

"Two years older than me."

"A year and a half — your birthday's next month."

I rolled my eyes at Gilley for splitting hairs. "Thanks for the reminder. Please go on."

Gil continued, "I found some records that show that Steven spent his childhood summers here. Looks like the old man had both Steven and his mother as his personal guests every summer until Steven went to college."

"Where's his mother now?"

"She died two years ago. Cancer."

"And now he's just lost Andrew, the only other family he's known."

"Which is why it's so important for him to get to the bottom of what happened to Andrew," Gilley mused.

"Anything else you could dig up about the father?"

"Lots. For starters, when Steven Senior returned from ducking the paternity suit he tried to have his old man declared incompetent so that he could take over the family fortune."

"Nice," I said sarcastically. "This guy just oozes warm and fuzzy. I'm assuming Andrew was able to thwart that effort?"

"He did one better. He gave power of attorney over to his grandson, then left the bulk of his estate — worth about ten million — to Junior."

"Game over," I said with a smile. "That'll teach Senior."

"The father could still contest the will," Gilley said.

"Yeah, but he runs the risk of having to succumb to another DNA test, and I doubt if Corrin would like to know for sure that her husband fathered someone else's child. For the moment she can float in a world of denial. The press would have a field day with it. Plus she might have forgiven him thirty years ago for his indiscretions, but it could be a whole new ball game this go-around. I don't know that I'd want to risk a divorce if I were him."

"Which explains why he hasn't challenged the will yet. And he's got those nasty IRS agents after him right now, but he does have the best defense team in town going to bat for him. He just hired Lanford and Groman, so he'll probably pay a hefty fine and be on his merry way."

"Did you find out anything on the recent break-ins at Steven's?"

"According to the police blotter a call came in from the alarm company a little over two weeks ago. Someone had broken a bathroom window and was apparently scared off by the alarm. Nothing appeared to have been stolen, and the police were quick to chalk it up to probable teen vandalism."

"Could be," I said. "But what about last night?"

"No one suspicious was seen in the neighborhood, but the incident was referred to the police captain to put a small task force on getting a neighborhood watch program going."

"I am continually amazed at what you're able to dig up," I mused as I looked affectionately over at Gil. "Good job, honey," I added, and Gilley beamed.

Just then from the backseat came a squawk. "Doc's up," Gilley said, and reached into the backseat to undo the door on Doc's cage.

Lifting him out, Gilley gently brought him up front and placed him on my steering wheel. "Hey, doll," I said, giving him a peck on the beak. "Who's a pretty boy?" I sang. "Who's a pretty, pretty boy?"

"Dr. Delicious!" Doc chirped.

"You think so?" I asked as Gilley laughed.

"Dr. Delicious! Get off the friggin' phone!" Doc squawked.

Just then we heard a car horn, and Gil and I turned to our left to see a black Aston Martin zoom past.

"Looks like he's off the phone," Gilley said.

"Great." I scowled. "He'll beat us there." And just to add insult to injury, another car, a gray sedan, zoomed past us as well. I gripped the steering wheel and punched the accelerator, determined to keep up with the good doctor. We trailed three cars behind for a few hours, and I noticed that the gray sedan seemed to be headed in the exact same direction as Sable and us, even through the three highway changes we had to make, but I didn't dwell on it. Finally our gas guzzling van forced us to exit off the highway in search of fuel and I figured I'd lost the race, but as it happened we caught up to Sable about two hours later, with no sign of the gray sedan.

We were cruising on Route 41, per the map that Steven had given us, when we sailed by a diner with a mud-splattered sign advertising, HOT GRINDERS! and we noticed the Aston parked out front.

I looked to Gilley, who read my mind and said, "Yeah, I could eat." Doubling back we cruised into the parking lot and, after securing Doc in his cage, headed inside.

We spotted Steven's profile right away. He was sitting at a table with a plate full of grinder and a beautiful blonde perched on the arm of a chair right across from him as the two giggled and flirted with each other like old chums. I felt my lips tighten and my fists ball just as Gilley said, "Uh-oh."

Turning toward the front counter I snapped, "Let's get that to go."

Silently Gilley followed me to the counter and we waited for someone to help us. After a short wait the beautiful blonde at Steven's table sidled up behind the counter and said, "What can I get for you?"

I looked at her for a beat before saying,

"That's okay. I'm not really hungry," and headed back out to the van. After wrenching open the door and sliding into the seat, I slammed it shut and jammed the key into the ignition. I was about to peel out of the parking lot when I noticed that Gilley wasn't in the van. Momentarily confused, I looked around the lot and saw no sign of him.

I drummed my fingers on the steering wheel for what felt like an eternity, irritated beyond belief that he had obviously stayed behind to order, leaving me to stew alone in the van. With a growl I leaned my head back on the seat and closed my eyes, trying to quell the attitude.

Just about the time I'd chilled, there was a tap on the window, and I opened one eye. Steven stood there with a bag up to the window and a big toothy grin. "Hungry?" he asked.

I rolled down the window and asked, "Where's Gilley?"

"I'm right here," Gilley said as the passenger-side door opened and he got in.

"It's good," Steven sang as he jiggled the to-go bag. "I used to come here as a boy with my grandfather. Best grinders in the world."

"It didn't look like you were eating much

127

in there," I snapped before I could stop myself.

Steven raised an eyebrow. "Really?" he said. "When did you come inside?"

Gilley coughed loudly next to me. "What?" I asked.

"Gilley said you were out in the van. He said you didn't like to experiment with diner food, but I convinced him that this was an exception."

"Ah," I said with a nod. "Yes, that's right. I was waiting out in the van."

"But you said you saw me in there," Steven said, his eyebrow still arched curiously.

"Yes. I had to use the restroom."

"I see," Steven said, a grin on his face that I badly wanted to remove. "Here is your dinner, then. Maybe Gilley can drive while you eat."

"That's okay," I said, taking the bag. "I'll let Gil eat first."

There was another cough next to me and Gil said, "Uh . . . I ate in the diner."

I swiveled my head over to him and narrowed my eyes. *Really?*

"I don't mind driving," Gilley said meekly. "Honest, you should eat, M.J. We've probably got a long night ahead of us."

I stuck out my tongue at him and turned

back to see Steven looking at me expectantly. "Fine," I said, getting out of the van. As I was about to step down, two strong arms encircled my waist.

"Let me help you there," Steven said, lifting me out of the van.

"Thanks," I said quickly, and tried to move past him, though his arms lingered on my waist. "You gonna let me go?" I asked after a moment.

"I am concerned for you," Steven said, his eyes searching my face.

"Really?" I asked, rolling my eyes. "And why would you be concerned?"

"Your face is red," he said, arching a brow. "Perhaps you should ride in my car, where I can keep an eye on you."

"Perhaps I shouldn't," I said, and pushed out of his embrace. When I got back in, Gilley gave me a look. "What?" I asked as I fastened my seat belt.

"Sweetie," he said, shaking his head, "if someone that gorgeous ever wanted me to take a ride in his very cool car, I'd certainly waste no time yelling, 'Shotgun.' "

"Just drive, Gilley," I growled.

"It's amazing you're not still a virgin," he mumbled as he started the van and pulled out after Steven.

We continued down 41 for a while and I

ate my turkey-and-cheese grinder, which was surprisingly good. After finishing the sandwich I watched the scenery glide by and tried to relax. The farther we drove on this stretch of highway, the less traffic we encountered. Houses were becoming sparse, and the woodland was thick on either side of us. The minutes ticked by as I noticed the afternoon sun giving way to dusk.

By the time Steven pulled off the road, the last threads of light were barely streaming across the sky. We saw Steven's car make a right and we followed, entering a long, winding driveway.

We were immediately enveloped by trees on either side of us, which formed a long, dark tunnel. The trees were huge maples, many of them thick, with knotty trunks and low-hanging branches that brushed our car. Finally the trees parted to reveal an enormous lawn. We traveled alongside it, the trees on one side, the lawn on the other, until we came upon the Sable hunting lodge.

As I took in the structure, I would have been the last to call it a "lodge." It looked far more like a castle to me. The house was huge — three full stories with light gray mason walls, a black slate roof, and an imposing wrought-iron gate. A circular driveway looped in front of the building.

Gilley pulled up right behind Steven, and as we got out our mouths hung open in awe. "You like?" Steven said as he came up beside us.

"It's magnificent," Gilley said.

"What's that?" I asked, pointing to a window on the third floor.

"Looks like a television's on," Gilley said, looking to where I was pointing.

"Uh-oh," Steven said.

"What's 'uh-oh'?" I asked.

"Watch for it," he answered cryptically.

We waited a few seconds until suddenly a light flashed in another window. Then another window lit up, then a few more all simultaneously. Despite my experience, I'd never seen anything like this, and I felt the hair on my arms stand up on end.

"Whoa," Gilley said, gulping as he gripped my arm. "That's spooky."

"When I first inherited this house, I hired a local woman to help . . . eh . . . inventory my grandfather's things. The day after she started she called and said she would not be returning because the televisions kept turning on by themselves."

"We've seen something similar in the past," Gilley said, and I knew he was referring to a house we did in Bellingham where a radio in the kitchen kept turning on by itself. "But never so many devices all at once."

I counted each flickering light and asked, "How many TVs are in the house?"

"If I remember correctly, there are twelve."

"I count eleven," I said, and just then, as if on cue, another light flickered on at the ground-floor level off to my right. "Okay, all twelve are working and accounted for. Come on, guys; let's go save some electricity."

I turned back to the van and pulled open the door. Grabbing my backpack and my duffel bag full of equipment, I marched up the steps. Gilley and Steven followed me, Gilley looking rather pale. After fiddling with his keys, Steven unlocked the door.

As the door swung open, the first thing to hit us was the sound of twelve televisions turned up full blast all throughout the house. The odd thing was, they all seemed to be on the same channel, something to do with bass fishing. I set the duffel and my backpack down and motioned with my head toward my right. Gilley and Steven followed me as I headed toward the nearest blaring set.

Flipping on a few lights as I went, we made our way to the kitchen to turn off the first TV. To be sure, I also unplugged it, then turned to Gilley and Steven and said, "It might be best if we split up and turn each set off. I'll take the ground floor; Gil, you take the second; and Steven, why don't you take the third and fourth. I only noticed one TV the top floor anyway."

"Split up?" Gilley said anxiously. "Do you think that's wise, M.J.?"

I blinked at him. "What do you mean, do I think it's wise?"

"Could be dangerous," Steven said, and I noticed he'd gone a little white too. "For you," he added quickly as his eyes darted around the kitchen. "I would hate to think of something happening to you as a guest in my house."

"I see," I said. "So, you think it's better if we stay together in an empty house and take three times as long to turn off all the televisions?"

"Well, he's got a point, M.J. It *could* be dangerous," Gilley said anxiously, looking with longing toward the van outside.

I scowled at the two of them. This was exactly why I didn't want Steven along in the first place. "Fine, gentlemen. Come along then. Let's turn the sets off so we can focus on your grandfather, Steven."

We moved from room to room searching out the televisions as Steven navigated the house for us. In a way it did work out, because the place had a gazillion rooms and one of us was bound to get lost.

When the last set was turned off and unplugged I said, "That does it! Now we can get to our baseline test and get the equipment set up and —" I was cut off by a noise that sounded like a loud motor coming from downstairs. We looked at one another quizzically, listening.

"What *is* that?" Gilley said.

"I don't know," Steven answered, moving out of the room. We followed him to the staircase and listened again. We could hear voices talking over the motor, and it grew louder, as if it were amplified and coming closer. And suddenly we knew what the noise was, just as it started coming out of the room we had just vacated.

"That's impossible," Steven whispered, and we turned back to the room, where a TV was blaring at full volume. On the screen two men drove a boat and discussed casting techniques. Even more unsettling, the television's plug was out of the electrical socket and sitting on the floor.

"M.J.," Gilley whined. "Do something!"

"What exactly would you like me to do, Gil?" I asked him. I'd never seen anything like this before. "It's not like I can just snap my fingers and —" I stopped. Just as I'd actually snapped my fingers, every set seemed to have shut off. We all looked at one another, listening for any sign that a set was still on somewhere in the house. "Shit," I whispered. "This is going to be a tricky bust."

"I don't think I like this," Gilley whined, moving closer to me and reaching out to snag my jacket as if I might leave his side.

"Perhaps we should go to a hotel for the night and come back in the morning?" Steven suggested. "I mean," he added, clearing his throat, "you two must be very tired from the trip."

"Great idea!" Gilley said, letting go of my jacket and dashing out of the room. "Come on, M.J.! Let's go get some rest!" And with that he bolted down the stairs.

Steven smiled at me, then went after Gilley. I had no choice but to follow them. By the time I'd made it downstairs, Gilley and Steven had grabbed all of the equipment and my backpack and were lugging it out to the van. Faster than you can say, "Boo!" they had it tossed in and were ready to roll. "Guys," I said, trying to slow them down, "I think we should stay."

Gilley looked at me to see if I was serious, then made a huge show of stretching his

135

arms wide above his head and yawning. "Man! I am beat! That was a much longer car ride than I expected. I don't think I could possibly stay up tonight to help you. I think we should come back tomorrow."

"I don't want you to think you need to work through the night," Steven added. "I'm not a . . . how do you say . . . driver of slaves. If Gilley's tired, I think it would be better to come back in the morning."

Just then the whole house lit up and the noise of twelve televisions could be heard blaring from inside. Gilley didn't wait for me to try to talk him into it; he simply jumped in the van and started the engine. Steven turned away from the house and moved to his car in a half walk, half jog. I rolled my eyes, took one last look at the house, and mumbled, "Fine."

CHAPTER 5

Steven led the way to town, about ten miles back from the way we'd come. A sign welcomed us to Uphamshire, population 4,056. Steven parked in front of a two-story Victorian, and we waited while he got out and walked up to Gilley's window. "We should stay here tonight," he said.

"Where are we?" I asked, peeking out at the house.

"Helen's Bed-and-Breakfast. She's an old friend of my grandfather. You two wait here while I make the arrangements." Gilley nodded agreeably, and Steven headed inside.

When he was out of earshot I gave Gilley a small whap on the shoulder. "We should have stayed, Gil."

"M.J.," Gilley began, "you know what my job is. I'm a van man. It was your idea to get me to go inside and help out, so you have only yourself to blame."

"Whose idea was it to allow Steven

along?" I retorted.

"Oh, come on!" Gilley insisted. "Those TVs were freaking me out!"

"They can't hurt you, and you know it," I insisted. "Geez, Gil! If I'd known you were going to act like a sissy girl, I would have come alone."

"I wasn't the only one who fled the premises," Gilley groused. "Your Dr. Delicious bolted too."

"He's not *my* Dr. Delicious," I snapped.

"Whatever," Gil said, turning away from me as he muttered, "Please let there be a minibar in the room."

We waited in silence for the next ten minutes until Steven came trotting out. "I've gotten us a couple of rooms. Helen is preparing them now, and they will be ready in about a half hour. Anyone up for a drink?"

"I am!" Gilley said.

"Great," Steven said, not waiting for me to answer. "There's a bar within walking distance. We can leave the cars here."

Gilley was out of the car in a flash. "Let's go!" he said happily.

I sat for a minute and debated going for a drink with the two of them or sitting it out in the van. "M.J.?" Steven said when he noticed I hadn't gotten out of the van. "You are following?"

I sighed, looked at Doc, who had his head tucked under his wing and was fast asleep, and decided maybe a drink wasn't such a bad idea. "Yeah," I said.

With Steven leading the way, we walked to a bar just down the street called Down the Hatch. "Quaint," I said as I read the sign.

"Not on the inside," Steven countered. He was right. Inside the place was definitely a dive bar, with wood-paneled walls, dirty floors, and the smell of grease and old beer hanging in the air.

We found a booth and settled in. Steven flagged a waitress, and, after we gave her our order, I scoped out the place while Gilley and Steven struck up a conversation. I didn't join in on their banter. I was still a little miffed at Gilley for bolting so quickly. We had a reputation to protect, and if word got out that one-half of our team was a big fat chicken, then our referral business could be in jeopardy.

My eyes wandered around the bar from patron to patron, taking in the locals, when I felt a thud against my energy.

The way I'm able to pick up the presence of someone who has crossed over is by feeling a sense of pressure against my energy.

Think of it as if your eyes were closed and you felt someone invade your personal space. For me the feeling is a hundred times more pronounced, and there's no way to turn away from it once it happens.

When I feel this, I have two choices: I can acknowledge the energy and strike up a telepathic conversation with it, or I can ignore it and hope it goes away. I tried the latter route, as all I wanted to do was have a drink, head back to the B and B, and do a face plant into a pillow, but the energy thumping against mine wasn't having any of it.

Finally, after taking a sip of my cranberry and vodka, I opened up and thought, *I am open. What is it you need to say to me?*

Immediately I felt a powerful shattering sensation around my chest. My eye was drawn to the doorway and a dark stain imbedded in the wood floor. Getting up from the table I walked over to get a better look, and when I came close to the stain I saw in my mind's eye the body of a man lying on the floor.

Coming back to the table where Gilley and Steven were both watching me warily, I asked, "Who was the young man murdered over there?"

"What?" Steven asked as he looked from

me to where I was pointing.

"There was a young man murdered in that doorway. He says someone shot him."

"You're telling me this place is haunted too?" Steven asked, his eyes large.

"Get used to it," Gilley explained. "Any structure older than fifty years usually has something walking around inside of it."

"I have never heard of a murder here," Steven said.

"His name begins with an L," I said, still conversing with the young man. "Larry, like the Three Stooges."

"He's talking about the Three Stooges?" Steven asked me.

"You know them?"

"Of course. I have watched them in both Argentina and Germany. They are very funny men."

"I think so too!" Gilley said with a dreamy look at Steven.

"As I was saying," I said, wanting to pull them back to the murder here at the bar. "If he's able to reference the Three Stooges then that would give us a time frame of within the last seventy-five years or so."

Steven got up suddenly and headed over to the bar. We watched as he motioned for the bartender and spoke to him briefly while pointing to our table. The bartender nodded and headed into the back. Steven then returned to our table and said, "The owner's a guy named Chris. His family has owned this place for fifty years."

A minute later a short and extremely rotund man with white hair and pronounced jowls waddled over to us. He looked like one of the Weebles I had when I was a kid. Stopping at our table he said, "Good to see you back in town, Dr. Sable. Jeb said you wanted to ask me about the history of this place?"

The thud against my energy increased tenfold, and I blurted out, "Who was killed over there?"

Chris's milky eyes swiveled to me. "Excuse me?"

"That old stain on the floor," I said, pointing to it. "Someone named Larry was shot over there, wasn't he?"

"You a reporter?" he snapped, suddenly defensive.

"No," I answered. "I'm a medium."

"I don't care about your size, honey. How do you know about Larry?"

I smiled. "I wasn't referring to my size. I'm the kind of person who talks to dead people, and right now this guy Larry is saying he was shot in your doorway."

Chris's jaw dropped slightly, and he

looked from me back to Sable. He barked, "This some kind of joke?"

"No, this is no joke. I have seen it for myself. She really can talk to the dead."

Chris waited a moment, perhaps to see if any of us would burst out laughing at the prank we were pulling. Larry buzzed in with another message. "Larry says you've been talking about putting in a new floor, but it won't help. You'll always see a stain over there," I said, pointing with emphasis back to the bloodstain.

Chris looked to where I pointed, then narrowed his eyes at me. I looked him straight in the eye, my expression calm but serious. After a moment he seemed to make up his mind and turned away from our table to waddle a few steps and drag a chair back to us before taking his seat.

"That was over forty-five years ago," he began. "My dad had just bought this place. There was this group of young punks in town, good-for-nothin's. They had been causing a lot of trouble for the local businesses, smashing windows, breaking and entering. They'd rob you blind, then go that one step further and trash up the place. Back then, not a lot of people carried insurance, so it was even harder to recover from something like that. A few folks even went out of business.

"The police weren't much help; our sheriff had been injured in WW Two, and he was useless. My dad knew it was just a matter of time before the gang targeted him, so he spread the word that he wasn't going to let the punks get away with it. He and I camped out every night for a whole week with our hunting rifles, taking turns on watch as we waited for them to strike. Sure enough, one night the gang broke a window and three of 'em piled in."

Larry had stopped banging on my energy. It seemed he was listening to Chris too.

"There were only three?" Gilley asked.

"Yeah," Chris said. "We learned later that they called themselves the Stooges. I guess they were big fans of Larry, Moe, and Curly."

Steven looked sharply at me and mouthed, *Whoa.*

I winked at him as Chris continued. "Dad and I watched from behind the bar as they came in and were about to trash the place. Then Dad yelled, 'Freeze!' and they did for a second, but then one of them picked up a chair and tossed it at us. We ducked and came up shooting. I was so scared; I mean, I was only about nineteen at the time."

"And Larry was killed," I said.

"Yeah. When the dust settled one was injured, the other had run off, and the third was dead on the floor, right where you pointed. To this day I'm not sure if it was my bullet that killed him," Chris said sadly.

Larry buzzed a thought into my head. The message had a sense of urgency. "Larry says he's sorry, Chris."

"So he's really here? You can hear him, for real?"

"I can," I said. "He keeps repeating, 'Tell him I'm sorry,' over and over. I think that's the reason he's been hanging out, refusing to cross over. He wants to apologize."

"Please tell him I said all's forgiven, and I'm sorry for the way it worked out."

I felt Larry's energy begin to recede — he'd heard. "He's stepping back," I said. Before Larry had a chance to completely disconnect from me, I encouraged him to leave this dimension. "He's gone," I said when he severed the connection.

"This is some friend you've got here, Steven," Chris said.

"She's been one surprise after another," Steven replied.

I felt my cheeks grow hot. "It's nothing," I said.

"Sorry about your granddaddy, by the way," Chris said to Steven, then added,

"Say, you should have your friend see if she can talk to him."

Steven gave a wink to me. "That's the plan."

"You on your way to the lodge?" Chris asked.

"We just came from there," Gilley answered.

"Oh? Felt the need to check out the town while you're at it, then?" Chris again.

"Actually," Steven said as he swirled his drink, "we're staying at Helen's for the night. There have been some rather . . . uh . . . unusual things going on at my grandfather's which we plan to investigate in the daylight."

"Yeah?" said Chris, motioning to one of his waitresses. After she brought him a draft, which he took a huge swig of, he continued, "I heard there've been some weird lights and noises coming from the house ever since Andrew died, and I know Maria gave you her notice. She get spooked and quit?"

"The housekeeper?" Gilley asked. I smirked, because the only way Gil could have known that was by eavesdropping on the conversation I'd had "privately" with Steven in my office.

Steven nodded at Gilley and answered

146

Chris. "I'm not sure it was that. She told me that now that she had her retirement fund, and there was no one to look after at the house, she was better off moving in with her sister closer to town."

Chris chugged the last of his draft like water, giving me a good indication of where his significant girth came from. "Well, I better get back to work. Your tab's on the house, Steven. And thanks to you, miss. That was quite a performance."

I smiled at him, knowing he'd probably felt guilty about Larry's death for decades. "Anytime, and thanks for the drinks."

After Chris had gone, Steven said, "Come on, it's getting late, and I'm thinking Miss Holliday will want to get an early start."

"Miss Holliday wanted to get started earlier, but was hampered by her two fleeing accomplices," I said with a chuckle; then I got serious. "Listen, fellas," I said to Steven and Gilley. "If we're going to do this, I need your solemn vow that no matter what happens, we're not leaving until we've done our best to make contact with Andrew. Deal?"

"Deal," Steven said firmly.

Gilley fiddled with the zipper of his jacket for a moment until I poked him; then he finally gave in. "Yeah, okay. But I still reserve the right to head to the van and monitor the equipment if things get too dicey."

I sighed, patting Gilley on the back, and settled for that.

The next morning I came downstairs with Doc on my shoulder and was greeted by a tall, rather plump woman who looked to be in her late fifties, with tight, curly blond hair and smooth, creamy skin. "Good morning!" she said cheerfully. "I'm Helen Scottsdale, the proprietor."

"Nice to meet you," I said as I shook her hand and introduced myself. Doc gave a whistle and cocked his head.

"Oh, what a pretty bird," she said, noting Doc.

"Doc's delicious!" he chirped. "Doc's a pretty, pretty bird!"

"Parrots," I said with a chuckle. "They have such big egos."

Helen giggled. "Steven's in the dining room. There's scrambled eggs, bacon, and toast. Would your bird like some fruit?"

"Doc's a pretty bird!" Doc said, bobbing his head.

"One order of fruit for the Froot Loop," I quipped, giving Doc a playful tug on his tail. He turned in a circle on my shoulder to show me he was all that and a bag of chips.

I headed into the dining room and found Steven seated at the head of the table reading a paper. "Morning," I said as I took my seat.

He looked over the top of the paper and said, "Good morning, M.J. Did you rest well?"

"Not really," I said honestly. "It's hard for me in strange places."

"Hard for you?"

I took a scoopful of eggs from a dish in the center of the table before explaining. "Let's just say I'm like a pay phone, and on the other side pay phones like me are really rare. So when I show up in a neighborhood, there's a line of people waiting to make a call."

Steven set the paper down completely. "I don't think I am understanding this pay phone analog."

"*Analogy,*" I corrected, and took a bite of eggs as I thought about how to better describe my struggle to get some sleep. "Helen's deceased relatives all wanted to talk to her last night. As if they were trying through me to make a long-distance phone call. They were all fighting to be heard, from a woman named Betty or

Betsy, who I think is Helen's mother, to a brother figure named Brian. And some guy named Arnold was truly obnoxious. He would *not* let me sleep. He kept going on and on about going to the lake, and he didn't know it would happen while he was on his fishing trip. Whatever that means."

As I finished that sentence there was a loud crash from behind me and Steven; we jumped at the noise. I turned in my chair and saw Helen standing there, a shocked expression on her face, and a shattered plate that had held fruit for Doc on the floor. "Did you say Arnold?" she asked breathlessly.

"Uh . . ." I said, looking at Steven. I hadn't realized she was right behind me. "Yes. Did Steven tell you that I can hear people who've died?"

"He mentioned it," she said as she bent over to pick up the pieces of porcelain. I set Doc on the arm of my chair and came over to help her.

"I'm sorry," I said as I bent beside her. "I'm not the most sensitive person sometimes."

"No, that's fine," she said quickly, and I noticed her hands were shaking. "But could I just ask you . . . what did Arnold say again?"

I met her eyes — there was something there that clearly tormented her — and without warning I felt Arnold come thumping into my energy. I got up holding some of the porcelain and fruit, and she stood too. "He says that he never would have gone to the lake if he'd known something was coming soon. He says he never should have left you alone."

A tear formed in Helen's eye and slid down her cheek. She gulped and turned away into the kitchen, and I stood there stupidly for a beat or two, still holding the broken plate and fruit. Steven came up behind me and held out his hands. "Give me those," he said gently, and I handed him the shards. He followed after Helen as I went back to my seat feeling totally ashamed of myself. Me and my big mouth. "Good job, M.J.," I said, swirling the eggs around on my plate.

"Good job at what?" Gilley asked as he took up a chair across from me.

"Nothing," I said dismissively. "Just making an ass of myself."

"Again?" he quipped. "I would have thought you'd had enough of that by now."

"Gee, Gil, gonna take that comedy routine on the road anytime soon?" I snapped.

"Hey," Gilley said, becoming serious. "M.J., don't be like that. I thought we were making fun. What happened?"

Before I got a chance to answer, Steven came back into the room. Taking his seat, he put his hand over mine and said, "She's fine. Just taken by surprise. Arnold was her late husband. When she was pregnant with their son, he went to the lake to do some fishing and Helen went into early labor. A neighbor took her to the hospital and word finally made its way out to Arnold. While he was rushing back he lost control of his car and was killed."

"That's terrible," I said. No wonder Arnold was bombarding me. I'd have been doing the same thing. "I feel like crap. I had no idea she was behind me."

"No harm, no foul ball, M.J.," he said to me, and gave my hand a squeeze.

I smiled at his blunder as from behind us we heard a sniffle, and Helen came back into the room carrying a fresh plate of fruit for Doc. "Sorry about that," she said, setting the plate down in front of him. "It was just a shock. . . ." Her voice trailed off. She gave me a small pat on my shoulder and hurried out of the room.

"*What* did you say to her?" Gilley asked.

Before I had a chance to respond, Steven

cut in. "What's the plan for attacking today?"

Gil flashed me a grin, and I was grateful for the change of subject. "The plan of attack is this," I said confidently. "The first thing I think we should do is remove all of the televisions from the house. Normally, I'd prefer to keep them to monitor the ghost's movements from floor to floor, but with so many for him to play with, I think it could get a bit chaotic."

"Good," Steven said with a nod. "Then what?"

"Then Gilley and I will need to do a baseline test."

"What is this baseline test?"

"We record the dimensions, temperature, layout, and electromagnetic energy in every room of the house."

"What is that for?" Steven asked.

"So that we can monitor changes throughout the day. A sudden drop or increase in temperature can indicate a ghost is afoot," I explained. "We also put some trigger objects in those rooms we think are most active — and before you ask, a trigger object is something that can be easily moved by a spirit and may attract their curiosity. We use things like a small dish of sand, or a house of cards, or a book stood on end. We know we've got spectral activity when one of these objects has been moved or shows signs of being tampered with," I explained.

"We'll also need to take a digital photograph of each room," Gilley said.

"I know I sound repeating," Steven said with a grin. "But why?"

"We'll be looking for orbs, corkscrews, vortexes, and sparks," Gilley said, and just as Steven opened his mouth to ask for another clarification he said, "Orbs are small balls of light that are the easiest form a ghost can take. Corkscrews are swirling bands of light, indicative of a ghost or spirit coming in from another dimension to ours. Vortexes are the portals spirits travel through when they go from this dimension to the other."

"Yes, M.J. told me of these portals earlier. Do you think my grandfather is using one?" I knew why he looked worried. I had told him that only bad energies needed them.

"No, I don't think he's using one. But there may be another energy in the house, and we definitely want to clear the lodge of all grounded spirits, both good and bad."

"If my colleagues back in Germany could see me having this conversation," he said as he shook his head. "I am afraid they would pull my medical license."

I smiled. "It can be a little surreal. That is, until you've experienced what I have."

"You two ready to get going?" Gilley said, wiping his mouth and scooting back his chair.

"Ready," I said, standing up and taking Doc off the arm of the chair. "Do you think someone should check on Helen?" I asked.

"I think it's best to leave her alone for now. I'll call later and make sure she's okay," Steven said.

We decided to leave Doc at the B and B, thinking that with a mischievous and energetic poltergeist loose it might make sense to keep him tucked away at the inn. Twenty minutes later we'd made it back to the Sable hunting lodge without incident. Gilley drove with a white-knuckled grip on the wheel as we came down the long driveway. "You sure you're up to this?" I asked him seriously.

"Yeah," he said grimly. "But I'm still reserving the right to head to the van if things get too freaky."

I laughed and gave him a pat on the back. "Poor Gil. Look what having a crush on an unavailable man has brought you to."

"Say what?" he said, cutting me a look.

"Dr. Delicious. You have a crush."

"No, not that," Gil said. "I was asking about the unavailable part."

I laughed at the serious look on his face. "He's straight, buddy."

"He's European; it's the same as being gay."

"He's *Latin*," I said.

"Oh, I stand *corrected,* he's not gay . . . he's bi."

"Whatever you need to tell yourself, honey," I said, surrendering.

We parked the van behind Steven again and got out to unload. Once we had all of the equipment piled onto the front steps, Steven opened the front door. The three of us walked in, listening intently for the sound of a blaring TV. We were met with only silence, so I turned and began to bring in the equipment. Gil and Steven joined me, though more than once I caught them pausing to listen again.

"Televisions?" Gilley asked once we'd hauled in all our stuff.

Nodding, I turned to Steven. "Is there someplace we can store the TVs so they won't get damaged?"

"There's a wine cellar below the kitchen. They should be okay down there."

I motioned with my hand in an *after you* gesture, and we began with the nearest TVs on the ground floor. While we worked I got a chance to scope out the place in the daylight. It was incredibly impressive for a "hunting lodge." I counted fourteen rooms on the main floor alone, complete with gourmet-sized kitchen, drawing room, solarium, library, formal dining room, sun-room, and indoor pool. The furnishings were opulent, mostly French antiques, and suited the place well.

As Gilley and Steven carefully took the first TV to the wine cellar, I had a moment to myself in the kitchen. Testing the sur-roundings for spiritual energy, I closed my eyes and sent out my radar. I got a hit right away, but it was elusive. Male energy. Older. A sense of confusion seemed to surround him, and then I felt it drift away. I opened my eyes and looked out the window. The view over the sink showed the grounds, and to the right, the side of the indoor pool's wall extended out from the house.

My intuition was drawn to that area; in fact, I felt a great sense of urgency to go there. Looking left I saw a door that led outside. "Guys?" I called down the stairs. "I'll be right back." I headed out the door.

Outside I held my hand up to block the sun — I'd left my sunglasses inside. I blinked a few times and followed my intuitive instinct, stopping in front of the far wall of the indoor pool. I bent down and touched the ground, which was covered with leaves and debris. In my mind's eye I saw a rake, and smiled. Yeah, this spot definitely needed a little attention. Standing up, I couldn't understand why I'd been tugged out here to this spot, so I looked around. Maybe I'd gotten it wrong?

Behind me was a short lawn before thick woods, which spanned as far as the eye could see. I felt compelled to go to the woods, but decided I'd better wait until after we'd done our baseline test. I turned back toward the house just as I felt another, much stronger pull to my right, and paused for a moment to assess that pull on my energy. When a spirit wants me to go in a certain direction, I often feel a sense of being tugged right or left. The more forceful the tugging feeling, the more urgently the spirit wants to get my attention.

This particular pull was incredibly intense, much stronger than to the woods or by the pool. Curious, I followed the tug and ended up in front of a large window. Peering through the window, I could see that I was next to the library. I stepped away and felt another tug, this one straight up. I put my hand on my brow again to shield my eyes from the bright sun and looked up. Something caught my attention in a window on the third floor. I could have sworn I saw a curtain move. I backed up and kept staring at the window. It didn't look open, so no breeze should have ruffled the curtain. Then, one floor below it, I saw one of the sheer curtains give a distinct swish of movement, followed by a dark, shadowy figure passing behind it.

"M.J.!" Gilley called, and I jumped.

"What?" I asked as I tore my gaze away from the window to see Steven and Gilley standing by the kitchen door.

"What's up?" Gil said.

"I thought I saw something up there," I said, pointing to the window. "Steven, whose bedroom is that?"

He took a moment to answer, a look of shock on his face. Finally he said, "That is my grandfather's bedroom. And that spot you're standing on is right where they found my grandfather's body."

I moved over in spite of myself. Steven and Gilley walked over, and the three of us looked from the ground back up to the bedroom.

"I thought your grandfather fell from the third story," Gilley said.

"He did. His shoe was found on the ledge

just above his bedroom, and the window was open from that bedroom," Steven said, pointing to the bedroom directly over Andrew's room.

"Weird," I said as my eyes moved back up to the window above Andrew's. "I could have sworn I saw movement up there, too."

"You saw someone?" Steven asked me.

I shrugged my shoulders. "I saw some-*thing*. Not sure what, at this point."

Gilley said, "What did you see?"

"I saw the curtain move first on the third floor, then on the second, and then a dark shadow passed in front of your grandfather's bedroom window. My guess is that either someone's in your house or it's Andrew making his presence known."

Turning toward the house, Steven said, "Only one way to find out."

We followed Steven back inside and through the maze of rooms to the front staircase. Climbing the stairs, we made our way to the second floor. "I can't believe your grandfather took all these stairs," Gilley said as he puffed his way up.

"There's an elevator leading from the kitchen to his suite."

"Well, why didn't we take the elevator?" Gilley complained.

"It takes forever and makes a horrible

160

racket." Just as Steven finished we heard it for ourselves, as a loud clanging noise came from a room at the end of the hallway on the second floor.

We ran to the room just as the elevator doors closed. "Come on; it's headed back to the kitchen!" Steven said, and raced back out of the room. We chased after him at full tilt down the stairs as we tried to beat the elevator. As we ran we could still faintly hear the racket of the elevator as it groaned down. Panting fiercely, we reached the landing and ran back to the kitchen just as the elevator came to a stop.

Steven halted in front of the elevator, holding an arm out across my stomach in a protective motion. Gilley came up on his other side and we braced ourselves as the doors slowly opened.

CHAPTER 6

With a terrific groaning sound the twin doors separated while I prepared myself for battle against any nasty poltergeist. As the opening became larger my eyes darted about the interior, looking for anything that could jump out at us, but when the doors finally stopped moving we all stared at an empty interior. Gilley blew out the breath he'd been holding, "Ohmigod! That is so weird!"

Steven stepped forward into the elevator. I saw him shiver and asked, "What?"

"It is like ice in here," he said, and turned in a circle with his arms outstretched.

Gilley whipped a digital thermometer out of his back pocket and turned it on. He extended his arm into the elevator and read the gauge. "He's right," he said, moving the thermometer in and out of the elevator. "Fifty-two degrees inside the boxcar," he announced, then took two steps back and reset the gauge. "And seventy-four out here. Definite poltergeist activity," he said, setting his jaw.

"We can't assume anything yet, Gil," I cautioned, and just as I said this I saw Steven wobble a little inside the elevator. "Steven?" I asked, stepping toward him. I watched as his eyes rolled back slightly in his head and he took an unsteady step back against the boxcar. "Shit!" I swore, and rushed to his side, catching him around the waist as his knees buckled and the icy cold hit me.

"I feel weird," Steven said weakly, and put his hand to his head.

"Help me!" I said to Gilley. "We need to get him outside, *now!*"

"What's happening to him?" Gilley asked as he ran to the other side of Steven and we began to move him out of the elevator.

"He's absorbing too much energy — he could black out any second if we're not quick!" I yelled.

We managed to get Steven outside, which was no mean feat, since the man was substantially taller than both of us. Once out on the lawn we eased him down to a sitting position, and I quickly straddled his legs and grabbed his head, which seemed to be bobbing around on his shoulders. "Steven!"

I commanded in a stern voice as I looked into his unfocused eyes. "Listen to me! You've absorbed some of the energy in the elevator. You need to listen to my voice and mentally come to it. Do you understand?"

"Mmm . . . uhmmm . . . mmmm?" Steven mumbled incoherently.

"What's wrong with him?" Gilley asked me in a high-pitched voice.

"I think that was his grandfather in the elevator, and I think he just came in from the mist. Steven's absorbed some of that residual energy, and he's feeling really spacey right now. In a minute he'll either lose consciousness or come back to us and start to feel nauseous."

Gilley edged back ever so slightly. "What do we do?"

"Try to talk him back. Buddy, can you get me some water from inside?"

"You want me to go back in there . . . *alone?*" he asked me, his voice still squeaky.

"Damn it, Gil! Get me some friggin' water!" I snapped impatiently.

"Okay, okay," Gil said, and jumped up to head toward the house.

I continued to hold Steven's head in my hands as I talked to him. "Steven," I said, "you must hear me. I need for you to mentally come forward to my voice. Think about the words that I'm saying. Try to make sense of them. I need you to feel the sunshine over your head and the ground you're sitting on. Here," I said, taking one hand off his face to place his palm on the ground. "Do you feel the texture of the grass? Can you smell the flowers close by? Really try to sense those things for me, okay?" Steven mumbled again, but after a few blinks I could see his eyes begin to focus. "That's it," I said. "You're doing great. There's a breeze. Can you feel that? And there are birds; do you hear them?"

Steven gave me a tiny nod.

"Good job; you're doing great. Just keep focusing on my voice, and feel everything around you."

"Here's the water," Gil said quietly from my side.

"Thanks, honey," I said softly to him, feeling bad about snapping.

"What else can I do?"

"He's coming back on his own, but it won't hurt to rub his hands and feet."

"I'm on it," Gil said, and quickly moved to take off Steven's shoes.

A few minutes later Steven seemed to be just about back to normal. "That was terrible," he said, holding his stomach. "I feel awful."

"Give it a little time yet," I coaxed. "The nausea will pass in a minute."

"What happened to me?"

"The elevator probably contained a great deal of your grandfather's energy. It's a small, confined space that can fill up quickly. So when you went rushing in there you absorbed a lot of it, and your grandfather had just come in from the mist, or that middle plane. So when you soaked up that energy you would have felt like you, yourself, were going to that plane."

Steven looked at Gil. "I must be woozy — I can't understand a thing she's saying."

"You're not alone," Gil said with a wink to me.

"In other words, Steven, you probably felt like you were fading right out of your body," I clarified.

Steven nodded. "Yes," he said. "That is a very good way to say what I felt. It was like a balloon. I was feeling like a balloon drifting away."

"Exactly. Now try to take a sip of the water."

He did and then looked down at his feet, where my partner was giving him one hell of a foot massage. "Gilley," he said with a slight wave. "That is feeling very good, but I think you can stop now."

Gil flushed slightly. "Just doing my duty," he said with a smile.

"I feel better," Steven said after another minute. "The sickness has passed. Why did I feel that?"

"No one really knows for sure. But a lot of people who have your experience often feel sick to their stomachs for a short period afterward."

"Will this happen to me again?" Steven asked.

"There's a trick that you can do the moment you feel that frosty, in-your-bones cold. Just imagine that your legs are like the trunk of a giant tree and that your roots go deeply into the ground. The term is called 'grounding,' and it works very well for keeping you firmly in your body."

"I shall do this from now on," Steven said, and took another sip of water.

"Can you stand?" I asked.

"Yes," Steven said, getting to his feet. "I actually feel fine now."

"Great, but I still think you should take it easy for a little while." I looked over at Gilley and said, "Come on, Gil. We've been off protocol since we started this thing. Let's get the rest of the TVs into the wine cellar and get to the baseline ASAP."

For the next half hour Gil and I focused

on moving the televisions into the wine cellar as Steven looked on. I worried as we took a very large flat-screen down the stairs that there wouldn't be enough room, but as we came down the steps I could see it was a much bigger space than I'd anticipated. "Wow," I said as we set the television down against a back wall. "This is huge."

"My grandfather loved fine wine," Steven said, following us down. "In his later years, some of his medications prevented him from drinking any, so he gave much of his collection away to his good friends."

I walked over to a rack that still held a few bottles. "I see he kept the best for himself."

"Actually, those are wines from Argentina and Germany. My grandfather liked me to feel at home when I visited."

"Ah," I said, and set the bottle down, looked off to my right, and noticed three steps down leading to a closed door. "Where does that go?" I asked. Steven came over to my side. "I don't know," he mused. "I think it leads to more storage."

"Oh, my aching back," Gilley whined behind us. "How many more of these things are there?"

"Three," Steven said, turning away from the door and heading up the stairs. "And only two are as heavy as that one."

"Remind me next time to stay home and do paperwork," Gilley grumbled, and followed after Steven.

I stayed behind for a moment, gazing at the door. I suddenly felt as if I were missing something.

"M.J.?" Gilley called from the kitchen.

"Coming!" I said, and turned away from the door. I'd worry about it after the baseline.

It took us the rest of the day to get the baseline test done. We broke for a quick lunch of canned soup, then went back to work, mapping out each room and taking measurements. For all my protests at having Steven along, I was actually grateful for a distraction from my constantly complaining partner. Gilley definitely wasn't cut out for this kind of job. He was used to sitting in his van and jotting down the measurements I called out to him over the walkie-talkie. Our baselines usually took an hour or two, due to the normal-sized houses we worked on.

By contrast, the Sable lodge, or "the Manse," as Gil had come to call it, held thirty-seven rooms not including the cellar. Dusk was beginning to settle as we finished up on the third floor. Wanting to concentrate solely on the baseline, I had avoided opening my energy to any tugs, pushes, pulls, or thumps, though I'd certainly been jerked around in several rooms. Andrew's bedroom was the strongest, along with one of the guest bedrooms, but I'd also felt a few tickles in the solarium and the library.

"That's everything," Gilley said, finishing the last measurement. "Can we go eat now?"

"I think we must," Steven said to him. "By the number of times you've asked about food, you may need a shot of insulin if we don't feed you soon."

"I happen to be hypoglycemic," Gilley said defensively.

"Should we eat here?" I asked.

"No, we should not. There is a wonderful place in town that I'm quite fond of. Is it all right to leave the equipment here, or should we pack it?"

"Let's leave it. I can haul in two of the monitors from the van to record any weird activity while we're at dinner." As if on cue, the lights in the room flickered on.

"Whoa," Gil said, as we all looked at the light fixture over our heads. "Come on," he said, tucking a pencil behind his ear. "Let's get the monitors hooked up before we miss anything."

We had the monitors moved inside and

the DVR set to record about twenty minutes later, just as the last threads of dusk were coating the sky with shades of purple. Gilley and I got in the van, and Steven came to my window before getting in his Aston. "Will you need to check on your bird before we go to the restaurant?"

I smiled at his thoughtfulness. "No, thank you. Doc's got plenty of food and water, and I put him in front of a window, so he should have plenty to look at. He's fast asleep by now, anyway."

"Okay, then, just follow me."

We drove behind him back through town to the west side, opposite Helen's B and B, and pulled into a driveway at Annie's Steakhouse. Gilley parked, and we got out to catch up with Steven. On the way we passed a gray sedan that looked very familiar, and I paused briefly in front of it. "What's up?" Gil said, looking back at me.

"I could have sworn this was the car that passed us on the way up here today."

"The one you thought was trailing Steven?" Gilley said, coming back to take a look.

"Yeah," I said.

"Well, that makes sense," Gil said. "See the rim of the license plate? Uphamshire Motors. It's a local car."

"Ah," I said with a nod. "That explains it. Come on, then; let's get some grub." We met Steven at the front door, and I was surprised that there was a line waiting to get in. "Wait here," Steven said, and slipped inside. He returned a moment later and gave us each a wink. "Shouldn't be long," he said confidently.

Sure enough, not five minutes later Sable, party of three, was called to the front, and we were escorted to our table. "How'd you manage to cut in front of all those people?" I asked.

Steven smiled as he opened his menu. "The owner has a heart condition. A year ago he flew to Berlin and my team operated on him. I might have let him know on the drive from the lodge that I was in town, and very hungry."

I shook my head with a grin and began perusing when I felt a cold prickle on the back of my neck. I shivered, but the feeling wouldn't leave. Finally I looked up and spotted a very handsome gentleman across the restaurant, with gray hair, fine features, and piercing blue eyes that were currently shooting daggers at our table. Alarmed, I put my hand on Steven's arm.

"Yes?" Steven asked me.

I didn't take my eyes off the man across

the way as I asked, "Who's that?"

Steven turned to look, and there was a pause before he made a hissing noise and said something that sounded an awful lot like a German swear word.

Alarmed, Gilley and I both looked at him. "What?" I asked.

"Ohmigod!" Gilley squeaked. "That's Dr. Steven Sable *Senior!*"

My head snapped back to the man at the table. "You're kidding!"

"No. It's him," Steven said with venom in his voice.

Sable Senior was seated at a booth with another gentleman. As we watched them watch us, I saw Senior say something to his companion, then reach for his wallet. After slapping some bills down on the table he stood, along with the other gentleman, and left the restaurant.

"Wow," I said as they exited. "I guess he's heading home to polish his father-of-the-year trophies."

Steven snorted. "More like asshole-of-the-year."

"And we can see there's no love lost on this side of the fence, either," Gil stated.

"Damn trumpet," Steven replied.

Gilley's face curled up as he attempted to hold in a laugh at Steven's continued attempts at American colloquialisms. "Uh . . . I think you mean, 'damn tootin'.' "

"This means something different?"

"Can I ask a relevant question?" I said, wanting to bring them back to the subject. "What's your father doing here?" We were nearly four hours outside of Boston. Somehow I doubted Senior was the kind of guy who liked to take a drive in the country.

"I have no idea," Steven said as he stood up. "But I'll be damned tooting if I'm not going to find out. Can you order me a steak, medium-rare, with a bakery potato?"

I nodded. "Definitely."

"You two get whatever you like," Steven said over his shoulder as he walked away. "I'll be back soon."

We ordered dinner for the three of us and ate most of the appetizer, saving some, since we thought Steven would be back at any moment. Our food arrived without any sign of him, and I asked the waitress to take his steak back and keep it warm. Looking around the restaurant, I began to worry and said, "Where could he be?"

"Should we go look for him?" Gil suggested.

I sighed and turned back to my food. "None of our business. We're on a need-to-know basis."

Gil dove happily into his steak, untroubled by the appearance of the senior Sable. I wasn't so easily distracted, and cut up my steak while stealing glances around the restaurant, hoping Steven would reappear.

Gilley had finished his steak and was polishing off his baked potato when Steven came back to the table. "Sorry about that," he said as he scooted into his seat.

"I sent your food back under the heat lamp," I told him. "It's probably dried out by now."

He smiled gratefully at me and motioned to our waitress. "No worry; they'll cook me another."

Gilley asked, "Did you find out anything?"

"Yes, and no," Steven said as he pulled his salad forward and raised his fork. "Many of the locals and employees here have seen my father in town since my grandfather's death."

"What's he doing up this way?" I asked.

"No one knows. He's always with the same gentleman, and they speak in . . . how you say, quiet speaking?"

"Hushed tones," I offered.

"Yes, that, and whenever one of the waitresses goes to the table, my father and his associate stop talking. People think he is up to no good things."

"Do you think it has to do with the Manse?" I asked, using Gilley's nickname.

"If you are asking if I think he wants to take it from me, no."

"Why not? The place is huge; it's got to be worth a bundle."

Steven stopped chewing to look at me thoughtfully. After swallowing he said, "M.J., out here that house is worth about two million dollars and is the most expensive property for fifty miles. My father's estate on the water in Boston is worth about twenty million alone. I can't see him bothering with my grandfather's lodge because it would be away from his friends and his work, and it would be very hard to sell."

"Maybe for the fond memories, then," Gilley remarked.

Steven scoffed and pushed his salad away as our waitress reappeared with a freshly cooked steak. After she'd gone he said, "I doubt it. My grandfather and my father didn't get on so good. Especially after my father tried to get my grandfather declared mentally incompetent."

"Sounds like they had a pretty contentious relationship," I said.

"To say the least. In fact, if it weren't for my grandfather, the courts might not have granted the paternal suit my mother filed."

"Your grandfather intervened in a paternity suit?" Gil said, trying not to give away that we already knew the whole history behind the Sables.

"Yes. My father had fled to Europe when he was summoned to court with a blood sample to determine paternity for me. My grandfather heard of the case, met my mother and me, and decided I was his grandson. He submitted his own blood and settled the suit himself. He was very generous to my mother and me."

"Are there any kids between your father and his wife?" I asked.

"No. My grandfather would not talk very much about my father and his wife, but one day he did say that Mrs. Sable did not like children."

"And your father never wanted children either?"

"I don't know," Steven said as he cleaned his plate. "We've never spoken."

"You're kidding," I said. "Never? Not even once?"

"No," he said, shaking his head.

"And the fact that you've inherited most of your grand father's holdings probably isn't helping you two grow closer," I said, as I felt Gilley give me a little kick under the table.

"How did you know I'd inherited most of my grandfather's holdings?"

I smiled sweetly at him. "Lucky guess?"

Steven gave me an even look, then swiveled his gaze to Gilley. "Didn't you tell me at your office that you do this . . . how you say," he asked as he made a chopping motion, "on the computer?"

"It's called hacking. I'm a computer hacker, and if the information exists, there's no reason why I shouldn't at least attempt to learn about it," Gil explained. Steven's look grew dark. "What can I say? We're thorough about checking out our clients."

"I see. Well, in the future, please feel free to ask me instead of doing this hacking thing, okay?"

Gilley saluted. "Noted."

Turning back to me, Steven asked, "Now that your baseball test is complete, what will you do tomorrow?"

I held in a giggle. "Baseline test, and the thing that we'll do is your ghost," I said simply.

Steven looked exasperated. Turning to Gilley he asked, "How do I make her tell me with the details?"

Gil turned to me. "I think he wants to know *specifically* how you will go about that."

I gave both of them a smile. "When we were recording the baseline, I felt a few twinges in some of the rooms. My first step will be to go back to those rooms, place some trigger objects, and set up some laser movement detectors. Gil can monitor those remotely, and when we get something I can head to that location and try to make contact."

"I know about these trigger things, but what are these moving detectors for?"

"Ghosts love things that make noise. Think of the televisions that kept turning on. Once we've isolated through the trigger objects where the highest levels of activity are, we'll place motion detectors in those rooms and see if our ghost likes to set off the alarms. Ghosts tend to be habitual. They repeat behaviors over and over. My thinking is, there are one or two rooms this spirit thinks of as home base, and it's in those rooms where I need to identify and try to make contact with it."

"What will you do once you find the ghost?" he wanted to know.

"I'll attempt to confirm that it's your grandfather, and if it is, the reason why he's stuck between worlds. If we get lucky, and he's willing to talk to me, he'll be able to give us some good information."

Steven nodded as he sat back in the booth and considered the game plan. "Should we go back to the lodge now?"

Gilley gave a tremendous yawn and patted his tummy. "M.J., I'm exhausted. Can't we let the monitors do their thing and get some recordings, then go back tomorrow?"

I considered the idea, and had to concede that with all the walking around the huge mansion and carrying televisions, I was pretty whipped myself. "You know, Gil, that's not a bad idea."

Gilley seemed to perk up as he beamed his thanks at me. "That's fantastic. We can get started first thing in the morning."

I nodded, then thought of something and said, "It might be better to wait until afternoon. Do you remember listening to the weather report on our ride here? It said afternoon thunderstorms are expected."

Steven gave me a confused look. "Why does that affect the plan?" he asked.

"Ghosts like it damp," Gilley said.

"Huh?" Steven said.

"It's easier for ghosts to make an appearance when there is moisture in the air. Rain is terrific ghost-hunting weather, and thunderstorms are even better. It charges the air with electrostatic energy and is the equivalent of giving a ghost a power shake," I explained.

"Haven't you ever seen an old scary movie where it's thundering and lightning outside and everyone's running from the things that go bump in the night?" Gil added.

Steven chuckled. "I thought that was just your American Hollywood thing."

Folding my napkin and setting it on the table, I said, "There's definitely truth to it. What it means for us is that tomorrow could get very long. Because no matter how freaked out you two get, I'm not leaving that house until I've attempted to make contact."

Steven and Gilley both looked down at the tabletop. Gilley cleared his throat, then whispered to Steven, "We can always hang out in the van."

I rolled my eyes and said, "You two are pathetic. Come on. We'll need to get a good night's sleep tonight to gear up for tomorrow."

Steven paid the bill and we got up to leave. As we were heading out, Gilley excused himself to the restroom and told us to head back together and he'd catch up later. I gave him a small, panicked look, as that meant I'd have to ride in Steven's car and be alone with him, but he dashed into the men's room before I had a chance to argue.

"After you," Steven said as he held open the door for me to exit.

"Where're you parked?" I asked, trying not to sound nervous. I didn't know how I felt about Steven. I could admit that we'd shared a moment when he'd dropped me off at my apartment the other night, but the more time I spent with him, the more I thought it was better to keep my distance. He was the kind of guy who could certainly tempt you into falling for him, but the moment you got too involved he'd break your heart. And if there's anything I'm a big clucking chicken about, it's heartbreak.

"Around back," he answered, and took my hand to lead me through the lot.

I subtly pulled it back and said, "Oh, I see it. Right over there." I quickened my pace.

Behind me I heard him snicker. I ignored him and made it to his car, where I stood next to the passenger-side door, waiting for him to release the locks. He didn't, but continued to walk toward the car. Giving him a hint, I said, "Want to hit the lock?"

He didn't answer. Instead he sidled up next to me, holding his keys up for me to see as he said, "The button is not working so good."

"Ah," I said, edging closer to the car door. "So you've got to manually unlock it?"

"Mm-hmm," he said as he pressed his body closer to mine and reached around me to insert the key. "I need to get it fixed," he murmured close to my ear.

I gulped and leaned back against the car in an effort to create a little distance between us. It was fruitless — the more I leaned away, the more he leaned in. Wedged between him and the car, I found myself trying not to notice how my senses were filling up with him. He smelled like sandalwood soap. His body was lean and firm against mine, and his breath felt warm against my neck. Slowly he placed the key in the lock and began to turn it, drawing out the moment as I squirmed, trying to keep hold of my hormones.

"Damn," he said as he stopped turning the key and lowered his lips to my neck.

My breath caught as I felt the warmth of his mouth on my skin. "What's wrong?" I asked, my voice on the edge of panic.

Pulling his lips away from my neck, he moved to my earlobe and said, "The key's stuck."

Trying to stop myself from pressing against him, I said, "Let me have a go at it," as I twisted away from him.

"Great idea," he said, and pulled me back to face him as he kissed me with such passion I gave in.

Reflexively my arms went up to encircle his neck, and my fingers tangled themselves into his hair. He reached down to my waist and pulled my hips into his. Either he had a double roll of quarters in his pocket or he was damned glad to see me.

Our kiss deepened, and so did our need. I let go of the locks of hair wrapped around my fingers and trailed one hand down his spine, inserting it into the back of his pants and grinding my hips farther into his.

Steven pulled away from my lips as he sucked in a breath. Reaching up he moved his hand under my blouse and cupped my breast. He then lowered his lips to my collarbone and traced the length of it with his tongue. I gripped his buttocks and gave a small gasp as his fingers slid down my waist and into my jeans.

He groaned and moved his lips back to nibble on my earlobe. My eyes rolled up, and in the back of my mind a tiny voice whispered the last vestige of common sense I had left, begging me to be aware of where I was and what I was doing. I blinked and shook my head, trying to clear it. Steven's hand moved to tease my left breast, and with effort I managed to say, "We can't do this here."

Steven raised his head and gave a look around the parking lot. Luckily, no one seemed to be around, but as if on cue we heard voices coming around the corner of the building toward us. With a heavy sigh he nodded, stepped back, and closed my blouse. "Yes. You are right. Let's return to Helen's." He then reached around me, turned the key, and winked as he pulled it out and opened the door for me to get in. "Guess it wasn't stuck after all."

I gave him a look as I got in and quickly straightened my clothing. As we pulled out of the parking lot, we spotted Gilley coming out. He gave us a curious look as we waved at him, as if to say, *You're still here?*

I groaned. "He's going to grill me on what took us so long."

"Tell him I banged into a friend," Steven said with a sly grin.

I laughed. "You mean bumped," I corrected, and then grew serious, choosing my words carefully. "Listen, I think we should cool it until after we're through here." Steven didn't answer. "It's just that I need to concentrate on the task at hand. It takes a lot of my energy to make contact with a spirit, and even more when that spirit is a ghost. I can't afford to become distracted. Do you understand?"

"It was just a kiss, M.J.," he scoffed. "Hardly worth having a discussion over."

I inhaled sharply. Of all the things I'd expected him to say, a verbal slap like that one wasn't on the list. After a moment, and with ice in my voice, I said, "Well, then. As long as we're clear."

Steven and I drove the rest of the way back to the B and B in silence. The moment his car came to a stop I was out the door, anger from his rebuke building as I climbed the front steps. Pushing through the front entrance I didn't wait for him, and moved quickly to the stairs leading to my room. I could hear him behind me as I reached the landing. "M.J.," he called, but I ignored him.

"Miss Holliday," he said a little louder, as I turned to walk down the hallway.

I stiffened, and without turning I snapped, "What?"

"I'm sorry."

I took a deep breath, waited a beat, then began walking again. "Good night, Dr. Sable," I said, not looking back.

The next morning Doc woke me at the first sign of light. "YMCA!" he sang. "It's fun to stay at the YMCA-A!"

"Doc," I hissed as my eyes snapped open.

"Shhhh! You'll wake everybody up."

"Young man, get your butt over here!" Doc continued, undaunted by my efforts to shush him.

"Doc!" I hissed.

"I said young man! It's okay to be queer!" Doc sang, bobbing his head and moving sideways back and forth across his perch.

Groaning, I scooted out of bed and hurried over to his cage. He continued with the song as I made a mental note to thump Gilley soundly for teaching Doc his publicly embarrassing rendition. Opening the cage, I retrieved my bird and stroked his feathers. Doc stopped long enough to whistle and say, "Doc wants a cracker!"

"Doc *is* a cracker." I chuckled. Walking with him over to my duffel bag, I pulled out a container of treats. "Here," I said as I gave him one. "This should tide you over until breakfast."

Doc gave me a head bob as he crunched on the treat. "Nice bum; where you from?" he squawked in between nibbles.

I giggled and walked him back over to the window, where I sat down in a chair overlooking the front driveway. I stared blearily out at the first red rays playing across the sky. I was reminded of a phrase my father used to say: "Red sky at night, sailor's delight. Red sky at morning, sailor take warning." I squinted at the edge of the horizon, where I could see the first signs of cloud cover rolling in from the southeast. Doc chirped and I looked down at him. "What's up, sweetie?"

"Who you gonna call?" Doc asked me. "Ghostbusters!"

I rolled my eyes. When I'd first suggested the idea of professional ghostbusting to Gilley, he'd rented the movie *Ghostbusters,* and he and Doc had watched it over and over. At first I'd thought it was cute when Doc began parroting quotes from the movie. Now it grated on my nerves, and was downright humiliating in public.

"Doc, don't say that," I said to him, knowing full well he'd ignore me.

"Look at the ass on that hunka man!" he quipped. Gilley loved to people watch with Doc from our office window.

I laughed. It had been a very long time since he'd used that one. Doc whistled. "Hey, sailor! Why don't you come to my port?"

"Great," I mumbled. "I've got a gay sidekick and a gayer bird."

"Dr. Delicious goes bye-bye!"

I looked at my bird curiously. I'd never heard him put that particular combo together before, and intuitively I looked outside. Sure enough, I noticed Steven's car wasn't where he'd parked it the night before. Setting Doc on the back of the chair I went to the other window for a better view of the driveway.

Our van was there, and next to it was an empty space, followed by a row of other guests' cars. "Weird," I whispered. Turning back to Doc I said, "Do you think we should check it out?"

Doc gave me a head bob and a whistle.

"Me too." I got dressed and loaded Doc onto my shoulder, thinking that if I left him alone in the room, he'd continue to make a lot of noise and wake the other guests. We crept out of my room and into the hallway and I made my way to Gilley's room. Pressing my ear against the door, I could faintly hear the sound of soft snores. "Gilley's still asleep," I said to Doc. He gave me another head bob and we moved down the hall.

I remembered that Steven's bedroom was at the end of the hall next to the bathroom. I walked quietly to his room and hovered just outside, wondering what I'd say if he suddenly opened his door and saw me standing there at five in the morning. Glancing at the bathroom, I decided to go with the obvious. Putting my ear to the door, I listened intently, but no sounds could be heard. Steven was either a quiet sleeper or he wasn't in his room.

He must have gone somewhere in the middle of the night. He was a doctor, after all — maybe he'd had an emergency. Then again, what if he was in his room, and his car had been stolen? I didn't know the current price of an Aston Martin, but my gut said it was north of anything I could ever afford. Maybe some thief had taken it.

I stepped back from the door, debating about what to do next. Finally, I figured that if there was a chance my car had been stolen, I'd want to be woken up. I gave the door a small knock. After a few moments of silence, I knocked again. Still nothing. "Okay, so no one's home . . ." I whispered. "Or he's a heavy sleeper. Maybe I should try the door and see if it's open?"

Doc reached up with his beak and tugged gently on my ear. "Yeah, I'm with you," I said, reaching for the door handle. My heart pounding at my invasion of his privacy, I turned the knob, and the door clicked open. "Open, sesame," I whispered. I gently eased the door open far enough to take a peek inside. The room was empty.

I pushed a little farther and stepped into the room, just to make sure. The bed was rumpled, and looked slept in. Steven's duffel wasn't in sight, and neither were any of his personal belongings. "Okay," I said to Doc. "Where do you think he's run off to?"

"Doc's a pretty boy!" he squawked.

"Shhhh!" I said, putting a gentle hand on his beak. "Come on, pal. You're gonna get me in trouble." We left the room and headed back down the hallway.

Making my way downstairs, I heard sounds coming from the kitchen. Curious, I went to investigate and found Helen in her bathrobe humming as she sliced up fruit by the sink. "Morning," I said as I came into the kitchen.

"Eeek!" she shrieked, dropping the knife and raising a hand to her chest.

"Sorry!" I said, as I came over to her. "I didn't mean to scare you."

Helen took deep breaths as she tried to calm herself. After a moment she regained her composure and picked up the knife. "I didn't realize someone was up this early."

"It's my bird," I said, indicating Doc perched on my shoulder. "He was hungry."

"Hi, Doc," Helen said, holding up a piece of cantaloupe. Doc whistled.

"You've got a friend for life," I said as he took the fruit.

"Can I get you some coffee?" she asked me.

"I'd love some, thanks." I took a seat in one of the chairs at a small table in the kitchen, and Helen brought me my coffee.

"I hope you got a better night's sleep last night," she said. "My late husband wasn't keeping you up again, was he?"

"Arnold? No. He's been quiet ever since I gave you his message."

Helen nodded and got back to chopping fruit. She put several pieces of cantaloupe in a bowl and set that down in front of me and Doc with a smile. Doc whistled and I fed him a few pieces, enjoying the companionable silence and a good cup of coffee.

After a moment I asked casually, "Did Steven happen to mention anything about heading back to Boston this morning?"

"No," she said as she reached for a carton of eggs. "Why, has he left?"

I nodded. "His car's not in the driveway, and he didn't answer my knock on his bedroom door this morning." I decided it was best to leave out the part about opening said door and taking a looky-loo inside.

"I wouldn't worry over it, M.J.," she said, cracking an egg on the side of a large bowl. "I'm sure he's fine."

I nodded. "I think I'll go for a run before

breakfast."

"Sounds good," she said. "I start serving right at six o'clock."

I took Doc back to my room and put him in his cage. Now that he'd been fed, he was content to look quietly out the window.

I changed into sweats and headed back downstairs, poking my nose into the kitchen again, where Helen was putting the finishing touches on breakfast, and told her to tell Gilley that I was out for a run in case he woke up and was looking for me.

"Have a good jog," Helen said. "If Steven comes back, I'll let him know too."

"Thanks," I said, careful not to let my irritation about his absence show.

I headed outside into the cool morning light and inhaled deeply. It was the perfect temperature for a run, not too hot and not too cold. I did a few stretches for a warm-up, then sprinted down the pavement.

I took the main road through town, aptly named Main Street, sticking to familiar territory at first, then got bolder and jogged down a side street that led to a more residential part of town. The houses here were neat and simple. Many of them had white picket fences, and reminded me of back home in Georgia. Some of the residents were up, gathering papers, watering lawns, walking their dogs. Other houses were still and quiet as their owners squeezed in one more hour of sleep.

After running parallel to Main Street, I cut back up toward it through another side street and ran right past a black Aston Martin parked in someone's driveway. My head whipped back to take a second look as I realized it must be Steven's car. Panting, I trotted back to check it out, and sure enough I saw his little MD tag on the license plate.

After ogling the car for a few seconds I looked up at the house it was parked in front of, a small one-story ranch with white trim and light blue shutters. The blinds were closed and there was no way to tell if anyone was awake inside.

I stood next to the car for a few seconds, wondering what Steven could be doing here at six in the morning. Curious about his arrival time, I moved to the hood and felt it. It was cool to the touch. That meant he'd been here for a while, or all night.

I scowled at that thought and looked back up at the house. Just then the front door opened, and with a start I crouched down behind the car, afraid I'd be seen. With my heart pounding, I duck-walked over to a row of bushes and moved behind them for cover. I could hear two people talking, one female voice light and amused, the other much deeper and accented. Their conversation came to me in little bits and pieces, not enough to put together and tell what they were talking about.

Taking a huge chance, I peeked up over the bushes, spotting Steven and a young woman talking and laughing as they walked over to his car. The woman was pretty, with long blond hair tied up in a ponytail. She looked familiar, and it took me a second to realize that she was the waitress at the grinder restaurant. Once Steven put his arm around her and gave her a kiss on the forehead, I didn't bother to hang around and watch the show. Instead, with my stomach in a tangle of knots, I inched back down and waddled along the row of bushes to the backyard. From there I cut through another lawn to the street behind the one I'd been on and started jogging again.

I ran much farther and harder than I'd planned, trying to work out what it meant that Steven had spent the night with another woman after kissing me so passionately the evening before. I finally came to the conclusion that I'd been right all along — he was a rat bastard and it was in my best interests to keep my distance from him. Once I finished this job, he would become a distant memory.

An hour and a half later I returned to the B and B. Gilley met me as I came through the door, out of breath and sweaty. "Good Lord, girl," he said when he saw me. "What'd you run, a marathon?"

"Morning," I said as I waved him off and turned toward the stairs. "If anyone needs me, I'll be in the shower."

I went up to my room, gathered some toiletries and clean clothes, and headed into the hallway. After closing my door I turned and bumped right into a broad chest. "Good morning," Steven said as I backed up.

"Hey," I said, looking anywhere but at him.

He reached forward and ran a finger along my wet hairline. "Been out for a run?"

I snapped my head away. "I need a shower," I said, and moved around him.

"I'll say." He chuckled.

I turned back and gave him a frigid look before walking to the bathroom at the end of the hall. "Are you still mad at me?" he asked.

I didn't answer him. Instead I went into the bathroom and shut the door behind me without looking back. "Jerk," I muttered.

After taking a steamy hot shower and dressing, I headed downstairs. Gilley was still at the kitchen table, slurping coffee and reading the local paper. "Hey," I said as I got a plate from the buffet Helen had set up.

"Morning, sunshine," Gilley said. "Sleep well?"

"Pretty good."

"Want to tell me why you're in a mood?"

"Who says I'm in a mood?" I asked, grabbing some toast.

"You never run like that unless something or someone has pissed you off. I'm guessing it has to do with the fact that a certain someone rolled in here this morning after apparently being out all night?"

"I hate that you're so freakishly perceptive," I grumbled, sitting down.

"It's a gift," Gilley said, setting down the paper while he waited for me to talk.

"Did you ask where he'd gone?" I asked him, taking a bite of bacon.

"Steven? No. It's none of my business," Gilley said.

"I saw him," I admitted. "I was out running and saw his car parked in some driveway. And I may have paused to check it out and caught him and that pretty waitress from the grinder restaurant coming out the door all friendly-like."

Gilley arched an eyebrow. "Define friendly."

"They had their arms wrapped around each other."

"And — I'm just guessing here — but my bet is that you two got a little friendly with each other last night in the restaurant parking lot, too?"

"How could you know that?" I demanded.

"I was doing a little flirt-flirt with one of the waiters inside the restaurant after you two left. We talked for a good fifteen minutes, and when I came out you two were just pulling out of the lot. Plus you had that look on your face," he said smugly.

"What look?"

"That 'Oh, no! Gilley's going to know what I've been doing' look."

"Whatever," I said, waving my hand and trying to brush the whole thing off. "It's no big deal. He's a player. I could've told you that when we started this gig."

"But you like him," Gilley said to me.

"You like whom?" Steven said from behind me.

Gilley and I both jumped and then gave a panicked look to each other. Gil saved the day when he said, "Bradley. This guy I just started dating. I introduced him to M.J. the other morning and I was getting her opinion about him."

"Do you know what I think?" Steven said, taking his seat next to me.

Discreetly I edged my chair a little farther away, while Gilley said, "No, but I'm thinking you're about to tell us."

"I think you should date whomever you want. Don't wait for someone to give you the okay. If you like this guy, then that's all that matters."

I rolled my eyes and set my fork and knife down. I'd lost my appetite. "Thank you, Dr. Phil," I said, and got up from the table. "Now, if you'll excuse me, I think I'll try to take a little nap before we hit the house later on."

As I made my way up the stairs, I could hear Steven ask Gilley, "What's her problem?"

I didn't wait to listen for Gilley's response. Instead I made my way back to my room and plopped down face-first on the bed. "What's up, Doc?" my bird chirped from his perch by the window.

Turning to look at him, I said, "Men suck." Doc whistled and cocked his head. There was a pause as I saw him trying to work out the sound. After a moment he repeated, "Men suck!"

"Great," I mumbled as I turned my face back into the pillow.

CHAPTER 7

The crashing sound of thunder woke me. That, coupled with Doc's frantic squawking. "Help! I've been shot!" he said as a loud crack echoed across the sky. I blinked the sleep out of my eyes and got up quickly. Doc hated thunderstorms, and I'd forgotten to take him away from the window.

"Shhhh," I cooed to him, moving his cage across the room. My bedroom was dim, and I could hear the pounding sound of rain against the windowpane. "It's okay, Doc. You'll be okay."

"I've been shot!" he said, and flapped his wings. He was clearly agitated, since he used that phrase whenever any loud noise scared him.

"You have not been shot, Doc. Come on now; it's okay. Just a little storm, nothing to be frightened about." Behind me we saw a flash, followed by the sound of a loud rumble, closer than the last one. Doc flapped his wings and turned in a circle on his perch.

Just then there was a knock on my door. "M.J.?" I heard Gilley call from the hallway.

"Doc's been shot!" my parrot squawked. "Gilley! Doc needs help!"

Gilley opened the door and came in. "He upset by the storm?"

"Yeah. I forgot to take him out of the window before I fell asleep."

"YMCA!" Doc sang, fluttering his tail when Gilley came over. "Doc's a pretty boy!"

"I came up to get you from your nap," Gilley said. "It's midafternoon, and the storm started early. I think it's a good time to head over to the lodge."

"Sure. Let me just get Doc settled and I'll meet you downstairs." After Gilley left the room I stroked and talked softly to my bird until he settled down. When he stopped squawking at every little burst of thunder, I put a cover over his cage, grabbed my duffel bag, and tiptoed out of the room.

I found Helen back in the kitchen again and asked her if she'd look in on Doc a little later. She happily agreed.

I met Gil and Steven on the front porch. It was raining something fierce, and the storm showed no signs of subsiding.

"Ready?" Steven asked me. I nodded. Gil winked at me and took off down the steps in the direction of the van. I was about to follow him when Steven grabbed my arm. "Why are you giving me this cold elbow?" he asked.

"Say what?" I said, trying to ease my arm out of his grip.

He let go of my arm and said, "You're avoiding me. Why?"

"Ah," I said as I realized what he meant. "The cold *shoulder*. I've been giving you the cold shoulder."

"Yes, the cold elbow and the cold shoulder and the cold arm. Why have you been doing this?"

I stood there for a moment, wondering how to play it. Should I tell him the truth? Or avoid the fact that I'd seen him coming out of that house this morning? I opted for the latter. "I've been focusing on the job, that's all. Like I said, I can't afford to become distracted. You do want me to help your grandfather, don't you?"

Steven eyed me for a long couple of seconds. He wasn't buying it. I thought he was going to press the point, but instead he nodded and motioned for me to go ahead to the van.

I raced through the rain and got in with

Gilley. "What was that all about?" he asked me.

"Nothing. Just laying the ground rules again. Come on," I coaxed. "We know the way. Let's go."

Gilley shook his head as if to say, *I'll never understand women,* and pulled out of the driveway. For the most part we rode in silence to the house, only commenting here and there about the strength of the storm.

When we pulled into the long driveway, I could feel my adrenaline pumping the way it always did when I hunted ghosts. It was partly the thrill of the chase, partly the challenge of making contact, and partly the satisfaction of helping a trapped spirit cross over.

As we got closer to the house, I noticed something odd. Gilley saw it too and asked, "Whose car is that?" before I had a chance.

"Don't know. But I hope Steven didn't think bringing in reinforcements was a good idea."

"Reinforcements? What kind of reinforcements would he bring?"

"Good point," I said, still looking at the car. As we pulled up beside it, we could see there was no one inside. Just then I looked up to see a few lights on inside the Sable house.

Gil parked next to the car, and we waited for Steven to pull in before getting out and making a dash to the front steps. "Who's here?" I asked, shaking the rain off me.

"Maria," Steven said.

"The housekeeper?" I asked.

Steven nodded, and Gil asked, "What's she doing here?"

"I'm not knowing," Steven said as he tried the door. It was open and we walked into the front hall. "Maria?" Steven called.

We waited a few beats and finally heard, "Coming!" from somewhere on the second floor. We watched the stairs until a lovely-looking older woman with black hair and brown eyes appeared at the top of the stairway. She carried a book and a blue mohair afghan in one hand, and with the other she gripped the railing as she made her way down the stairs. "Steven!" she said when she saw him. "Hello! I didn't expect to see you here. How've you been?" she asked as she walked forward with a pronounced limp.

"I'm fine," he said as she opened her arms wide to embrace him. "What are you doing here?" he asked her after they'd given each other a firm hug.

"Oh, it's silly, really," she said, a flush going to her cheeks. "After your grandfather died I was so upset, just had a terrible time. And I left behind some of my personal belongings. This is my grandmother's afghan," she said, holding it up for us to see. "I wanted to come back and get it before you sold this place off."

"Who says I'm selling?" Steven asked her.

"You want to keep it?" she asked. "Well, that's wonderful! Oh, Steven, I know Andrew would be so proud of you."

"Thank you. How is your hip? I noticed your limp is worse."

She waved him off. "Now that I don't have all these stairs to climb, it's not so bad. Just hurts more when it rains."

Steven nodded. "There may be some arthritis setting in. An old injury like that can be prone to arthritis."

Maria said, "Can you believe it's been twenty-five years since I took that tumble? That was the first year we had you here with us, and you were such a good boy to help me with all my chores when my hip was so sore. I should have known better too. These stairs have always given me a run for my money — I've slipped down them more than once, you know."

"You should be taking the elevator," Steven said.

"That old bucket of bolts? Naw, the thing

takes forever and makes far too much noise. I'm much more careful now in my old age. Don't want to end up like my sister. She spends most of her time in bed nursing a bad knee."

"Are you two getting along well together?"

"Yes, yes. We need each other now that we're the only family left."

"Good to know you're with family," Steven said kindly. Then, remembering us, he said, "I'd like you to meet Miss M. J. Holliday and Gilley . . ."

"Gillespie," Gil said, and extended his hand forward. Maria shook our hands and said, "Pleased to meet you."

"They are here to do some busting," Steven said with a smile, like he was Mr. Cool.

"Some what?" Maria asked.

"We're ghostbusters," Gilley said proudly. "Dr. Sable here says that you've had some strange occurrences happening in this house, and M.J. and I are here to get to the bottom of them."

Maria looked worried. "Is that why there aren't any televisions in the bedrooms?"

"All of the TVs have been moved to the basement," I said. "They were becoming distracting."

Maria's pensive expression didn't change.

Turning to Steven she said, "You'll be careful, won't you, Steven?"

"Of course, Maria, of course."

Maria nodded, her eyes large and sorrowful. Reaching up to touch Steven's face she said, "You look so much like Andrew, you know?" Steven beamed; then Maria said, "Let me get out of your way, then." She tucked the book she'd been carrying under her arm as, on Steven's arm, she limped to the door.

"Good to see you, Maria," Steven said, and the two hugged again.

"Nice woman," Gilley said when she left.

"She is," Steven said. "She was so upset when my grandfather died. It's good to see her smile again."

Clapping my hands together to get their attention, I said, "Okay, gentlemen, time to focus. Gilley, let's take a look at what the monitors recorded first."

The three of us moved over into the doorway that led to the study where we'd propped the monitors. They had been programmed to pick up the readings from the spectrometer, the thermometer, and the night-vision camera we'd mounted in the master bedroom. As we got close to them my heart sank; the monitors were off. Gil noticed it too and moved around to the plugs, which were removed from the socket they had been plugged into.

"Crap," he said, holding up the plugs for us to see.

"Plug them back in, Gil, and see if they got anything."

Gilley did, and slowly the monitors and the DVR came to life. Gilley hit the rewind button and almost instantly it clicked, then stopped. "That is not a good sound, I'm thinking," Steven said.

Gil hit the play button to reveal about ten recorded seconds of still-empty bedroom, and then all we got was fuzz.

"So basically, the moment we hit the button and stepped outside the plugs came out of the socket," I said, disappointment evident in my voice.

"Now what?" Steven asked.

Irritated with the wasted effort, I turned to Gilley and said, "Buddy, can you bring the floor plan we drew for the baseline to the kitchen and we'll talk about roles and responsibilities?"

Gilley saluted and clicked his heels. "Aye-aye, *Capitán!*"

"Can you please leave the sarcasm behind?" I asked as I led the way to the kitchen.

"It's not in my nature," Gilley said, picking up the floor plan and following after us.

"Here's good," I said as we reached the breakfast table in the kitchen. Gilley spread out the floor plan and I got out my pen. "This is the area I think we should start in," I said, circling the master bedroom. "We definitely want to set up a vigil in there for a while. I'll open up my intuition and see if Andrew wants to make contact. I also think it's a good idea to spend some time here." I circled the guest bedroom on the third floor. "And here," I added as I circled the library.

Steven nodded as he watched me circle rooms and point arrows to locations for the trigger objects and motion detectors. "Sounds good," he said agreeably.

Looking to make sure Gilley was also on board, I continued, "After I conduct my search in the master bedroom, I can move on to the other rooms to see if I can pick up anything there."

"And if none of those places proves good hunting ground, is there anywhere else you'd like to try?"

"I also got a tug outside, near the woods, but with this weather, maybe we should wait for it to clear up a bit before we check it out."

Steven nodded. "Good. Gilley, why don't you take the master bedroom and I'll take the library?"

"*What?*" Gilley screeched. "Wait a second, we're supposed to do these vigils *alone?* I thought we were going to do them in groups!"

"That would take three times as long," I said. "And besides, at the first hint of anything weird just yell out, and the other two of us will come running."

"M.J., are you *crazy?* I could be dead by the time you get to me!" I rolled my eyes and gave Gil a look. "You cannot be that scared," I said to him.

"I am, M.J.! I am!" he said, his voice sharp and panicked.

"Oh, for Pete's sake, Gil!" I said, throwing up my hands. "*Fine.* Come with me then. We can hang out in the master bedroom together."

"I'd rather go to the library with Steven," Gilley said meekly.

I scowled. "I'll bet you would," I retorted. To Steven I said, "He can show you how to work the digital thermometer and spectrometer. If after a while nothing weird is happening, come on upstairs and hang with me in the master bedroom. Then we can all go up to the third-floor guest room."

"Sounds good," Steven said, and patted Gilley on the back. "Come on, Gilley. Let's bust some feathers."

"Bust some *tail*," I heard Gilley say as the two moved out of the kitchen.

I made my way upstairs to the master bedroom as quietly as possible. I had my EMF reader out and pointed in front of me to see if there was already some activity going on. All readings were normal.

When I reached the second floor I heard something. *Thump, thump, thump,* sounded over my head, close to the ceiling, though not necessarily coming from the floor above. I cocked my head and listened, and after a few seconds it sounded again, but this time it was a little farther down the hall from where I was standing.

I looked back down the staircase, wondering if I should alert the fellas, but decided to investigate on my own. I crept up the stairs to the third floor and watched the needle on my meter jump as the noise it emitted became a high squeal. "Someone's afoot," I said.

When I reached the third floor I clicked the meter off and listened. For a long time I heard nothing, when suddenly there was a thunderous *bam!* right behind me. I jumped a foot and backed up against a wall, my heart pounding and my breathing shallow.

"M.J.?" I heard Gilley call from downstairs. "Was that you?"

"No," I yelled back. "I was getting some readings up here and came up to investigate. I have the distinct impression that someone doesn't want us snooping around."

I heard footsteps on the stairs and looked over the edge to see Steven jogging up. When he got to me he put a concerned hand on my shoulder. "You okay?" he asked.

"Fine," I said, shrugging it off. "Sometimes you'll run into an energy that is particularly confrontational."

"My grandfather was a gentle man," he said, looking puzzled. "I can't imagine he'd want to hurt you."

"Good to know."

"I can't believe you left me down there!" Gilley panted as he reached the top of the stairs. "From now on, nobody takes off aloooooone — Ahhhhh!"

Steven and I watched as Gilley seemed to be yanked by the shoulders from an invisible force. His eyes opened wide as his body arced, arms flailing and mouth open as he balanced precariously on the stair's edge for a nanosecond before flying backward down several stairs. The staircase shuddered as his back hit it. Like an awful movie playing in slow motion, we saw his lower body curl up over his head as he tumbled like a rag doll down the rest of the stairs.

"Gilley!" I screamed as I shot after him, jumping down several stairs at a time to try in vain to stop his awful head-over-heels tumble. I could hear Steven right behind me.

We caught up to Gilley as he hit the bottom of the stairwell with another frightening thud, landing on the marble floor flat on his rump. "Unnnnh!" he cried as he rolled onto his side.

"Oh, my God!" I said as I bent down, my hands shaking as I placed them gently on his shoulders. "Gil! Where are you hurt?"

Gilley tried to take a breath, but the wind seemed to be knocked out of him. In a flash Steven was at his side. "It's going to be all right," he said in a low, calm voice. "M.J., let go of Gilley and let me take a look."

I moved aside just as Gilley finally took a shuddering breath, followed quickly with a wheezing plea: "Get me outta here!"

"In just a moment, Gilley. First I must make sure it is all right to move you." I waited anxiously while Steven felt all along Gilley's body, checking for any signs that something was broken. Gilley's breathing was returning to normal and so was his voice.

"It hurts!" he cried. "Oh, my bum, it

hurts! Please just get me outta here!"

Finally Steven gave me a nod. "M.J., can you help me get him up to the bed?"

"Nooooooooo!" Gilley squealed, and both Steven and I winced. "Don't take me up there! Please just get me out of this house!"

Steven grimaced, "Gilley, we need you to lie down and —"

"No!" Gilley screamed. "Don't take me up there! M.J., *please!*"

"Let's get him to the front porch and we can talk about what to do with him next," I said. I was so racked with guilt about having forced Gilley along that I was willing to offer him any comfort I could.

Steven gave a reluctant nod, and we moved Gilley out the door. We set him down gently, and I hurried back inside to grab an armload of cushions off the sofas in the solarium and a throw that was draped over a chair. Running back outside, I made a small makeshift bed for Gilley, easing him onto the pillows.

Steven continued to feel along Gil's body and asked him questions about where the pain was. While the rain poured down I stood helplessly by, wringing my hands and praying that Gil would be okay.

Finally Steven seemed satisfied with his exam of Gilley. "Well," he said, standing up.

"I have good news and bad news. Which do you want first?"

"The good news," Gilley said, looking up at us with such a pathetic puppy-dog look that I wanted to cry.

"Your injury is not terminal."

The comment was so unexpected that it caught me completely by surprise. I felt the corners of my mouth turn up, and began to giggle. I took a deep breath and tried to shake it off, but the more I tried to stifle the giggle the more I couldn't help it. Steven too let out a small chuckle, but he quickly stopped as Gilley shot us both a dirty look.

"And the bad news?" Gil asked, his eyes narrowing at me as my shoulders shook with silent laughter.

"I think your coccyx has a fracture."

Gilley gave him a blank look. "My *coccyx* has a *fracture?*"

"Yes," Steven said gravely, then gave me a subtle wink and added, "You seem to have broken your fairy tail."

That did it; I began to howl with laughter. Steven chuckled right along with me, and the more we laughed the harder it was to stop.

"I'm so glad you're enjoying yourselves at my expense!" Gilley snapped. "Would you still be laughing if I'd broken my neck?"

That sobered me. I took another deep breath, wiped the tears of laughter from my eyes, and cleared my throat. "No, Gil. And I'm sorry. It was just . . . seeing you tumble down those stairs shook me up, and I suppose I'm just relieving some of that tension."

Gilley gave me half an eye roll. "It really hurts, M.J."

"I know," I said, squatting down next to him, truly ashamed of my behavior. "And I couldn't be more sorry for insisting that you come along into the house on this bust."

"I told you, I'm a van guy!"

"Agreed," I said, and rubbed his arm. Looking up at Steven I asked, "Do we need to call an ambulance or take him to the hospital?"

"We can. Gilley, do you have insurance?"

Gil and I shared an uncomfortable look with each other. "The premiums are over five hundred dollars a month," Gil said. "M.J. and I can't swing that kind of expenditure right now."

"How much would it cost?" I asked while I mentally added up the available credit on the plastic in my purse.

"That's why I asked if you had insurance. With this type of injury the hospital would take X-rays and probably prescribe bed rest.

It would cost you about a . . . how do you say the slang for money over hundreds . . . big?"

"Grand," I moaned.

"Yes, a grand, and the result would be the same. I am thinking that I will write you a prescription for the pain and take you back to Helen's for bed rest."

"How long will I have to stay in bed?" Gil asked.

"Until the pain subsides enough that you can move around freely. You should be back to normal in four to six weeks."

"Four to six weeks?! But I have a hot date next Friday!"

"With whom?" I asked. Other than Bradley, whom Gilley had herded out of his life with the fire drill, he hadn't told me about any hot new prospects on his dance card.

"I don't know yet!" he snapped. "But if I can't walk around, how am I going to find one?"

I gave him a sympathetic pat on the back and focused on Steven. "We'll need to get him back to the B and B; then you and I can come back here."

"You cannot be serious!" Gilley said. "M.J., it's far too dangerous in there! Something pushed me down those stairs!"

I looked back at the house for a moment,

swearing I had glimpsed a dark shadow passing in front of the window. Then I looked up at Steven to see his reaction.

"I'm still in," he said firmly.

I tried to hide my relief. There were places that even I'd been nervous to walk into, and this house was quickly becoming one of them. "Good. If we hurry, we can make it back before it gets dark."

"It's a plan. Can you help me get him into your van?"

We got Gilley loaded into the back, where he could lie down on a stack of fluffy cushions. As he muttered about murderous poltergeists we drove back to Helen's. After explaining that Gilley had tripped on the stairs (we didn't want to frighten her), we got him to his room, and for company I put Doc in with him while Steven went to the pharmacy and filled a prescription for painkillers.

"M.J.," Gilley said to me as I turned to leave the room.

"Yes, Gil?"

"I don't like this job one bit."

"I know," I said to him. "I'll be careful."

Steven came back a short while later and gave Gilley a pain pill. When we were sure Gil was okay, we made our way back to the van and drove in silence for a while until he asked, "Have you ever seen anything like that?"

"Yes," I said. "And I've heard about many cases where people have been tripped or pushed down steps before. It's more common than people think."

"So these ghosts can be quite dangerous?"

I nodded. "Absolutely. That's why it's a good thing to have someone like me around. When a poltergeist becomes angry, they can funnel that anger into affecting physical objects. I once got a call from a frantic mother whose son was pushed down their basement steps. It turned out the house was haunted by a little boy who was jealous of the woman's son. He was a doozy to cross over, but I eventually got him there."

"You know what is so odd?" Steven mused. "Maria's fall twenty-five years ago. My mother and I had just arrived from Argentina for the summer, and Maria spoke Spanish. She told me how she had been going up the stairs with the . . . clothes from washing?"

"Laundry."

"Yes, with laundry, and she felt something pull at her."

"Were you here when she fell?"

"No. We arrived a few days later. Her hip was fractured, and my grandfather set up a bed for her in the study. The old man fussed over her the whole summer. It was quite sweet, actually."

"That mixes things up a bit," I said.

"What do you mean with mix up?"

"It sounds like Maria was pushed by the same poltergeist that shoved Gilley. And I swear I felt a female energy on the stairs when I was going up them. In other words, it couldn't have been your grandfather the first time it happened; he was still alive when Maria was injured. It seems we have a second ghost in that house."

"I am thinking that it is best if we glue together, for safety."

"Your take on English slang is really quite charming, you know?"

"I am a charming guy," he said, wiggling his eyebrows.

"I'm surprised that it's not a bit better, though. Didn't you speak English with your grandfather?"

"No, we mostly spoke German. My grand-father served in World War Two — he was a German translator — so after I went to boarding school there, he and I could talk very well."

"Ah, that makes sense. So, pretty much you'd pick up what you could hear during the summer until you were what? Eighteen?"

"Sixteen. I graduated early."

We pulled into the driveway of the lodge. After parking the car we entered the front door, both a little more on guard than the last time we'd come into the entrance hall. "Where would you like to focus first?"

"Scene of the crime," I said, gesturing toward the stairs. "I think it's better not to focus on trigger objects and motion sensors when we have a ghost more than willing to make contact. Come on; let's head up and see what we see."

"Keep hold of the railing," Steven cautioned as we climbed the stairs.

I did, and we made our way up without incident. When we reached the third floor we moved away from the stairs and stood with our backs against the wall, waiting and watching. After a few moments Steven gave me an expectant look, and I said, "Give me a sec." I closed my eyes and focused my energy outward, searching for signs of our not so friendly spectral tenant.

After concentrating on the area for a little bit, I felt a very small tug in the direction of the guest room I'd first noted on the floor plan. Motioning to Steven, I headed there, continuing to feel for activity on my radar.

When we got to the bedroom I looked around. The room was painted a soft lavender, with a cream-colored bedspread embroidered with violets. There was a framed photo on the nightstand, and it called to me. I picked it up and looked at the image of a woman of about thirty with wavy brown hair and ruby lips. She was laughing as she held up a jar to the camera.

"Who's this?" I asked as I offered the photo to Steven.

He studied it. "I don't know," he said.

"Your grandmother, perhaps?" I asked.

"No. She was blond and much heavier and, from what I remember of her before she died, unhappy."

"A sourpuss, huh?"

"Just like her son," Steven said. "Hmmm," he continued as he flipped the frame over and pulled it apart to reveal the back of the photo. " 'Maureen, nineteen sixty-two.' "

"Who's Maureen?" Even as I said it I felt a cold prickle at the back of my neck. The temperature around Steven and me seemed to plummet, and when I exhaled I saw my breath.

"What the . . ." Steven said as he looked sharply at me, his eyes nervous.

I put my finger to my lips and whispered, "Someone's here." I then opened up my intuition again to feel a strong pull toward a rocking chair across the room. I put my hand on Steven's arm and motioned toward the chair. "Over there," I whispered.

"The ghost?" he asked me.

As if in answer the chair began to creak back and forth, all by itself. I was wary of it at first. If this was the ghost that hit Gilley then it had a temper. Intuitively I reached out in the direction of the chair. *Who are you?* I asked in my mind.

The chair picked up speed and began to rock in earnest. "Holy Mother of God!" Steven hissed, his whisper urgent and frightened. "M.J.! Who is it?"

"I'm workin' on it," I said softly. This time I dispensed with using telepathy. Maybe this ghost wanted to hear me speak. "We've come peacefully," I began, my tone low and measured. "We're here to help. We simply need to know who you are and why you're here, and we can help you."

The chair stopped rocking abruptly. I felt the initial M in my head loud and clear, and then small, round orbs of light began buzzing around the top of the chair, zipping back and forth like flies. "Whoa . . ." Steven said. "Look at that!"

"Maureen?" I called to the chair. "Maureen, is that you?" My answer was the chair flipping backward onto its back as the orbs of light scattered to the four corners of the room. Steven and I ducked as one or two came straight at us.

As we looked up from our crouched positions, I noticed the temperature had returned to normal again. "Is it gone?" he wanted to know.

"For now," I said, sending my radar out again just to be sure.

"You asked if that was Maureen. You do not think that was my grandfather?"

"No. The energy was too light to be male."

"Pardon?"

"Male versus female energy. Male energy weighs more."

"I am not understanding this thing that you are saying. Please explain how it *weighs* more?"

I smiled patiently and said, "To me male energy is thicker and heavier than female energy. This ghost had light energy. It definitely felt female. Plus, the initial I got was an M."

"You talked to her?" Steven asked me. "What did she say?"

I shook my head and held up my hand in a stop motion. "I didn't have a chance to really talk to her. She was too agitated. She's angry about something, and I'm not sure what it is. Angry isn't good, just so you know. It makes reasoning with the ghost a lot harder."

"But where is my grandfather?"

"I don't know. Are you sure you heard his voice that night?"

"I'm positive," he said firmly. "It was as if he were standing right behind me."

"Well, it would be nice of him to show up. Maybe I could get a straight answer out of him. . . ." My voice trailed off as I felt the smallest tug on my energy from the direction of the window. Distracted, I moved closer to get a look outside.

Steven followed me as he asked, "What is it? Is Maureen here again?"

"No," I said, and pulled back the sheer curtain. "Something else . . ." And that was when we saw him. Three stories down an elderly man walked across the backyard, heading toward the woods. From this angle we couldn't see his face, but once he reached the edge of the woods he paused and turned slowly around to face the house. He lifted his chin and looked up, scanning the house, and stopped when he got to the window we were staring out of.

My breath caught, and I could feel Steven shaking beside me. "My God," he said breathlessly. "It's Papa. . . ."

Andrew lifted his finger, pointed to us, and then he vanished into thin air.

■ ■ ■ ■

Fifteen minutes later I was blowing on a cup of tea down in the kitchen. Steven sat numbly on one of the stools by the island, his thoughts clearly elsewhere. "Here," I said, putting the teacup under his nose. "Drink this. It'll help."

"It was him," he muttered as he took the tea. "That was my grandfather."

I nodded. "Looks like it. So what we have here are two ghosts that need our help to cross over."

"I need to know what happened to him first," Steven insisted.

I sighed and looked into my own cup of tea. "I told you I would try. But it isn't my top priority."

"Why can't we just wait until we get our answers and then you can cross him over?"

"Because, being trapped between worlds, Andrew is suffering. He's probably frightened or confused or even guilt-ridden. My top priority is seeing that he moves on as quickly as possible. If he did in fact kill himself, then this is the right thing to do. If someone pushed him off the roof, well, that may be one for the police."

Steven's head snapped up. "You said

227

pushed. Do you think Maureen could have pushed him like she pushed Gilley?"

"Anything's possible. And if she was responsible for Andrew's death, there's not a lot we can do about it."

"Can't you lock her up in her window?"

"You mean her portal? I just don't get the feeling she's a negative energy, Steven. I mean, I know she took a tug on Gilley, but I'm sensing there was more to this story than we know right now. I think she had a reason for doing what she did, but I can't figure out what it is yet."

"If she murdered my Papa, I want you to lock her up."

"What am I, the cosmic jailer?" I shot at him, and when he looked offended I softened my tone. "I really think it's better if we try to gather as many facts as possible before we make a conclusion. For now, I'm not going to look at Maureen as a negative entity, at least not until we know for certain one way or another, okay?"

Steven nodded. "Okay."

"Now," I said purposefully. "We need a plan of attack. My guess is that Maureen has exerted enough energy for the night. It takes quite a bit of strength to give us the little show she put on for us upstairs. And that goes for your grandfather as well."

"I'm confused," Steven said, scratching his head. "What is all this talk of exerting energy?"

I sighed. "Ghosts can walk around among us without being seen or felt at all. It doesn't take a lot of energy to do that, but once they try to take other forms, that's when they amp up the wattage, so to speak."

"Huh?"

I tried again. "There are three forms most ghosts take when they want to get our attention: orbs, shadows, and full view. Most ghosts, as I said, travel around unseen and unnoticed for a period of time, but eventually they may try to make contact. The first form they may try is a small ball of light, just like the ones we saw upstairs."

"Okay, I'm with you," Steven said.

"Then, if they're strong enough, they may go for appearing as a dark shadow. Often these shapes don't look human, just large black blobs moving across the wall. Other times their shadows can look quite real and appear even though there's no light to necessarily cast a shadow."

"Spooky."

"They often are. Now the third form, and the one that takes the most energy, is a full physical form. Most ghosts can sustain this for only a few moments before they tire and disappear, just like Andrew did tonight."

"So my grandfather used up all his energy to walk outside and point at us?"

"Absolutely. He should be quiet for several hours at least."

"But Maureen only took the orbital form. She might still be nearby."

"It's possible, but making physical objects move is also a tremendous exertion of energy. She gave that rocking chair a ride tonight. And if she also pushed Gilley . . . well, that had to take it out of her as well."

"Where does that leave us, then?"

"With some quiet time to set up a few more trigger objects and a couple more motion detectors."

Steven nodded. "Okay, let's get started."

For the next hour he and I methodically put the sensors and trigger objects in all the rooms I had identified as being hot, plus a few others that Steven said his grandfather liked to hang out in. Finally, the only room left was the wine cellar.

We opened the door leading downstairs, and Steven flipped on the lights. A blast of cold air hit us as we trooped down the stairs. "Hold it," Steven said as he held his arm out, halting my progress. "Feel that?"

"Yes," I said as I felt the temperature shift. "That's weird," I muttered.

"What?"

"My radar isn't buzzing. Normally when I'm entering a room where there's an energy, I'll get this sensation that lets me know I'm not alone. I'm not getting that here."

Steven pulled his arm back and asked, "Should we check it out?"

"Most definitely," I said, and moved past him.

When I got to the bottom of the stairwell I let my eyes rove the area while my radar continued to search out the entity causing the temperature change. Still, nothing bumped my energy field.

Steven sidled up next to me and said, "I think I know why you're not getting anything."

"You do?"

"Yes. Look over there."

I did and I was surprised to see the door leading to more storage space flung wide open. "Ah," I said as I put my hand out in that direction. "That's where the cold air is coming from. Someone opened the door."

"The question is, who?" Steven said.

"I didn't," I was quick to say.

"I know. I was the last person down here after we brought that final TV, and when I went back upstairs I remember that the door was closed."

"Well," I said ruefully, "ghosts do love to open doors."

"They do?" he asked. "Why? Don't they just walk through them?"

"Oh, they do that too. But if I had to guess as to why, I'd say that opening or closing doors makes them feel powerful. Command over the physical makes them feel connected to the space they occupy."

"You believe Maureen or my grandfather opened this door?"

"Looks that way."

"Come on," Steven said. "Let's take a look."

We walked to the door and paused in the doorway, squinting into the dim light as we looked through. I was surprised to discover that instead of a room, a long tunnel opened up in front of us. "Whoa," I said. "I thought you told me this was a room used for storage."

Steven looked just as surprised as I did. "That's what I thought was here."

"Do you know where it leads?" I asked.

"No," he said, peering into the darkness.

"Well," I said, moving forward into the tunnel. "There's only one way we're going to find out then."

"That's what I was afraid of," he

mumbled, and followed me.

The tunnel's walls were fortified by brick, and the floor was cement, just like in the cellar. Our footfalls echoed as we went forward, but after about ten feet we both stopped because the light was too dim. I put my hand on Steven's back and said, "I don't think it makes sense to go much farther without being able to see where we're going. There's a flashlight in the van, but I want to see if we can pick up something on camera, and the night-vision video cam is the best tool for that."

"Where is this cam?"

"Upstairs in one of the bedrooms."

"Let's get it," he said, and we both turned and headed back out of the tunnel.

Making our way up the stairs, Steven asked me, "Did you happen to pick up any spirits in the tunnel?"

"Nope. But then, I didn't exactly have my radar on when we made our way into it. I'll make sure I turn up the volume when we head back down."

A few minutes later, armed with the night-vision cam, we clattered back down the cellar steps. Steven was in front of me when he halted suddenly. "What the . . . ?" I heard him say.

Peeking around his shoulder I saw what

stopped him. The door to the tunnel was closed. "Did you shut the door when we went upstairs?" I asked.

"Nope," he said, and moved down the steps to the door. Putting his hand on the handle he turned the knob and tugged, but the door held fast.

"What's the matter?" I asked, coming to his side.

"It's locked," he said as he tried it again, and the door held firm.

"You're kidding," I said. Steven stepped aside and gave me an *after you,* gesture. I gave him a raised eyebrow and moved to try the door. It was locked tight. "Do you have a key?" I said.

"No, but I have a phone, and I know of a locksmith in town."

"Good idea. While you're calling on that I'm going to go outside and see if maybe there's a way into the tunnel from up top."

Steven nodded and followed me upstairs to the kitchen, where he took out the phone book and began to flip the pages. "I'll help you outside as soon as I'm done with the call," he said.

I gave him a thumbs-up and headed out the door. Luckily it had stopped raining, since water was hell on the camera. Night was falling as I went over to where I thought the tunnel was. I tried to gauge from the house where the tunnel might be, but I kept bumping into the wall of the indoor pool. I couldn't see any hidden stairs or trapdoors buried in the ground, and the more I looked, the more confusing the layout became.

Steven joined me a few minutes later, carrying a flashlight. "Locksmith will be here in the morning," he announced. "Did you find anything?"

"No, and it's the strangest thing. See that?" I said, pointing to a small window at ground level. "That's the window in the cellar that faces to the right of the stairwell. The door to the tunnel is to the left of that, which means . . ."

"It goes under the pool," Steven finished.

"Yeah. But that's got to be wrong. I mean, who would construct a tunnel under a pool?"

"Would be very dangerous," Steven said as he scratched his chin and looked from the window to the wall of the indoor pool.

"Exactly. Plus, I have to wonder why someone would build a tunnel in the first place. Your grandfather must have had a reason for its construction. Any ideas?"

Steven smiled and shook his head. "My grandfather was a bit on the . . . what is the word you use . . . ecstatic? Like the nice way of saying someone is unique?"

I smiled. "I think you mean eccentric."

"Yes, that is what he was. And there is no way to know what would have motivated him to do that."

"I guess, then, we wait until morning to find out."

"I guess we do. Did you want to go back to Helen's?"

"No," I said, reaching for his flashlight. "Thank you," I said when he gave it to me. "I think it's better if I stay here and try to make contact with your grandfather or Maureen."

"Good. There's a place in town called Angelo's. They have really good pizza, and they deliver. I'll go order for us. You coming in?"

"In a minute. I want to check around out here for a bit," I said as I switched on the beam and played it across the lawn.

"Give a scream if you find anything," he said, and moved off toward the house.

"You mean shout," I murmured as he walked away. I moved the flashlight beam around the lawn, searching for any outside opening to the tunnel. I had no way of knowing whether the tunnel even opened up aboveground, but my gut told me it did. The problem was that Steven and I had gone only a short distance into the tunnel when the light got too dim to see. That meant that I couldn't be sure about any twists or turns the tunnel might take after a certain point. Nor did I know how long it was, but somehow I knew I was in the right area.

As I walked across the lawn in the direction of the woods I suddenly had the very distinct feeling I was being watched. I stopped walking and looked around, thinking maybe Steven was watching me from inside the house, but when I checked I could see him through the kitchen window, punching in a number on the phone.

I turned in a circle, trying to feel where the sensation was coming from, and my eyes kept moving back toward the house. I scanned the kitchen window again and my breath caught in my throat. Right behind Steven was the shadowy figure of an older man standing in the entrance to the dining room. Steven was talking on the phone, completely unaware that anyone was behind him. I ran straight for the kitchen window, waving my arms to get Steven's attention. As I got within twenty feet or so of the window I saw Steven's head snap up and our eyes met. I stopped and pointed as I mouthed, *Behind you,* at him. He seemed confused, so I cupped my hands around my mouth and yelled, "Behind you!"

Steven turned, gave one hell of a shout, and dropped the phone. A split second later the ghost of Andrew Sable disappeared.

CHAPTER 8

"You're sure you're not picking him up?" Steven asked.

"Andrew Sable is one slippery ghost," I said as I moved back into the kitchen after searching the entire ground floor. "I keep reaching out, encouraging a reply, but he won't answer me."

"Maybe it's what you're wearing," Steven said, looking at my jeans-sweater-and-hiking-boots combo critically. "My grandfather liked the ladies. You should change back into that dress you wore for me."

I scowled at him. "First of all, what I'm wearing is perfectly acceptable ghostbusting attire. Second, I did not wear that dress *for you.*"

"You have worn it out with other men?" he asked me, and his confident grin told me he knew I hadn't.

"Maybe it's not me he's not responding to. Maybe he's just appalled that his grandson squeals like a little girl," I snipped.

"Ouch," Steven said, putting a hand over his heart. "I am wounded."

His unwavering smile said otherwise. "Sorry," I said anyway, feeling bad about the comment. "I get snappish when my blood sugar gets low. How long before our pizza arrives?"

"Let's hope they deliver it at all," Steven said with a small chuckle. "I believe the man who took the order was a little upset after I yelled in his ear."

"Got anything I can snack on?" I asked hopefully.

"There are some crackers in the pantry. You may help yourself," he said as he waved his hand in the direction of a set of double doors next to the fridge.

I went to the pantry, opened the door, and gasped. Steven must have heard me because he asked, "What is it? Is it him? Are you picking up my grandfather?"

"In a matter of speaking," I said. "Check it out."

Steven came over to me and looked in. His mouth hung open. "That is so freaking out!"

My head swiveled to Steven. "You really shouldn't try to use American slang just yet," I said.

Steven ignored me and continued to look at the pantry. "Have you ever seen anything like this?"

"No," I admitted. "We'll definitely want to take a picture; I think it's pretty unique, and Gilley and I have a collection of odd stuff on our Web site." The pantry didn't offer much in the way of food — some dry goods like cereal, flour, sugar, and pasta, along with some canned vegetables and soups. The unusual thing wasn't in the contents. It was in the way they were displayed.

Every item had been turned upside down, save one. A container of Quaker oatmeal, right side up, sat front and center, prominently displayed among all the other upside-down items. "What did I tell you?" Steven said as he lifted the container. "My grandfather wanted to live a healthy life. He didn't commit suicide, and this message from beyond his grave proves it."

"I'll never doubt you again," I said, and took the oatmeal from him to examine it more closely.

Just then there was a *bong* from the front of the house. "Pizza's here," Steven said, and went to get the door. I put the oatmeal back exactly as it had been and dug my digital camera out of my pocket. After taking a quick picture I closed the pantry door and turned around to face the area where I'd seen Andrew. Again I focused all of my energy on attempting to make contact. I closed my eyes and reached out in my mind. *Andrew! Andrew Sable, if you're here, please speak to me!*

I waited and finally, with the softest touch, I got a message that sounded like *M . . . was . . . trouble . . .* My eyes snapped open and I walked forward, attempting to make a stronger connection with him.

I'm sorry; I didn't catch that. Could you repeat that?

Andrew didn't reply. I got frustrated and said loudly, "M was trouble?"

"Who's trouble?" Steven said behind me.

I jumped because I hadn't heard him come up behind me. "You scared me!" I said as I whipped around.

"So then I'm trouble?" he said playfully. "Come on; we'll eat and you can tell me what I've done . . . this time."

"You haven't done anything," I said, following him over to the counter, where he put down the pizza and opened the lid. "Man, does that smell good!" I said as he got me a plate and a slice and handed me a soda. "What kind is it again?"

"Chicken parmesan."

"Kind of a weird combo for pizza," I said, picking up my slice and taking a bite. "Okay, so it's fantastic," I mumbled as the delicious mix of roasted chicken, parmesan cheese, and a hint of garlic played across my taste buds.

"When I came here for the summer holidays, my grandfather always let me order pizza whenever I wanted. It was one of the things I missed when I would go back to Germany," Steven said, taking his own slice. "Now, what is this about someone who is trouble?"

"While you were getting the door I did one last call-out to see if Andrew would answer me. He did."

Steven's piece of pizza paused midway to his mouth. "What did he say?"

I shook my head and scowled. "It was weird. It sounded like 'M was trouble.' "

"Who?"

"M. But clairaudient information isn't always crystal-clear. He could have meant the letter M, the letter N, or even the name Em, like Emma."

Steven scratched his head as he considered the possibilities. "How do we find out for sure?"

I chewed on the bite of pizza I'd just taken before answering. "I think we need to go with the obvious first. I think we need to continue to make contact with Maureen."

"She's the M," Steven said flatly.

"Not necessarily, but if Andrew was saying the letter M, then it fits. Along with the fact that she most likely pushed Gilley down the stairs."

"I am telling you this," Steven insisted. "She must have pushed my grandfather too. Off the roof."

"You can't keep jumping to conclusions here, Steven. And even if she did push him off the roof, we still need to find out what he was doing on the roof in the first place. I think we need to be cautious about —" I was interrupted by a loud clanging noise that made both of us jump.

"It's the elevator," Steven said as he set down his pizza. "Come on; it's going upstairs!"

We raced out of the kitchen and over to the staircase, where we dashed up the steps as fast as we could. Reaching the second floor we were both out of breath, but didn't pause as we ran to the master suite and stood in front of the elevator, waiting out the last tense moments before it inched up to our level. But instead of stopping the elevator passed the second floor and continued to climb. "It's headed to the third floor!" I said, and bolted out of the room with Steven hot on my heels.

Again Steven and I climbed the stairs and dashed down the hallway, unsure where the elevator would stop. "Where does it let out on this floor?" I asked.

Steven looked up and down the hallway. "I don't know," he said. "I've never seen it go past the second floor."

We had no choice but to wait for the creaking to get louder and louder as we listened intently, ready to dash into the room where it stopped. At first I thought the elevator would let out in the guest bedroom where we'd seen the orbs, but a quick peek in that direction showed us there were no doors for it to let out in.

Finally the creaking ceased, and we knew the elevator had come to a stop. It was hard to tell where, though, so Steven said, "The doors must be hidden. You look in that room and I'll look in this one. Scream if you find them."

I ran into the guest bedroom and listened intently, searching the room. I could hear the faintest whirring sound coming across the room from one of the closets. I hurried over to it and opened the door.

Behind the door I found an empty walk-in closet outfitted with elevator doors on the opposite side of the entrance. As I watched, the doors slid open and I felt the temperature plummet. "Steven!" I called as I opened up my radar. "In here!"

I heard Steven's footsteps come pounding toward me, but my attention had shifted to what was sitting on the floor of the boxcar. I stepped forward to retrieve the object, and just as I lifted it Steven was behind me, asking, "What's that?"

"Honey," I said as I twisted the glass jar around in my hands.

"What's it doing in the elevator?"

"That's what I'd like to know," I muttered.

"What do your six cents say?" he asked.

"My sixth sense," I corrected. "Hold this," I said, giving him the honey and closing my eyes. In my mind I reached out to the energy and asked it to come forward and talk with me. I had the sense that this energy was female, and in my mind I could picture her clearly. She had brown hair, about shoulder length, ending in a short curl at the bottom. Her eyes were hazel; her nose was long and narrow and matched her chin. I didn't think she was very tall, a few inches shorter than me. Her build was average to a little plump, and she wore a long skirt and a white blouse. I held the vision of her for only a second or two, long enough for me to identify her, and then she was gone.

"It's a woman," I said.

"You can see her?"

I opened my eyes and looked at Steven. "Yes. And she looks very familiar. Hang on," I said, and crossing the room I picked up the photo framed on the nightstand. "It's her," I said.

"You're sure?" he asked.

"Yes. I saw this woman, but older."

"How much older?"

"Twenty or thirty years, but I'm convinced it's her."

From behind us we heard a creaking noise, and Steven and I looked at each other for a beat, then looked to the corner of the room, where the rocking chair was again rocking back and forth. I called out in my mind to the chair, knowing the woman I'd seen was rocking it. *Who are you?* I asked.

Follow the bees. . . .

"What?" I said aloud as Steven looked at me curiously.

"I didn't say anything," he said, thinking I'd been speaking to him.

Follow the bees. . . .

Again I called out with my mind, *Okay, I'll do that, but please tell me who you are and why you don't want to move on. I can help you.*

The rocking chair stopped rocking abruptly, and the tiny flying orbs we'd seen earlier appeared again and began whizzing about the chair in little darting motions that looked exactly like a group of bees hovering around a beehive.

"There . . ." I said, pointing them out to Steven. We watched with our mouths wide while the little orbs seemed to buzz around the chair; then one by one they crossed to the window and out of the pane as if the glass weren't there at all.

"What *are* those?" Steven whispered.

"Ghost bees," I said as I looked out the pane to see where they went. They buzzed around in the darkness, white dots of relief against the darkness of the night. Steven came up beside me, and we looked on as the little group of them made their way down to ground level and across the lawn.

"Where are they going?" he asked me.

"I don't know, but we're supposed to follow them."

"How do you know?"

"Maureen told me," I said, and pointed to the cluster of orbs as they stopped just before the woods and buzzed in a tight little circle to and fro. "Come on," I said, grabbing his hand and pulling him away from the window. "We've got to follow them."

We ran back down the steps, and I stopped for a moment at the bottom, unsure what path was best to get to the ghost bees in time. "This way," Steven said, and headed off to my left.

We passed through the foyer, where Steven paused to grab the flashlight from the side table I'd set it on, then out through the library and into the yard through a French door. To my relief the ghost bees were still there. The moment we got within ten feet of them they stopped their swirling hovering and one by one made their way into the woods.

"Can you switch on the light?" I whispered to Steven.

He clicked it on and the beam pointed to the ground in front of us. With a sucked-in breath I realized the bees had been hovering above a well-worn path in the woods. "Look," I said, pointing it out to him.

"Come on," he said, moving forward onto the path. "Let's not lose the bees."

Even though the rain had stopped, the sky above was still thick with clouds, and no moon shone through. The air was cool and damp, and I shivered just a little in my light sweater, hoping we weren't in for a long trek through the woods. The ghost bees led us in a winding direction that exactly mirrored the path we were walking on. I followed right behind Steven as he focused the beam of the flashlight on the path while keeping an eye on the orbs just ahead. We walked into what felt like the heart of the woods as the eerie darkness enveloped us.

I could see Steven bristle with every twig snap and rustle of leaves, and once or twice he paused and looked behind us. I wasn't as nervous, but had to admit to myself that I wasn't happy about going so deeply into the woods at night, especially given the cool temperature.

We had walked for a while when one particularly loud twig snap got the best of Steven. He stopped and turned toward me. "Someone is following us," he whispered.

"It's your imagination," I coaxed. "It's spooky out here."

"No, M.J.," he said flatly. "Someone *is* following us."

I was about to chuckle and try to convince him that he was simply imagining things when I heard the unmistakable sound of what was clearly footsteps not fifteen yards behind us. My eyes widened at the noise, and silently I nodded to Steven. He heard it too and pulled the beam up, flashing it in the direction the noise had come from.

Nothing but woods appeared in the light of the beam. "Who's there?" he demanded as he moved the beam across the area.

There was no reply.

I looked back toward where the ghost bees had been and let out a small gasp.

"What?" he whispered.

"The orbs are gone," I said, pointing behind him.

Steven whirled around, and I watched his shoulders slump as he saw for himself. "Where'd they go?"

"I don't know," I said, squinting into the dark for any hint of the little lights. "Maybe farther down the path?"

"Come on," he said, and pointed the beam down on the ground again. "Maybe we can catch up."

We continued along the path for a way, searching for the orbs in vain. Finally Steven stopped and said, "This is no good. The little things are gone."

"Does it make sense to assume they continued down the path?"

"Not in the dark," he said, and dropped his voice to a whisper. "And not while we're being followed."

I discreetly stole a glance behind me. "You're right. Let's head back and pick this trail up in the morning."

I gave Steven an *after you* arm motion, and he gave me a playful nudge as he passed me on the path. I giggled as I came off balance a little and stepped backward, and that was when we clearly heard someone run through the brush to our left.

Steven whipped the beam in that direction, and for an instant someone or something gray seemed to dart out of sight. "What the . . ." he said, and stepped off the path in the direction of whatever it was.

"Hey!" I said as he began to crash through the woods toward it. "Wait up!"

I hurried after him, but he had much longer legs and could leap over foliage with far more ease, not to mention that he had the flashlight, while I was left guessing where to go in the darkness.

One of my guesses, in fact, was way off, because after bounding forward, my left leg was held in check by a branch that sent me tumbling. "Ooomph!" I said as I crashed to the ground, my shin striking a stump that sent shooting pains all the way up to my hip. I grabbed my leg and groaned for a minute or two as my eyes stung with tears. "Shit!" I hissed under my breath as I rubbed my shin.

When the pain had stopped throbbing

enough for me to sit up, I looked around and couldn't see Steven or the flashlight's beam anywhere. "Great," I said into the darkness. "Thanks, buddy. Nice job looking out for your partner."

Slowly I got to my feet and took a tentative step forward, igniting fresh pain into my leg. "Son of a . . ." I said as I bent to clasp my shin again. When it subsided, I stood up, hovering on one leg and feeling in the dark for some support. Close by was a small tree, and I hobbled closer to it and held on, trying to shake off the throbbing pain.

"Come on, M.J.," I said to myself. "You can do this. It's not that bad." My voice shook not so much from the pain as from the realization that I was alone, in the middle of a strange dark forest, with no way of knowing how to get my injured butt out and back to the house. Plus, what had been a damp, chilly night had now turned into a full-on teeth chatterer. There was no way I'd be warm enough to make it through the night.

"Great," I groused, as I began to shiver in earnest. "This is just great." At that moment a little breeze blew a strand of hair into my eye, and with an impatient wave I brushed it away. The breeze came back and did the exact same thing. Annoyed, I pushed the strand away again, and just then I noticed a tiny little orb of light dancing in front of my eyes.

I blinked twice and said, "Hello. Where'd you come from?"

In answer the orb did a loop-d-loop and swirled a few feet away. I smiled because the movement reminded me of Tinker Bell. The little orb danced back to me, did another loop-d-loop, and whizzed away. "You want me to follow you?" I asked.

The orb moved up and down, mimicking a head nod, then zoomed another few feet away. Slowly I limped after it, and after just a few yards of having my feet slip on roots and foliage, the ground smoothed out underneath my feet. I paused and felt down with my hands. It appeared the orb had led me back to the path.

I smiled and continued to limp forward, careful not to trip again as I followed the orb until I could see the lights from the house. Just as I looked from the house back to the orb it disappeared with the tiniest of popping sounds. "Thanks, Tinker Bell," I said as I limped out of the woods.

I headed painfully inside and called out as I entered the kitchen, "Steven?"

No one answered. I went into the main

hall and tried again: "Steven? Are you here?" Still no answer.

I frowned and limped back to the kitchen, where I set the teakettle on the stove for a cup of tea to warm my bones and pulled a stool up to the sink so I could tend to my shin.

Pulling the leg of my jeans up, I examined the huge welt forming a few inches below my kneecap, and a long, angry scratch on the right side.

I grabbed a paper towel from the dispenser and dabbed the scratch with cool water just as the teakettle began to whistle. I carefully hopped off the stool and got a cup and tea bag from the cupboard. As I was pouring the hot water I looked up through the window to see the wild bob of a flashlight beam bouncing up and down through the woods. I could also faintly hear Steven calling my name.

If I hadn't been so ticked off that he'd left me behind, I would have gone right to the door and called him inside. Instead, I let him flounder around in the woods until I saw the beam pause just at the edge of the lawn.

Knowing he had seen me from the lit window I did a little hand wave and took a sip of tea. The beam moved up to the window for a second, then down to the ground, where it swayed with determination across the lawn. In a few moments I saw Steven's outline as he came closer to the lights of the house.

He banged open the kitchen door and demanded, "Where have you been?"

I turned to face him, the leg of my pants still rolled up above my knee. "You left me in the woods, Pedro, and if it weren't for those orbs I'd still be out there lost and cold, so if I were you I'd be relieved that my partner managed to get back here safe and sound, instead of being so pissy."

Steven's eyes focused on my injured shin. "What happened to you?" he asked flatly.

"I was trying to keep up with you when I tripped on a root and smacked my shin on a stump."

Steven set the flashlight on the counter and came over to me. "Sit down and let me look at it."

"It's fine," I said.

Steven took another step closer, invading my personal space. "Sit down," he said softly.

With his body so close, my heart began to thump a little faster in my chest, and I felt the first tickles of perspiration along my brow. "I've already rinsed the dirt out; all it needs is a little ice," I said.

Steven gave me the same kind of look a parent gives a child when their patience has run out; then he took the mug of tea still in my hand, placed it on the counter, and in one quick move bent low, scooped me up into his arms, and carried me the few steps back over to the bar stool. "Hey!" I said as I was being lifted up.

"Shhhh," he said as he deposited me on the stool. "Settle down and let me look."

I could feel heat come into my face as his warm hands felt along my shin. I winced a few times as he pressed on my skin where most of the swelling was happening, and let out one big "Yeowch!" when he tapped on the spot that took the brunt of the blow. Stepping back he said, "It's not broken, but you're going to have a bad bruise."

"Thanks," I said, and began to roll down my pant leg.

"Hold on," he said, placing his fingers around my wrist. "It's better to ice it first." I waited while he went to the freezer and extracted a package of peas. He grabbed the other bar stool and propped my leg on it before gently placing the peas on my injury.

"Yikes." I winced.

Steven smiled. "I'll be right back. Hold

this in place until I tell you to, okay?"

I nodded as he walked out of the kitchen, and a moment later I heard the front door open. After a few more seconds he came back inside, carrying a little black duffel bag, which he deposited on the counter next to me, and from it extracted a vial of some antiseptic, some gauze, and a few cotton balls. Next, he sat down next to me and cleaned the nasty scratch the stump had made. He placed a bandage on it, then gently eased the package of peas back on top.

"Feeling better?" he asked after he'd put his first-aid kit back together.

I nodded, still uncomfortable at his close proximity. "Yeah, it's starting to numb up."

"Keep your weight off of it for the rest of the night," he said, reaching for my cup of tea.

"Got it," I said, extending my free hand for the cup. Before giving it to me Steven took a sip and held my eyes over the brim. The look he gave me was a smoldering one, and without thinking I bit my lower lip and squirmed ever so slightly.

One corner of Steven's mouth lifted, and he set the tea down on the counter again, just out of my reach.

"Can I have that back?" I asked.

Steven's eyes still held mine as he said, "Caffeine will keep you up. As your doctor I think it would be better for you to sleep."

I rolled my eyes and leaned forward to retrieve the cup, which Steven moved farther out of reach again, playing with me. I shot him an irritated glare and leaned way over, trying to snatch the mug before he had a chance to move it. He was too quick for me, and picked it up with a chuckle, took one long slurp, and said, "You really want it that bad, eh?"

"I'm cold, and I'd like to warm myself up before you drink it all down," I snapped.

"Well, why didn't you say so?" Steven said as he moved toward me again and set the cup down right next to me.

I turned to pick it up when I felt a finger under my chin, lifting my gaze back up and away from the cup as he bent low and kissed me. "I didn't know you were cold," he cooed as his lips moved to my ear and he began to nibble on the lobe.

"All I need is the tea," I said hoarsely, trying hard not to gasp as his lips moved down the side of my neck.

"Shhhh," he said softly, and moved back to my lips.

The package of peas fell out of my hand and onto the floor with a slap as my hands went up to his neck. He pulled his face away from mine for one brief second at the sound of the peas hitting the floor; then he kissed me more deeply, and this time I moaned. After a few more seconds Steven picked me up again and carried me to the stairs. I looked up the long staircase and said to him, "I can make it, you know."

"Good to know," he answered, and marched up the steps. We reached the first floor and he headed down the corridor to the master suite. There he laid me gently on the bed, then crawled on the bed, his hips resting lightly on mine and his torso hovering over me as he propped up on his elbows to stare into my eyes. He spent a moment combing my hair out onto the bedspread and looking at me so hard that I squirmed against him. "God, you're sexy," he said.

I would have returned the compliment but he'd already lowered his mouth again to cover mine. His kiss deepened as my pulse quickened.

My fingers slid down his back and gripped his ass, which was small and firm and oh, so sexy. Steven pushed his hips forward into mine, and I moaned again as I felt the firmness of him between my legs. A second later he was off me and standing next to the bed, and I held a whimper in check as his warmth and weight moved away.

As he shrugged out of his shirt I could see what a fabulous body he had. Broad shoulders and defined pectoral muscles tapered down to a flat stomach and small waist. His upper chest was crested with black hair that formed a T down along his breastbone and meandered in a path that disappeared below his belt. I heard a low chuckle and looked up to see his eyes dancing with merriment. "Like what you see?"

I raised one eyebrow. "What else you got?"

Steven laughed. "Plenty," he said with confidence.

"I'll believe that after I've seen the full monty," I quipped.

Steven gave me a sexy grin and began to slowly unbutton his jeans. Just as I was about to see if monty was in fact a python, a huge crash rang out right below our bedroom. "Holy crap!" I squealed as I jumped off the bed and hurried through the door, Steven close on my heels.

"What room did it come from?" I asked as we got to the stairs.

"The library," he said, and started ahead of me. We crested the landing and turned the corner into the library, surveying the scene. One of the giant bookcases that lined the wall had toppled over, strewing books all over the room and smashing a wing chair. "My God," Steven whispered.

My antenna was up and scanning the room. I felt the vestiges of something paranormal, but it was hard to tell whether it was male or female. For some reason it felt mixed. "Who did this?" Steven asked as he turned to me.

"They both did," I said.

"Grandfather and Maureen?"

"Feels like it," I said. "They both seem a little pissy, but I think it's with each other, not at us."

"Are we in danger of another temper trampoline?"

I grinned. "Temper tantrum. And no, once they pushed over this bookcase they both zipped back into the mist. I don't feel them hanging around here."

Steven bent over and picked up a book. "What a mess," he said.

"Yep. We'd better get started," I replied, and bent down to pick up an armful of books.

"Or we can go back upstairs and worry about this in the morning," he coaxed.

I avoided looking at him. The truth was that I'd been damn close to jumping his bones just now, and honestly, I'm just not that kind of girl. "I think we should pick this room up and keep a vigil. Andrew and Maureen are very active, and I believe they may take a short breather and come back to cause some more mischief."

"My idea sounds like more fun," Steven said.

"My idea will keep us safe," I replied as I put a stack of books on the nearby desk and turned to him. "Besides, you already had your fun this morning." The comment slipped out before I'd had a chance to think about saying it, and I immediately regretted it.

"I'm sorry, what?" he asked.

"I was out for a jog this morning," I said, blowing out a sigh. There was no way out of it now. "I saw you coming out of that woman's house. You two looked quite chummy together."

Steven actually laughed. "And did you recognize the woman I was with?"

I looked at him, and it was my turn to cock my head. "Yes," I said. "She was the waitress at that grinder restaurant."

"Annalise is a very old friend of mine," he began.

"I'll bet."

He smiled, as if he were amused by an inside joke I wasn't privy to, then moved over to where I was leaning against the desk and traced a line from my cheek to my collarbone with his finger. The move was so light it made me want to shudder, but I stiffened instead. "During the summer holidays when I visited my grandfather, he would pay her to watch after me to give my mother some time for herself," he explained.

"She was your babysitter?" I asked, a little surprised by how far back they'd known each other.

"Yes," he said with a broad smile. "That first summer I was eleven and she was sixteen. I had a . . . er . . . crash into her? You know, to like someone older than you?"

"You had a crush on her," I supplied.

"Yes, I was crushing. It feels the same when you are a young boy and suddenly these urges develop, you know?"

"Did she ever reciprocate?" A forward question to ask, but he seemed to be opening up, and I wanted to know.

"No, I wasn't the Sable she was interested in," Steven said, and there was the smallest bit of venom in his voice.

"What?"

"She was much fonder of my father," he said.

"You're kidding," I said, watching him closely for any hint of deception. "But I thought he stuck to Boston?"

"My grandfather was a forgiving man. He always held on to the hope that my father would come around. So he would invite dear old Dad up for a weekend, but my father would refuse to come to the lodge while I was here. They would meet in town at Helen's and talk, and after a few days Steven Sr. would go back home."

"So, what happened between Annalise and your dad?"

"Annalise is Helen's niece. She worked at the bed-and-breakfast for a few years, and that's how she met my father. My mother heard from some of the locals that she and my father had an affair, and this upset my mother, because she had thought he might still love her. That was when I was fifteen, and after that my mother refused to come here during the summers."

"So, Annalise and your father had an affair, and then he ended it and that was it, right?" I had a feeling there was more to it, but I wanted to see what Steven would tell me.

"No, unfortunately not. Annalise became pregnant and had a baby girl."

"Your father had *another* illegitimate child?"

"I don't know for sure," Steven said as he went back to stroking my collarbone. "Annalise never told me or anyone who the father was. But twelve years ago she gave birth to a little girl she named Shanah."

"Doesn't Shanah wonder who her father is?" I asked.

"Shanah doesn't wonder much at all. She's mentally handicapped. Annalise tried to give birth at home, but the baby was deprived of oxygen. Shanah nearly died."

"That's so sad," I said, feeling ashamed of myself for prying.

"Yes, it is. Now Annalise works two jobs and does the best she can to take care of her daughter. She knew I was in town, since we stopped for a grinder, and last night she called me in a panic because Shanah wasn't breathing properly — one of her many health conditions. I went over to help and stayed until this morning."

"I see," I said, looking back down at my feet again and feeling like an idiot. "Sorry about getting snippy, then."

"On the contrary," Steven said as he lifted my chin with his finger. "I like it that you're interested." And with that he kissed me deep and long, then picked me up and put me in the matching wing chair across the room. "Now stay off your leg. I will clean this mess up. You can keep me company with your great charm and wit."

That made me laugh, and I did keep him company, with a minor interruption when I made a call to check on Gil, until about three a.m., when we both curled up on the long sofa in the room and fell asleep.

CHAPTER 9

Over coffee the next morning, Steven and I discussed what we thought we'd seen in the woods. "I've seen all kinds of ghosts, phantoms, and things that go bump in the night, but that flash of gray wasn't one of those. I think it was human," I said flatly.

"You think some person was actually following us?"

"Could be."

We both puzzled on that for a bit, wondering what someone would be doing in the middle of the woods following the two of us. "But why are we so interesting?" I asked.

"That would depend on who's doing the following."

I continued to ponder the situation before saying, "Plus, after all that, we never did find where those orbs wanted to lead us."

"Odd how they disappeared the moment we heard someone behind us," Steven mused.

"Or maybe not," I said, looking pointedly at him. "Maybe wherever the orbs were leading us was for our eyes only."

"That's what I am thinking," Steven said. "But how do we get the orbs to come back and lead us to where they were taking us?"

"Maybe we can find it on our own," I said.

"You are thinking about the path in the woods?"

I nodded. "Yep, Toto, I think that's the yellow brick road. And if we really look at the starting point, I'll bet you ten bucks it's the same spot your grandfather walked to when we saw him from the upstairs window the other day."

"Okay, then," he said. "We'll go after the locksmith gets here."

"Say," I said, curious about something. "You spent lots of time here as a kid — you never noticed this path in the woods?"

Steven blushed slightly. "I never went near the woods," he admitted.

"What kid doesn't want to explore the woods?" I asked.

"The kind that nearly gets bitten by a coyote in the first week that he visits here," he said. "They were a real problem around here when I was young, and they are very scary-looking creatures."

I nodded. "I'm with you on that one," I

said with a shudder. "And the noise they make — is that awful or what?"

"It can be quite frightening," Steven said. "But I haven't seen one around since we got here, so maybe they're not as much of a problem as before."

"Let's hope so. Anyway, I'd like to check out that tunnel if we can," I said. "Once we get that door open, I don't think it's a good idea to let it close on us again without knowing where it leads."

Steven smiled. "Okay, have it your way. Creepy dark tunnel first, scary woods full of ugly coyotes second."

I giggled. "Your English is improving," I said.

"I am jigsaw with that," he quipped. I didn't have the heart to tell him that he'd gotten Gilley's "jiggy" mixed up with a puzzle.

We waited an hour for the locksmith to show, which allowed us enough time to shower, get dressed, and munch on some dry cereal. The doorbell finally rang around nine thirty, and an older gentleman with a patch on his shirt that read, MICKEY, was at the door. "You two call for a locksmith?" he asked.

"Come in," Steven said as he held the door wide.

Mickey entered and took in the large hall. He let out a low whistle of appreciation and said, "This is some place you got here, Dr. Sable."

"Thank you," Steven said. "The door we need help with is this way," he called as he led Mickey through the hallway to the kitchen and down the steps to the cellar.

I followed dutifully behind, watching the stairs as I went down, when I nearly crashed into Mickey because the front of the line had halted. "What's up?" I asked Steven, who was holding up the line.

Mickey said, "Doesn't look like you'll need a locksmith after all."

I poked my head around Mickey and saw what the holdup was. The door to the tunnel was wide open.

"Mickey," Steven said, turning to the locksmith but giving me a look. "I need you to change the lock on this door. And I'll want an extra key."

"No problem," Mickey said, and moved around Steven to get to work.

I came down the last few steps to stand next to him and said, "You know, I'd really like to know where this tunnel ends."

Steven nodded. "Me too. When he's done, I think we should go in."

"Works for me."

We waited for the locksmith to complete the switch on the lock, and Steven paid him, then showed him out. While he and Mickey headed up the stairs, I took the liberty of venturing into the tunnel a bit, but it was too dark for me to go more than a few feet. Trooping upstairs, I grabbed the flashlight and my night-vision camera and went back down. Steven joined me a moment later. "You ready?" he asked me.

"Yes. Here, you keep the flashlight, but don't turn it on. We'll find our way through the viewfinder of this," I said, holding up the camera. "It should pick up any weird spectral stuff that we wouldn't be able to see with the flashlight on."

"Got it," Steven said, and together we proceeded into the tunnel, each of us keeping a hand on the wall to help guide us. We'd walked about five or six yards when I heard dripping. Pointing the camera up, I noticed what looked like several beads of water coming off the ceiling.

"Steven, click the flashlight on a sec and point it up there," I directed, my voice echoing through the tunnel. He did, and what we saw made us both gulp. "We're under the pool," I said nervously.

Steven reached up and touched one of the spots as he considered my question. "Yes," he agreed as he traced not just one crack but several as they snaked their way across the ceiling of the tunnel. As he checked the largest cluster of cracks in the middle of the ceiling to make sure we were fairly safe before heading in farther, I noticed a black box taped to the corner of the ceiling with a wire coming from it. Thinking it must be some sort of electrical box, I was grateful it didn't appear to be connected to anything currently conducting electricity. It would be scary to have a live wire down here with so much water.

"This is not good," Steven said as he pointed the beam at the ceiling.

"How bad is it?" I asked as alarm bells went off in my head.

"Bad enough for me to say that I think we should find out what's at the end of this thing, then get out of here and close that door for good."

"Do you think it's safe enough even for that?"

Steven knocked on the ceiling with his fist. No additional water leaked out. "I think it will hold long enough. These cracks aren't good, but I don't think they're going to give way soon. Let's keep going, but make it quick."

Steven clicked off the flashlight and I held

up the viewfinder again as we went on. At one point the tight space came to a sharp corner that was impossible to see around. Steven hesitated as he got to the turn and surprised me by gripping my shoulder tightly.

"What?" I asked turning the viewfinder on him so I could see him. He moved his finger to his lips and made a shushing sound; then he cupped a hand to his ear, letting me know he'd heard something. I kept my mouth shut and listened hard, and sure enough we could hear distinct footsteps from around the corner.

I looked back up at Steven, his eyes wide as he determined what the noise was. Leaning forward he whispered in my ear, "We're not alone down here."

I nodded and whispered back, "I can't sense who it is."

"No?"

"No. I'm reaching out with my antennae, but I'm not hitting any kind of spirit energy."

"Maybe it's not a spirit," he whispered back. There was a pause between us, and I blinked in the dark, unable to see anything unless I held up the viewfinder. That gave me an idea, and I whispered to Steven, "We can point the camera around the corner and look through the viewfinder. Hopefully whoever is there won't be too far out of camera range and we'll be able to see who it is."

"Good idea," Steven said, and moved me around in front of him. With Steven's chest at my back I held the camera up at an angle where we could both see through the viewfinder and pointed the lens around the corner. Just out of clear view there appeared to be a figure moving deeper into the tunnel. I was convinced it wasn't spectral, as there was no energy coming from it that felt spiritual. "It's a man," I whispered back to Steven.

"Could be a woman," he said. "We can't tell from back here."

"I say we follow slow and quiet-like until we can get a better view."

"After you," he said into my ear.

I moved soundlessly around the sharp corner, which was a tight fit for me and an even tighter one for Steven. Once we'd cleared the turn, I held the camera in front of us and we both moved forward on tiptoe. My palms grew sweaty as we inched closer to the shape in front of us, which was gradually turning from a gray blob into something decidedly human. Step by step we closed the space between us, and we watched as the figure stopped walking and bent down to the ground. I felt Steven's grip on my shoulder tighten. Suddenly in front of us a light flickered, causing me to squint into the viewfinder, and I quickly looked up from it to the real light ahead. We could just make out the bent form of someone crouched down and facing away from us. I lowered the camera as we headed toward the light, until Steven tripped on my heel and I let out a small gasp.

The light immediately went out, plunging us all into darkness again. I quickly raised the camera and looked through the viewfinder, but all we could see were the legs of our intruder running up what looked like steps at the end of the tunnel.

"Stop!" Steven yelled, knowing we'd been heard. "Who are you?" he said as we jogged forward. A blinding light shone in the darkness. We both stopped to shield our eyes; then we heard a bang as we were plunged back into total darkness. "Hello!" Steven said again, but there was no reply, and I knew that we were now alone in the tunnel. "Steven," I said urgently. "Turn on the flashlight and let's run after him!"

Steven did, but at that exact instant there was a tremendous explosion. The sound was like lightning striking right next to us. The explosion and resulting tremor reverberated through the tunnel and knocked us to the ground. I landed on top of Steven, who rolled me underneath him and covered me with his bulk as dust and debris showered down seconds before water came pouring in all around us.

We scrambled up and I grabbed the flashlight from the ground, where the water was quickly rising about our feet. "The pool!" I yelled. "He's blown a hole in the pool!"

Steven took my arm and yanked me behind him as we ran ahead to the stairs. We dashed up but stopped short as the flashlight's beam reflected off a large wooden door. Steven pulled at the handle, but it was locked tight. "Damn it!" he said as he backed down a few of the stairs, then raced up and threw his shoulder against the door. It shuddered, but held firm. "That bastard's shut us in here!" he yelled, pounding on the door with his fist.

I joined him in pounding, both of us calling for help. Panting, I turned around and nervously aimed the flashlight back down the steps and noticed that the second stair was quickly disappearing as the water continued to pour in. "What do we do?" I asked, trying to keep the panic out of my voice.

Steven answered by throwing himself again against the door one last time, but it held firm. He was silent for a moment as he rubbed his shoulder; then he seemed to make up his mind and he said, "We go back."

"We *what?*"

"How is your backstroking, M.J.?" he said, and dashed down the stairs, taking my hand and pulling me along.

"But, Steven!" I squealed as I waded now in knee-deep water. "We could drown going this way!"

"Yes, that is true," he said over his shoulder. "But if we stay here, we will definitely drown. That pool is Olympic-sized and fourteen feet deep. There is enough water to fill two of these tunnels."

"Shit!" I said, working hard to steady the beam of the flashlight, which kept getting wet as I struggled to walk through the rising water. "Could the odds be any more against us?"

As if on cue the flashlight went out. Next to me I heard Steven say, "That would be a yes."

CHAPTER 10

I trudged forward in the darkness as the water rose above my chest and I was quickly forced to swim while trying desperately not to panic. I could feel Steven next to me, periodically pulling on my shirt to make sure I was keeping pace with him as we followed along the wall of the tunnel. As my labored breathing reverberated off the walls, I could sense the ceiling just above my head, and knew we had very little time. "Steven," I sputtered as I kicked and paddled.

"I'm here," he said with another tug on my shirt.

"How are we going to get out of this?"

"We need to reach the beach," he said, his voice remarkably calm for a guy about to drown.

My mind worked on that for a minute. "What *beach?*" I asked.

"You know," he said, his voice bouncing

off the sides of the tunnel. "Where the hole is."

"You mean *breach*," I panted as I continued to kick with my legs and pull with my arms.

"Yes, that too," he said. "When the water reaches the ceiling it will stop coming in, and if the hole is big enough we can swim through it to the pool."

"Just like that? We swim through the hole?" I asked, my hope rising.

"Yes. Unless the pool collapses on top of us; then our goose will be . . . how you do say . . . burned?"

I groaned. "How much time do you think we have to make it?" My legs and arms were quickly becoming tired.

"I don't know, so you must swim as fast as you can, okay?" he said, and gave my arm a pull forward.

I gulped and concentrated on making it down the tunnel. Fortunately, about the time my hand could easily touch the ceiling, we made it to the sharp corner. "Hurry!" Steven urged, pulling me in the dark around to the other side. This section of the tunnel was now dimly lit, as twenty yards ahead of us we could see the water pouring in through a three-foot gap in the ceiling. "We're close!" Steven said, and we both pushed ourselves hard the last few yards to the hole. We treaded water around it as the water inched up farther and farther.

"What now?" I asked.

Steven moved behind me and grabbed me around the waist. Breathing hard in my ear from the difficult swim, he said, "We must wait for the tunnel to fill all the way up. Then we swim through the hole and get out of the pool as fast as we can. The rest of the floor could collapse at any moment, so don't walk on it. Just swim to the edge and pull yourself out."

I nodded and waited those last anxious moments while water moved ever closer to the ceiling. Steven and I strained to stay close to the hole and breathe the remaining air until we were completely submerged. Finally, noses touching the ceiling, we took one last gulp of air and moved closer to the hole, waiting for the pressure to equalize so that we could swim up through it. Seconds ticked by, my heart pounded hard in my chest, and finally I felt Steven give me a great shove forward and up through the hole.

Kicking and stroking as hard as I could, I plunged up out of the tunnel and into the pool. With a few more kicks I cleared the surface as my lungs were about to burst. I gulped the air hungrily before I noticed that Steven hadn't come up yet.

Looking down I could see the hole, and in the center of it he seemed to be struggling. Alarmed, I took another gulp of air and swam back down to him. He was tugging at something around his waist, and I saw that the back of his belt was caught on one of the jagged edges of steel sticking out of the concrete. Reaching for him, I pushed his waist down and worked to unhook the belt. It took me a few tries, but I finally got him free and that was when I felt him go limp.

Turning around in the water, I hooked my arms under his shoulders and clasped my hands across his chest, then kicked my legs with all my might. We moved a fraction of an inch. My lungs screamed for air, and my heart pounded hard in my ears as I looked up at the surface, which seemed a thousand feet away. I glanced back down at the pool's bottom, just a foot or two below. Still holding tight to Steven with one arm, I used the other to push us back down, trying to get as far away from the hole as I could, then crouched and with all of my remaining strength pushed off from the floor of the pool. We coasted several feet up, and I kicked and used one arm to make it to the top.

I gasped as I cleared the surface, struggling to pull Steven's head above water too. I had no idea if he was able to take a breath, but I'd worry about that in a moment. Rolling onto my side, I held him with one arm and used the other, along with my legs, to make it to the shallow end. Finally my feet found the floor, and I dragged Steven's limp body forward until I had him in about a foot of water. I heard a loud gurgle back in the deep end, and knew that the hole was giving way and the whole floor of the pool was about to collapse.

Panting and exhausted, I tugged Steven over to the ladder, trying hard not to focus on the fact that his lips were turning blue. I climbed quickly out of the pool and lay down on my stomach, and, reaching for him, I hooked my hands under his shoulders and pulled with a strength born of sheer adrenaline. Another gurgle came from the deep end just as I nearly lost my grip on him, and with a tremendous growl I heaved him from the lip of the pool onto the deck. As his feet came over the edge the hole in the bottom of the pool expanded with a rumble that shook the foundation, and a gigantic gap opened straight up the middle of the pool.

My breathing was so labored I could

barely remain conscious, and my limbs felt like lead. More than anything I just wanted to lie down for a moment and catch my breath, but the light blue tinge to Steven's lips had spread now to his cheeks, and I knew I had very little time left. I crawled to his head and tilted it back, thankful that I'd had lifeguard training in high school. Pinching his nose, I opened his mouth and took a huge gulp of air. I blew down into his airway but felt it constricted. I tried again, and again, and finally he convulsed and a great gulp of water came up out of his mouth. I turned him sideways as he began to cough and retch. "Thank God," I panted, easing him up to lean on me after he'd coughed up the worst of it.

It took several minutes before Steven was able to talk. Finally he managed to say, "I couldn't get out of that damn hole."

"It was your belt. It got caught."

He nodded and continued to hack and wheeze. I waited him out, holding on to his chest as we sat there dripping and regaining our strength. After a while he gave a pat to my hands and rasped, "Thank you."

I smiled. "You're just lucky I remembered my CPR training."

"You did chest compressions?"

"Uh . . . no," I said, suddenly remembering that I hadn't even thought about checking for a pulse.

"You just blew into my mouth and it worked, huh?"

"Let's not forget about pulling you to safety and getting your butt out of the pool," I reminded him.

Steven leaned to the side so that he could look into the pool. "We were almost toasted, huh?"

I smiled tiredly. "Yep. Our goose was almost burned."

Squeezing my knee he got slowly to his feet. "Come on," he said to me. "Let's get out of these wet clothes and go find the son of a bitch who tried to kill us."

An hour later, as our clothes tumbled around in the dryer, Steven was outside wrapping up his talk with the local sheriff. I remained inside sipping some hot tea, ensconced in a bathrobe that had come right out of Andrew's closet.

The smell of a spicy aftershave seemed to compete with the scent of chlorine still on my skin as I watched them through the window and thought about who could possibly have wanted us dead. On that front, Steven and I were both in agreement — someone had wanted to drown us, and had lured us to the basement with the open door to the tunnel.

Before the sheriff arrived we'd had a chance to talk about it, and Steven had said, "Whoever that was in the tunnel, it was definitely human."

I nodded. "Yep, that's a safe bet. Last time I checked, not even the cleverest, most active spirit I've ever come across could set off an explosive."

We fell into uncomfortable silence before Steven said, "So the question is, who and why?"

I was still pondering that as I saw the sheriff flip his notebook closed and hand Steven a card. A minute or two later Steven came back inside and the sheriff drove off. "So what'd he say?"

"He said we were two lucky people, especially after he got a look at the cellar and what's left of the pool." Water now nearly covered the basement steps. Besides calling the sheriff, Steven had also contacted his insurance company and a plumber. The plumber couldn't come out until the day after tomorrow, and the adjuster wanted to wait until all the water had been drained before assessing the damage and writing a check. We'd been advised to stay away from both the pool area and the cellar. Gee, and

Steven and I were so close to perfecting our synchronized swimming routine.

"So what now?" I asked as I walked with him through the front hall and back to the kitchen. Steven ducked my question until he'd gone into the laundry room off the kitchen to retrieve his pants and shirt. Coming back out, he tossed me my own clothes and said, "Now we get dressed and head back into those woods."

Once we were clothed we walked over to the edge of the woods, where the orbs had led us the night before. "Should be easier to follow the path in the daylight," I said as my eyes swept the brush in front of me, looking for the path.

"Not just yet," Steven said as he looked at the ground leading away from the house. Looking there too, I noticed an indentation in the lawn that came from the wall of the indoor pool and out across the lawn in a line, before turning sharply and entering the woods just down from where we stood. "This way," Steven said.

When we got to the spot where the lawn stopped and the woods began, we saw the indentation continue, but it was much harder to see, given all the foliage. We poked around in the general direction we thought the tunnel traveled, looking back at the house to check that we were on course. But the scrub became too dense, and we knew we were offtrack when no exit from the tunnel could be found.

"Where did we go wrong?" I asked, scratching my head.

Steven looked around him and placed his hands on his hips. "There must be something around here," he mused, and suddenly his face lit up. "M.J.!" he said excitedly, then pointed to our right. "Over there, look!"

I turned to where he indicated and saw what looked like a tiny stream leaking out from behind a tree directly across from us. Steven moved toward it and I followed him. Sure enough, when we rounded the tree we could see a narrow door, cleverly built into the side of the tree, as a steady flow of water leaked out of the tree and puddled around our feet. "This is wild," I said, trying the door. It was locked tight.

"Come on," Steven said, leading me away from the tree. "We know where that leads, but what we don't know is where this path goes."

I swiveled around to see that the stream was actually made possible by a path that led away from the tree. Water covered it in its path of least resistance, but as we walked along, the water eventually became side-tracked and nothing but the dry path remained.

We walked at least a half mile, until we came abruptly to a rather small cottage almost completely engulfed by the woods.

"Where are we?" I asked as we stepped out of the woods onto a small walkway leading to the front door of the cabin.

"I think we're at Willis's house," Steven said as he looked around.

"Your grandfather's groundskeeper?"

"Yes," Steven said, raising his hand to knock. "This must be the cabin my grandfather built for him last year."

I lowered my voice and asked, "Why haven't we seen him before now?"

Steven smiled at me without answering and knocked very hard, three times. We listened as someone called from inside, and after we opened the door I knew exactly why we hadn't seen Willis.

"Steven!" a frail-looking black man in a wheelchair said as we stepped inside.

"Hello, Willis," Steven said, moving to him and squatting down next to the wheelchair. "How is the leg?"

"Oh, it'll be all right," Willis said, smiling as he reached out to clasp Steven's hand. "That's the thing about diabetes: You can't let it get you down." He laughed.

I could see that Willis's right leg was propped up on a foot stool in front of the chair.

"Mind if I examine it?" Steven asked as he moved to inspect Willis's leg.

"You doctors are all alike," Willis said. "You know your daddy was just here about an hour ago, and he's already fussed over it."

Steven paused ever so slightly as he asked, "My father was here?"

"Yeah. Ever since we lost Andrew he's been coming up here to check on me. And I know the two of you don't get along, but I'll tell you, your father is a good man. We've been having ourselves some good talks, he and I."

"Really," Steven said, and I watched as his back seemed to stiffen.

"Yep. He's been trying to talk me into moving back to Jamaica Plain with my daughter; you remember her?" Willis said as he pointed to a series of photographs on the mantel above the fireplace.

"I remember. How is she getting along?" Steven asked.

"Janelle is doing great. She became a nurse, you know. Works in the same hospital as your father, in fact. And I'd love to move back with her, but there's no sense in being a burden on your children. That's why your father's been trying to get me well. He's been talking to me about this new drug he's working on that might be able to help out an old man like me," Willis said. "He says he thinks he can even get me back up and walkin'."

Steven looked hard at Willis. "Does my father come here . . . er . . . with frequency?"

Willis cocked his head inquisitively and thought about it for a moment. "I think just about every couple of days for the past two months or so."

"That's great," Steven said tightly, and stood up. "Listen," he said, walking over to sit on a nearby couch and patting the seat next to him for me. "We are having some big trouble at the lodge."

"Was that what I heard earlier this afternoon? I was taking a nap when I thought I heard thunder, but when I woke up there wasn't a cloud in the sky," Willis said.

Steven nodded and started to explain to Willis what had happened to us earlier. While he talked, I took a moment to look around the small cottage. The place had the look and feel of a log cabin, with log walls, hardwood floors, and an A-frame roof. A stone fireplace dominated the living room, and behind where we sat I had noticed a galley-style kitchen.

My eye finally settled on a small table by the front window, where a chessboard was set up with what looked like a game in process. As I looked at the arrangement I felt my radar begin to hum. The letter A drifted into my head, and something that sounded like *a . . . drew* buzzed around inside my mind.

I elbowed Steven, who stopped talking and turned to me. "What?"

I pointed to the chessboard. "Watch," I said.

Just as Steven turned to look, we could clearly see one of the black chess pieces move across the chessboard and knock over one of the white chess pieces. As that happened I felt a sense of celebration at the edge of my thoughts. "He says, 'I win,' " I said as I got up off the couch to take a look.

From behind me I heard chuckling and the squeak of a wheelchair as Willis followed me to the table, parking his wheelchair opposite the other chair there. "Well, would you look at that," Willis said. "That old man still knows how to play."

I knew nothing about chess, but understood as soon as Steven joined me and announced, "Checkmate."

"Andrew's here," I whispered.

"Of course he's here," Willis said. "He's been playing chess with me almost every day since he died."

Steven and I both turned to Willis with a mixture of shock and surprise. "Has he ever spoken to you?" I asked. Sometimes the average layperson could be a better conduit than a trained medium.

"Spoken? You mean have we had ourselves a conversation?"

"Yes," I said.

"Well, sure. But I'm afraid I've done all the talking and he's done all the listening. I can feel when he's around, which happens to be right around this time every day. That's how I knew something had happened to him, you see. We had a chess game planned and Andrew never showed. I could hardly believe it when they told me how he'd died," Willis said as his eyes became moist.

"We are not believing it either," Steven said. Turning to me, he asked, "M.J., can you talk with him?"

"I'm trying," I admitted. I'd been calling out to Andrew in my mind for several seconds, hoping he would acknowledge me, but he wouldn't come forward. Thinking of something, I said, "Willis, I need you to do me a favor."

"What's that?" he asked.

"I need you to tell Andrew that it's okay to talk with me. I'm here to help him make sense of things."

"Who are you, anyway?" Willis asked, really looking at me for the first time.

Steven blushed. "That's my fault," he said to me before turning to Willis and explaining. "I'm sorry for my manners. Willis, this is M. J. Holliday. She is here to try to find out what happened to my grandfather. She is an expert in talking with people like him. People who can't move on to where they belong."

"You mean she talks to ghosts," Willis said succinctly.

"Yes."

"Then why does she need me?"

I answered, "Because Andrew may not be able to see me until you point me out. You see, I think he is currently stuck in his daily routine. He can see you and knows to interact with you, but he may be unwilling to acknowledge anything outside of his comfort zone in his current state of confusion. It's my belief that he hasn't realized he's died, Willis."

Willis listened intently to me and seemed

to absorb what I was saying. "I'm with you," he said after a moment. "So what do I say, exactly?"

"Just call out his name, tell him you'd like him to talk to me for a bit. That I'm here to help him sort things out. I think he might listen to you."

Willis creaked backward away from the table and pointed his chair toward the big living room. "Andrew," he said in a commanding voice. "It's Willis. I have company today and I'd like you to join us for some conversation. You know your grandson is here to visit you, and he's brought along a lady friend. Her name is M.J., and she's here to talk with you."

I closed my eyes as Willis talked and opened my intuitive mind as wide as I could. Right after Willis stopped, I felt Andrew's energy come forward. *Hello, Andrew,* I called in my mind.

Hello. Have we met before? he asked, his energy strong and our connection very clear now that I had been introduced.

No. I'm a friend of Steven's. We've come to visit you and learn about your fall.

My fall?

Yes, Andrew. A little while ago you had oatmeal for breakfast; do you remember?

There was a pause, then: *Yes. That was*

this morning. I'm looking after my heart these days.

I smiled inwardly at the irony and continued, *So what happened after you had your breakfast; can you remember, Andrew?*

Another pause. *I went upstairs to make a phone call.*

Who did you call?

Roger. I wanted to make sure he took care of things.

Then what happened?

There was a long silence. Finally Andrew said faintly, *Something happened.*

"What happened?" I said out loud, my eyes tightly closed as I concentrated. I could feel Andrew pulling away from me, as it was harder and harder to hear him.

I don't . . . , he said. *I can't . . .*

"Andrew!" I insisted. "Don't go yet! You must tell me what happened!"

No . . . M . . . trouble . . . get help! With a suddenness that startled me, the connection broke. I could feel Andrew's energy sever from mine. I opened my eyes and stared right at Steven, who looked anxious. "What happened? What did he say?"

My shoulders drooped. "He wouldn't tell me everything, but I managed to get a little information out of him."

"Tell us," Willis said.

"He said that on the morning he died he finished his breakfast and went upstairs to call Roger to make sure he took care of things. Then someone with the first initial M or someone nicknamed Em, maybe an Emily, was either in trouble or was causing trouble, and he tried to get help, but then he jumped back into the mist and that's all I got."

Steven ran a hand through his hair and turned to Willis. "Do you know who my grandfather was talking about?"

Willis puckered his lips in thought, then slowly shook his head. "Your grandfather and I kept limited company, Steven. It's true I worked for him for almost forty-five years, but our friendship was restricted to this cabin and our daily chess games."

"So you're saying you didn't know any of his acquaintances or friends on a first-name basis?" I asked.

"In a nutshell," Willis said. "But I do know this: Every time I try to tell your father that Andrew wasn't the kind of man to commit suicide, he changes the subject. So I'm glad that you're looking into this, Steven. Something happened to him up there, and I know in my soul that Andrew couldn't have taken his own life."

A thought seemed to occur to Steven, and

he asked, "Willis, on the day of my grandfather's death, did my father come here?"

"No, I can't say that I remember him coming by that day," he said to us. "But he was here the week before. I remember because Andrew was angry when he came to our chess game. He wasn't one to hang his family's laundry out, even to me, but he was so angry from something that had just happened that he let it slip that your father was a fool, and it was time Andrew taught him right from wrong."

"And you have no idea what he was referring to," I said.

"I didn't press. It was none of my business."

Steven nodded and offered, "Is there anything you need before we leave?"

Willis smiled good-naturedly. "Naw, thank you, Steven, but Maria should be coming over a little later with some groceries for me."

"I'm glad to see you are taking care of each other," Steven said kindly. "It was good to see you, Willis. We'll be at the house if you need anything."

Steven and I took our leave. Once outside I noticed that the small dirt road led to a driveway to the side of the log cabin that I assumed was the way Willis and those who took care of him got to and from the cabin. I pointed to the drive and said, "Anyone could come down that road, park a little way away from the cottage, and make it onto your property."

"I was just thinking the similar thing," Steven said. "What I want to know is who knew about the tunnel, and why did my grandfather have it built?"

"You said you spent summers here as a kid; you never saw any hint of it?"

"None."

"Unfortunately, your grandfather isn't very talkative. He's still in serious denial."

"Denial?"

"He's not willing to accept that he's dead. He's acting as if nothing has happened to him, and he's just going through his daily routine."

"How do we get him to accept that he has died?" Steven asked.

"We find out what happened that morning on our own, and repeat it back to him."

Steven gave me a sideways glance and said, "I was afraid you were going to say that."

I smiled and continued, "We start by finding out who this Roger is. Come on; I happen to know someone who's perfect for this kind of job."

We walked back to the house, where I immediately went to the kitchen to retrieve my purse and dig out my cell phone. Punching in the speed dial I waited and was rewarded with a "Hi, M.J. How's it going over there?"

"Fine, fine," I said easily, not wanting to worry Gilley over the details of nearly getting killed. "How's the fairy tail?" I kidded.

"Hurts like a godmother, but I'm suffering through it."

"I have a job for you."

"Thank God, I was starting to get bored."

"I was able to connect very briefly with Andrew a little while ago, and all I could get out of him was something about a phone call he placed to someone named Roger. I need to know who this Roger is, and if and when you find out, I need you to try to get some info about what they might have talked about. Pull the phone records, ask around, figure it out."

"Got it. Anything else?"

"Yes. There's a second ghost in this house. Her name is Maureen. Andrew keeps referring to either the letter M or someone named Em, like Emily. Nose around; maybe some of the locals know who this Maureen was and what her connection was to Andrew. Also, see if there's a link to an Em or

Emily while you're at it, just to cover all the bases."

"I'm on it. I'll call you on your cell when I get something."

"Thanks, Gil. Hope the tush feels better soon."

I clicked off with Gilley and set the phone on the counter. "What'd he say?" Steven wanted to know.

"He's all over it."

"Do you think he'll find out something?"

"I do. Gilley's a whiz at this stuff. Trust me."

Steven nodded, then pushed away from the counter he'd been leaning on and said, "Time to go."

I cocked my head at him and asked, "Where to?"

"The second branch off the path. I believe it leads somewhere. Remember the little orbitals?"

"You mean the orbs?"

"Yes, those too. They were leading us somewhere on the second branch before we lost them. I think we need to find out where it goes to in the daytime."

Steven and I exited the kitchen door again and searched for a bit at the edge of the woods trying to find the path, as it was well hidden. We finally located it and moved forward on the trail, passing the tree with the hidden door and continuing on deeper within the forest.

After about twenty minutes we could see a break in the trees ahead. I tugged on Steven's sleeve to make sure he saw it too, and he looked back at me to say, "I see it. Come; we're almost there."

We broke through the woods a few moments later and saw that we stood on a hilltop that overlooked a large open field. Immediately visible was a small house, down the hill and to the right.

The house looked like something out of a storybook, painted a buttercup yellow with bright blue shutters and a large blue door with a heart-shaped wreath over it. Window boxes bloomed with spring flowers on every sill of the house, and a white picket fence enclosed a small yard around the perimeter. A walkway led from the door to the gate of the fence and was also lined with flowers. To the right of the house was a driveway that dumped out onto a dirt road that headed south and disappeared at the end of the field to tunnel through more woodland.

At the back of the house little white huts dotted the landscape every five yards or so. I wondered what they were, but my attention was redirected by Steven, who nudged me and pointed a few feet to our left. I looked over and saw a tombstone, and it was then that I realized that the path we'd been on led directly to the grave.

We walked over and squatted down to take a better look, noticing fresh flowers at the grave. Steven read the engraving and my mouth fell open. " 'Maureen Emerson. Born nineteen twenty-seven. Died nineteen seventy-four.' "

"The woman from the photo," I said.

"Who was she?" Steven asked, and I shrugged my shoulders. I had no idea.

"Let's walk down to the house. Maybe we can get some answers," I suggested.

Steven nodded, and we both headed down the hill. I was a little self-conscious, as I realized we might be trespassing on this person's property. "Do you think we should have come by the road?" I said. "You know, so that these people don't think we've been snooping around on their land?"

"It's not their land," Steven said. "It was my grandfather's, which means that it's now mine."

We arrived at the house, and Steven opened the little gate for me and bowed, allowing me to enter first. I smiled at his theatrics and walked to the front door, giving it a hearty knock. We waited several moments, listening to the silence before I knocked again. Still no response, so I turned to him and asked, "Now what?"

"Let's check around the back," he suggested, and we went to the rear of the house.

The backyard was just as tidy as the front, with close-cut green grass and a garden lining the house. There was also a small sitting area with two metal chairs and a table. Everything looked freshly painted, planted, and well maintained. Steven headed over to a window and cupped his eyes to peek inside. "Steven!" I hissed. "Don't do that!"

"Why not?" he said, still doing the Peeping Tom thing.

"What if someone's *in* there?"

"Then they'll come to the back door and yell at me, and we can ask them about Maureen and why they're on my property."

"Maybe your grandfather rented them this house?" I offered.

"If he did, then he didn't tell me about it," Steven said, backing away from the window.

"So what did you see?" I asked, curious about what the interior looked like.

"Oh-ho," Steven said, smiling at me. "It's not okay for me to look in, but it is okay for you to ask me what I saw?"

I narrowed my eyes. "Yeah, yeah, whatever.

Just tell me what you saw."

Steven thumbed toward the window. "That's the kitchen. Very neat and clean in there, just like out here. I am thinking that an older woman lives here, no kids and no husband."

"So now you're the psychic?" I said with a smirk.

Steven smiled broadly. "You do not need to be a psychic to put clues together and know about things."

"What kinda clues?"

"Well," he said, rubbing his chin, "there is one cup and one bowl in the dish rack. Curtains and the paper on the wall are . . . very female with lots of lace?"

"Frilly?" I supplied.

"Yes, that too. Also, there is no newspaper, just a book on the counter."

"What does that have to do with anything?"

"Men like the news with their morning coffee. Women, on the other arm, enjoy some romance with their tea."

I scowled at him. He was just too smug for his own good. "Great job, Sherlock, but while you were peering into windows, I was taking a gander at something far more interesting."

There was the smallest sag in Steven's

smug smile as he asked, "What?"

I gave a thumb wave over my shoulders. "Behind us. Those little huts? Those are beehives."

Steven squinted in the direction of the hives. "Yes, that is important. Come on; let's go see them."

We approached warily as I counted twelve hives. As we neared them, we could see that at least six were active hives, and these were all located on the left side of the group. They buzzed with the energy of thousands of little yellow-and-black honeybees.

Steven and I kept a safe distance from them, and stood silently for a little bit as we listened in awe to their collective hum. Motioning with his head, Steven moved closer to the six hives on the right, which were silent and obviously abandoned.

Upon inspection, I noticed that these hives were also more weather-beaten. Their paint was chipping and the wood was warped. I wondered if they were older than the other hives. Perhaps they had been the original six and the other group had been built to replace them.

Steven continued to walk forward while I hung back a bit, afraid that there might still be a bee or two hovering about inside them, ready to sting me. I watched as he walked in a circle around the first wooden box, and lost him around the backside as he knelt down. "Find something?" I called to him when he didn't reappear right away.

I waited another beat or two, wondering what he could be doing back there, when he popped back into view and held something up for me to see. It looked like a large rusted funnel and a plastic hose, both very old and very dirty. "What *is* that?"

"Private property," I heard a woman's voice say from behind me, right before I heard the distinct metallic sound of the cocking of a shotgun.

CHAPTER 11

Steven's eyes widened and his smile faltered just before he dropped the funnel and the hose and raised his arms above his head. I followed suit and turned ever so slowly around.

"State your business," a woman who looked very similar to Maureen's photo said, as she leveled the shotgun first at Steven, then at me.

"We're just looking," I heard Steven say.

"You're trespassing on private property," the woman snapped. "Give me one good reason not to shoot you."

"Okay, how about this. How about we're not trespassing," Steven said. "I own this land."

I was watching the woman closely, and I saw the gun lower a fraction as she took her eye off the sight to stare up at Steven. The moment passed and she lowered her eye to the sight again. "What's your name?" she asked.

"Dr. Steven Sable. My grandfather was Andrew Sable."

My heart was pounding in my chest by now, the tension of having a large gun pointed right at me sending adrenaline zipping along my veins. The woman held her position another moment, and just when I thought we were going to have ourselves a little standoff, she abruptly lowered the gun. "I'm sorry about your grandpa," she said.

"Thank you," Steven replied, lowering his arms and coming over to stand next to me. "This is M. J. Holliday," he added, and seeing that my arms were still raised high above my head, he put a hand on my arm and lowered it. "You can put your hands down. I don't think she's going to shoot us."

The woman cracked a smile at me. "You're completely pale," she said.

I noticed suddenly how rapid my breathing was. *"Can you blame me?"*

Steven wrapped an arm around my shoulders protectively while I focused very hard on getting it together. "So, who are you?" he boldly asked the woman.

She regarded us a moment before answering. "The name's Mirabelle. This is my house and my land."

"I am begging your difference," Steven said evenly.

I rolled my eyes when Mirabelle gave him a quizzical look. "He begs to differ," I translated.

"Yes, that too," Steven said impatiently. "My grandfather purchased six hundred acres here, and built the lodge in the middle. I believe you're on his land."

Mirabelle smiled, but it wasn't a friendly one. It reminded me more of a crocodile. "You are correct. This *was* Andrew's property. He deeded over twelve acres to my mother forty years ago. And when she passed on, Andrew made sure it went to me. You can check the county records if you like."

It was Steven's turn to smile tightly. "Why would he do that?" he asked. "What connection did your mother have to my grandfather?"

"Gin," Mirabelle said, the crocodile smile widening.

"As in rummy?" I asked, totally confused.

"No, as in bootleg. This section of Massachusetts used to be made up of dry counties for a couple hundred miles. Times were when you'd have to drive clear to Boston to buy a bottle of hooch. Andrew saw a need within the community, and he filled it via my mother, who made the best damn boot-leg gin around."

"So I'm confused about this twelve acres," Steven said.

Mirabelle hoisted the gun in her hand to her shoulder, and the sudden movement caused me to jump. "Easy, there, girl. I'm not gonna hurt you," she said with a chuckle. "Why don't you all come in for tea and I'll explain it to you nice and slow." And with that she turned on her heel and walked away toward the house.

I looked at Steven with wide eyes and said, "She can't be serious."

Steven seemed to study her for a moment. "She seems to be."

"I'm not going in there with that crazy woman!" I hissed, keeping my voice quiet lest I upset the gun-toting luna-chick.

"Okay. I'll fill you up later," he said, and began following.

My jaw fell open as he walked off. "Damn it!" I swore under my breath. "This is a bad idea, M.J.," I muttered to myself as I caught up to Steven. "I see one body part in her fridge and I'm *outta* there!"

"Agreed," he said, and ruffled my hair.

The inside of Mirabelle's house was much like the outside. The decor was bright and springlike without overdoing it. She motioned us into her living room, which was painted a granny apple green with dark wood accents and patterned slipcovers. Steven and I sat side by side on the couch, he in a relaxed position, me on the edge of the seat ready to bolt at the first hint of trouble.

"I have Earl Grey tea; will that suit you?" she asked from the kitchen.

"That's fine," Steven said for both of us, then looked at me and whispered, "Will you relax?"

I scowled at him and held my ground on the edge of the couch. I looked around the room and something caught my eye. I could have sworn I saw movement in the hallway just off the living room. It was then that I noticed my energy was humming and I got a tugging sensation from my solar plexus. "Someone's here," I said quietly to Steven.

"Huh?" he said, giving me a funny look.

I didn't respond to him; instead I closed my eyes and reached out intuitively to the shadowy figure I'd seen in the hallway. *Hello? Can you hear me? I'm M.J., and I won't hurt you but I'd like to know your name.*

Mirabelle's mom . . .

My eyes snapped open. I turned to Steven and said, "Maureen is here."

Steven sat forward and looked into the

hallway I indicated with a head nod. "I thought she was at the lodge?"

"They can travel quite easily," I said to him. "It's not that far away, after all."

"What's not that far away?" Mirabelle said as she carried in a tray of steaming tea and cookies.

"Nothing," Steven said, and gave me a look that said, *Shhhh.*

"This is a lovely home," I commented. In my head I heard, *Thank you.*

Mirabelle offered the tray of tea and ginger cookies first to me, then to Steven as she said, "Yes, it is, and quite popular these days."

"Pardon?" Steven said as he took the tea from the tray.

"There's a Realtor in town who says he has a couple from New York who want to buy it — lock, stock, and barrel — for a huge chunk of change."

Something about her statement made me feel worried. I puzzled over it, then asked, "How would a couple from New York even know about this place? I mean, it seems pretty far off the beaten path."

Mirabelle shook her head and made a tsk-ing sound. "The past year or so all sorts of out-of-towners have been coming up this way and snooping around. They're all from

New York, and they think they can throw their money around and us simple folk will jump to their every whim. In fact, that's who I thought you two were when I came home from my walk. I figured the gun was a good way to scare off any folks who thought they could wave a checkbook at me and get me to play nice."

She didn't answer my question, and I was about to push the point when Steven said, "You were telling us earlier about this booted gin and the deed to this property?"

"Ah, yes," Mirabelle said, taking a seat on the love seat directly across from us. "I don't know the full details of the bargain my mom and your granddad struck back in the day, because it was before I was born. But by the time I was five I was helping Mom with the sieves hidden in the beehives. Everyone in town thought she was scratching out her living making honey and selling it at the local markets, when in fact that was just a cover for the real operation.

"She and Andrew had quite the business. She'd make the gin, and maybe a little whiskey too; then in the middle of the night she and I would carry these big jars with honey labels through the forest, following a path that led to a tree not far from that big house Andrew had."

"How long did this go on for?" Steven said.

"Until she died in nineteen seventy-four. I had just turned seventeen then. In fact, I think it was a year or two before you showed up," Mirabelle said, giving him a little wave of her hand.

"You knew about me?"

"Sure did. Your grandfather talked about you all the time."

"He used to visit you, then?" Steven said, and I noticed how soft his voice had become.

"Couple times a week. He'd come through the woods and place flowers on Mom's grave, stay for tea, then leave. His visits got shorter and more sporadic as the years went by, but every once in a while I'd see him up there, placing flowers on her grave, and I knew he still cared."

Again I felt a tug in my solar plexus and I got the oddest thought. It sounded like, *Tell about the ball. . . .* In my mind's eye I saw a Christmas tree. I looked at Mirabelle and asked, "What's the deal with the Christmas ball?" thinking perhaps she had gotten a special present as a child for Christmas and this was some fond memory her mother wanted Mirabelle to talk about.

Mirabelle's reaction was unexpected. She

looked at me as if I'd said something so offensive that I deserved to be slapped. It was a moment before she said, "So, you've heard about how she died?"

I shook my head and said, "No. I'm sorry; perhaps I should explain. I'm a psychic medium, and right now your mother is behind you in that hallway asking me to have you talk about some sort of ball that has to do with Christmas."

I had to give Mirabelle credit. She seemed to take my profession in stride, because she nodded at my explanation and said, "Andrew threw a big party at Christmas in nineteen seventy-four and invited my mother and me. I wasn't feeling well, and decided to skip it. Mom almost stayed home too, but I insisted she go. She'd been so excited by the invitation, and she'd bought herself a special dress to wear. I remember how beautiful she looked standing in the doorway right before she left. She blew me a kiss and that was the last time I ever saw her."

"What happened?" I asked.

"The morning after the party the sheriff was at my door saying there'd been a terrible accident, and Mom had fallen down the stairs at the Sable lodge. Someone said they saw her heel catch on the top stair, and there was nothing anyone could do for her. Her neck had been snapped and she'd died instantly."

At that moment something pushed me hard from behind and I fell off the couch and onto the coffee table in front of me. Steven leaned forward and grabbed me under the shoulder, "M.J.? Are you all right?"

"I'm fine," I said, completely embarrassed. "I don't know what happened." I knew that the push had come from Maureen. Sitting back on the couch, I straightened my shirt and motioned for Mirabelle to continue.

"That's the end of it," she said sadly. "Mom died and a few weeks later Andrew came here and said that the house now belonged to me. He explained that Mom and he had struck a bargain many years before that made the house and twelve acres hers as payment for services rendered."

"So, she supplied him with gin; he resold it and paid her with land," I said.

"Yes."

"What was between your mother and my grandfather?" Steven asked. "Why is her picture in his house?"

Mirabelle blushed slightly and fussed with her napkin. "They had a long and secret romance," she said.

Curious, I asked, "Why was it so secret?"

"Because Andrew was married. His wife often stayed in Boston — word had it she didn't like it up here. Andrew would go hunting here on the weekends, and Mom would head over to his place. They broke up only once, and that was when she got tired of waiting for Andrew to divorce his wife, so she took up with my dad and married him. I was born a year later, and Dad left when I was two. From that point forward until she fell down the staircase, my mother and Andrew had a regular thing. To this day I'm convinced she was the love of his life."

"So, your parents divorced," Steven said, more statement than question.

"No," Mirabelle replied. "My mother was a devout Catholic. She thought it was okay for Andrew to divorce, but it wasn't a choice she was willing to make."

Turning to Steven I asked, "When did your grandmother die?"

"The late eighties. I never liked her."

"She was a bitter woman," Mirabelle said, then caught herself. "I'm sorry. I didn't mean to insult your family."

"Do not worry over it," Steven was quick to say. "It was common knowledge."

Mirabelle smiled and gave Steven a nod.

Then she glanced up at the clock and said, "I really do have to get a move on. The bees need some attention before it gets too late in the day. Come by anytime and we can chat again," she offered.

"As long as you don't greet us with the gun," Steven kidded.

Mirabelle giggled. "Promise." She showed us to the door.

We made our way back up the hill, and Steven asked me, "What happened in there when you fell forward?"

"Maureen pushed me."

"Pardon?"

"Maureen gave me a shove," I said, giving him a direct look that said I wasn't kidding.

"Why?"

"I don't know, but now we know who pushed Gilley down the stairs, and I'm guessing we know that Maria didn't trip on her little tumble either. Maureen's intent on pushing people."

"So she really could have pushed my grandfather off the roof," Steven said.

I considered that before answering him. "I know that it's possible, Steven, but in my gut I just can't see it happening that way. When Mirabelle was talking about Andrew and Maureen, there was something in Maureen's energy that told me she loved

Andrew very much. I can't see her murdering him."

"Then why all this pushing?" he asked me.

"I think she's trying to tell us something about what happened the night she died. I don't think her heel caught. I think she was pushed, and she's reenacting what happened to her." Steven looked at me thoughtfully, and just as he was about to speak, my cell phone bleeped.

"I've got dirt," Gilley said when I picked up the line.

"Dish," I said.

"I got a hit on your ghost Maureen, whose last name is Emerson. She owned some property smack-dab in the middle of the Sable land."

"That's old news," I said. "Steven and I discovered that, like, an hour ago."

Gilley made a snarfing noise on the line. *Hello!* he said. "Could you have told me?"

"Sorry, we were sort of in the middle of things. But let me ask you, did you happen to get any info on how she died?"

"Hang on," Gilley said, and I could hear him typing into the computer. "Her obit says she fell down a set of stairs on Christmas Eve. Wait a sec," he said, and I heard more typing. "Here we go, local paper has an online archive, thank God. Most of these small towns aren't that sophisticated. Maureen Emerson, longtime Uphamshire resident . . . blah, blah, blah . . . yadda, yadda . . . found it. Says she was attending the Andrew Sable Christmas Eve ball when her heel caught on the top stair and she took a tumble, snapping her neck and killing her instantly, according to an eyewitness."

"Does it say who the eyewitness was?"

There was a pause on Gilley's end as he skimmed the rest of the article. "Nope, just says it was one of the attendees."

I scowled. Why weren't things ever easy? "Gil, here's the drill. I think that Maureen was the ghost that pushed you down the stairs the other day, but I don't think she meant to hurt you. I think she was reliving the night she died. I think someone pushed her down the steps and then claimed to have seen her heel catch on the stair."

"That's a lot of assumptions, M.J."

"Yeah," I said. "But my gut says I'm right. Can you dig a little deeper into Maureen's death? Maybe find someone who might have been at that party that night?"

"M.J., that was over thirty years ago!"

"I know it's a long shot, Gil, but if anyone is going to work a little magic on that end of it, it's you."

"Just don't expect a miracle," he

grumbled.

"Also," I continued, "I need you to look into the background of Maureen's daughter, Mirabelle. I think she's clean, but the fact that she knows her way through the woods to the secret entrance of the Sable house has me a little bothered."

"What secret entrance?"

I'd forgotten that I hadn't filled Gilley in on the tunnel cave-in, and I didn't want to open up that can of worms right now. "Nothing, just work on both of those, would ya?"

"Along with working on this Roger guy, too, I suppose."

"Yep. Along with that," I said, smiling. I knew I was giving Gilley a lot of work, but it was his forte, after all.

I filled Steven in on Gilley's end of the conversation as we made our way back to the lodge through the woods. When we got home we were both famished, so we drove into town to eat. When we arrived at the local diner, Steven hesitated as we were about to walk in, looking through the window of the eatery. "What's up?" I asked.

"My father is in there."

"You're kidding," I said, looking through the window myself. "Did you want to go somewhere else?"

"No, this will be fine. Come on."

We headed inside, and several people looked up as we walked through the door. Steven's father wasn't one of them, and it was obvious that he was so engrossed in his conversation with another man that unless we made a point to call attention to ourselves, he would hardly notice our presence. Steven took advantage of this and walked around the back of the restaurant, then circled back and took a seat directly behind his father's booth.

My eyes widened and I shook my head at his boldness, but incredibly, his father took no notice of us.

"If the permits are signed within the next few months, how quickly can we break ground?" we heard Steven Senior say.

"We'll be able to move fast," the other man said. "I'd say by the following week, as long as there's no holdup at the county office."

"I'm working on making sure there are no unexpected delays," Steven Senior said with a hint of amusement in his voice.

"I'll bet you are, Dr. Sable," the man said with a dry laugh. "The only matter left is gaining the deeds for phase two. You know what'll happen if —"

"Why don't you let me worry about that,

Jim," Steven Senior interrupted. "Your focus should remain on the job at hand."

"Yes, Dr. Sable," the man said quickly. "I didn't mean to imply —"

"Of course you didn't," Steven Senior said as his cell phone chirped. I peeked over the top of my menu as he answered it curtly with, "Did you get it?" There was a pause, then, "Good. Meet me in the lobby this evening," and he hung up the phone. "Shall we go?" he said to his acquaintance as he stood up from the table and threw several bills down.

Just then our waitress came over and began talking about the specials, so any further conversation Steven and I could have heard was drowned out. With regret I watched the two men leave the diner.

After we'd placed our order I said, "Sounds like Daddy is working on a major project."

"Mmmmm," Steven said thoughtfully. "My father has always thought himself important."

"Seems like he's got some sort of construction project here in town."

"Curious, don't you think?" Steven said to me. "He's never been a very caring man, and yet he's been looking in on Willis. His profession is in medicine, yet he's now working on a construction project."

I cocked my head sideways. "You think he's up to something."

"Yes."

"Could be a coincidence," I suggested. "Maybe while he was up here checking on his old friend Willis, someone approached him about investing in a project that was too good to pass up?"

Steven seemed to consider that for a moment. "I just can't see that logic," he finally said. "My father has never cared about anyone but himself. This is why he got into trouble with the medical board three years ago."

"Your father had trouble with the medical board?"

"His license was suspended for . . . how do you say moving things in your favor?"

"Manipulating?"

"Yes, for manipulation of the results of a medical trial he was conducting."

"So tell me about the relationship between your father and your grandfather," I said. I was curious about this whole Sable family dynamic. "How did the two of them get along before you came around?"

Steven twirled his fork as he said, "My grandfather told me that when he was a boy, he dreamed of going to medical school and becoming a doctor. His father, however, would have none of it, and pushed my grandfather to take over the family business, mostly timber and mining. When my grandfather had a son, he pushed him to fulfill the dream he never could. But my father flunked out of medical school twice before finally graduating."

The waitress interrupted our conversation when she arrived with our lunch. After she'd gone Steven continued, "So my father graduates, but doesn't do anything with his training. Instead, he goes to South America and becomes a . . . eh . . . playing boy?"

"He becomes a playboy," I supplied.

"Yes, that too, and he finally comes to Argentina, where he meets my mother and begins a long affair with her. When he gets back to the United States, my grandfather is so furious with his behavior that he will not give him any more money. He advises him to use his medical training to earn his way in the world."

"Ouch," I said as I munched on a fry. "Talk about tough love."

"Exactly. So my father has just enough money to make it the few months to study for his medical boards, which he barely passes, and he begins practicing medicine. The trouble for him is that it takes time to build his practice, and my father was not known for his patience.

"Within six months of opening up his practice, he starts up again with his college girlfriend and proposes."

"He's married to Corrin Wharton, right?" I said.

"You've heard of her?"

"I've heard of her filthy-rich daddy," I said, giving my eyebrows a bounce.

"I think it was love at first sight," Steven mocked.

"So he marries Corrin; then what?"

"My father thinks he's in the clear, and goes back to the old lifestyle of long visits to Argentina and making false promises to my mother. This is about the time I was conceived, and as my mother tells it, everything was going along well until my father is caught with my mother by a friend of Corrin's."

"The plot thickens," I said.

"Pardon?" Steven asked. "What thickens?"

"Things become complicated," I explained.

"Very," he said. "My mother said that my father told her he had to go back to Boston to take care of the mess caused by his wife's friend, but that he would be back soon and the two of them would eventually marry."

"So let me guess where this is headed," I said, thinking that Steven lucked out when he got his apparent good sense from his mother. "Your mother never sees him again."

"Banjo," Steven said, pointing a pretend gun at me.

"Bingo," I corrected with a giggle. "The term is, 'Bingo.' "

"Banjo, bingo," Steven said, waving his hand. "Anyway, when my father gets back to Boston, his wife threatens to divorce him if he doesn't stop playboying, and to make sure he doesn't get into trouble again she makes him go back to his medical practice. She also hired and paid his nursing staff to keep watch on him and report directly to her."

"And did the relationship between your grandfather and your father ever improve after your father tried to declare him incompetent for acknowledging you as an heir?"

Steven nodded. "Yes, but only on the . . . er . . . like on the top of the water?"

"Surface," I said, then took a bite of sandwich.

"Yes, surface. After a few years my father became a regular visitor at the lodge, except, of course, during the summer, when I was here; then he would come up only once or twice and stay in town at Helen's. The two men would go out on their hunts, something I never enjoyed, but which both of them seemed to like. Still, I don't think my grandfather ever fully trusted my father again."

"You still believe Steven Senior was only playacting to get back into Andrew's good graces?"

"My father was on a very short dog leash," Steven said. "He could not do anything without his wife knowing about it. His only freedom was up here with my grandfather."

"But your grandfather wasn't buying it," I said, more fact than question.

"Exactly."

"So how is that you ended up in medicine? I mean, your father hardly sounds like the kind of man you'd want to follow in the footsteps of."

"That is the true . . . how do you say, like iron?"

"Irony," I supplied.

Steven nodded. "When I was a small boy, my mother tried very hard to give me the impression that my father was a great man of medicine, and that the reason he was not able to come live with us was because he was busy saving sick children around the world."

"Poor woman," I said sadly. "She must

have felt bad about your not having a father figure."

Steven nodded. "She did. By the time I came to visit my grandfather and learned the truth of my father's character, I already had it in my head that I wanted to be a great doctor too."

"Your grandfather must have loved that. The son he has to push into that career, but his grandson goes into it willingly."

"Yes. Anyway, my grandfather insisted I have the best education possible. He and my mother discuss this, and she suggests a boarding school in Germany. Her cousin married a German and they live close to the school, so I had family nearby to make me less lonely."

"You must have missed your mother," I said, watching Steven's face closely.

"Oh, believe me, I did. But I saw her on holidays and when she would come to stay with me during the summer to visit with my grandfather here. In the end, it was for the best. I got to learn German and English, and I can say that I've traveled the world."

"So you speak three languages?" I asked, rather fascinated by how worldly Steven was.

"Five. I also speak French and Italian, but English is my most rusty language."

I gave him a wink and asked, "Your father really never wanted anything to do with you? He never made any attempt at all to get to know you?"

"None. Which is why I believe that my grandfather left his fortune to me, and not my father. He knew that Steven would never acknowledge me as his rightful heir, so by naming me in his will, he could ensure that I was really a Sable."

"Did your father know you were going to inherit everything?"

Steven smiled. "Oh, I doubt it. Word leaked to me in Germany that he . . . uh . . . when you're so angry you go kaboom?"

"Exploded?"

"Yes, that too. He went kaboom and exploded at the reading of the will."

I laughed. "Come on. Let's go check in on Gilley and see if he's found out anything further about our list of interesting people."

We left the restaurant and got back in the car, heading toward Helen's bed-and-breakfast. I looked lazily out the car window. With my full stomach and the grueling events of that day I found my eyelids feeling heavy. We stopped at one of the town's three stoplights, and I forced my eyelids open, trying to stay awake. Just then I saw Steven's father come out of a small, stand-alone building with a marquee that read, ROGER DILLON, ATTORNEY-AT-LAW. "Wait," I said, reaching over to squeeze Steven's arm. "Look over there."

"He seems to be everywhere we are, no?" Steven remarked as his father turned the corner and headed to a Rolls-Royce parked down the side street. Behind us another car tooted its horn. Steven put the gearshift into first, and again I put my hand on his arm. "Yes, and take a look at the sign above the store."

The driver behind us laid on the horn slightly longer this time. I saw Steven's jaw tighten as he noticed the sign, and then he stepped on the gas and pulled over to the curb, parking in front of *Jeanie's Fabrics.* "Let's go," he said, and hopped out.

I followed suit, and we walked half a block to the building, pausing at the side street to see if the coast was clear of Steven Senior. It was, so we went in.

The interior of Roger Dillon's law office was a testament to taxidermy. A dozen or so stuffed and mounted animal heads laid claim to every wall and open surface of the lobby. No two heads were of the same species. There was a deer head, a bear head, and a fox head, along with more exotic creatures like a gazelle and a zebra. There was even the head of a rhinoceros, and I noticed that part of its horn had decayed with age and was starting to flake off.

The scene was like something out of an Alfred Hitchcock movie. It was truly creepy.

The small room was paneled in dark wood, and a threadbare gray carpet covered the floor. The air hung heavy with the smell of must and old paper. There were two battle-hardened chairs that looked about as comfortable as sitting on the floor.

A little bell above the door had jingled when we came in, and from the back we heard a voice say, "Be right with you!"

"What *is* this place?" Steven whispered.

"The front lobby to the Bates Motel," I said.

"Can I help you?" a tiny man with round features and olive skin said from behind the counter.

"Hello," Steven said, extending his hand to the man. "I'm Dr. Steven Sable. I thought I knew most of the townspeople, but I don't think we've ever met."

The man regarded Steven for a moment before shaking his hand. He couldn't be much taller than four and a half feet, but was colorfully dressed in a brown tweed suit and orange bow tie. He had large blue eyes and short white hair that stuck up in odd places. Overall, he reminded me of an Oompa Loompa.

"Good to finally meet you, Steven," the man said. "I knew your grandfather well. He and I had a few great hunting trips together, although I never could get him to come out on safari with me."

Steven smiled as he shook hands. "Are you the great hunter Roger my grandfather was always talking about?"

I could sense that Steven was lying. "Andrew talked about me?" Roger said, his little chest puffing up.

"He did. He said you were a very good hunter."

Roger smiled broadly. "I never knew he felt that way. He used to tease me a lot about all my trophies," he said, waving his hand at the walls. "But maybe it was just his way. Say, did you know you just missed your father?"

"Did we?" Steven replied casually. "That's too bad. I would have liked to catch up with him."

"I didn't know you two were speaking," Roger remarked. "But I suppose Andrew's death has brought you close after all these years."

"Mmmm," Steven said, allowing Roger to think what he liked.

"So what can I do you for?" Roger asked us.

Steven turned away from the counter and walked over to the closest wall to inspect the trophies there more closely. He said lightly, "I heard you were one of the last people to talk with my grandfather before he died. I was thinking you might wish to share what his final thoughts were, or what you two talked about."

A cloud seemed to cross over Roger's face. "I'm afraid I can't do that," he said. "It's confidential."

Steven turned away from the trophy wall. "How could it be confidential? My grandfather is dead. I don't think he would mind if you shared this with us."

"He might not mind, but the other party involved would."

Steven cut me a quick look, and said, "Ah. I see. Is that a grizzly bear?"

Roger beamed. "Why, yes, it is. But the real beauty is in my office. I got a polar bear about ten years ago up in Canada. They're one of the most ferocious predators on earth, you know."

"You are making a joke with me," Steven said. "You shot a polar bear?"

"Yep. Had him stuffed and mounted. That set me back one pretty penny, let me tell you!"

"Can I see it?" Steven asked excitedly.

"Sure, come on back and I'll show you." Roger waved his arm as he turned to walk back down the corridor.

Steven turned to me. "Coming?"

"Actually, I'm pooped, and I'd love to take a minute and just rest. I'll stay right here while you boys go have your fun." And with that I sat in one of the weathered chairs.

Steven and Roger disappeared down the hallway while I put my head back against the wall and closed my eyes. About the time I was beginning to nod off, I heard someone clear his throat.

Opening one eye, I saw Roger standing by the counter. "You two done swapping hunting stories?" I asked.

Roger beamed at me. "Your boyfriend says he doesn't hunt, which is a shame, because he sure seems interested in it. He's in the men's room. He told me to come check on you and make sure you weren't mad, since we took so long."

"I'm not mad," I said, sitting up and yawning.

Roger fiddled with his blazer as he seemed to struggle to come up with a topic that didn't involve guns, wild animals, or taxidermy. I stood up and stretched, hoping

Steven wouldn't be too much longer. "You and Andrew were close, huh?" I asked, trying to fill the uncomfortable silence.

"No, not really. We were both members of the Uphamshire Hunting Association, but he preferred duck and quail, while I like more challenging game. We didn't see each other regularly outside meetings."

"Ah," I said with a nod. This man was dull, dull, dull. "What kind of law do you practice?"

"I dabble in a little bit of everything," Roger said. "From real estate and tax law to divorce and separation, with a little bit of bankruptcy thrown in for good measure. I'm the only lawyer in town, so it's good to be well versed in a lot of different areas."

"I see. Say, Roger, maybe you can help me out. I really have to say that I love this area, and I'm considering purchasing a vacation home. Are there any Realtors you could recommend?" I was thinking about what Mirabelle had said, that she was being chased by a Realtor with an out-of-town couple who wanted to buy her home. Something about it seemed fishy, and I wanted to check it out.

"There's only one Realtor in this area, Curt Bancroft. He's on Main and Second

Street. We send each other business now and then."

"Thanks, Roger." Just then Steven reappeared, holding his stomach a little and wearing a sheepish look.

"Sorry," he said. "That chili I had for lunch had an argument with my stomach. M.J., you ready?"

"Sure am. Nice meeting you, Roger."

"Likewise," he said, and watched us go.

When we were clear of the building I said, "Chili, huh? I could have sworn I watched you down a burger."

"What time do you have?" Steven asked, avoiding my comment.

"Four thirty," I said. "Why?"

"Follow me," he said, and crossed the street into a hardware store.

"What are we doing here?" I said when we'd made it inside.

"How you say to make the minutes go by while you are waiting?"

"Passing time."

"Yes, we are passing time for now," he said as he pulled me down an aisle lined with garden hoses and lawn tools. I gave him a quizzical look, and all he said was, "I will explain to you in a half hour. Just follow my leadership for now."

We puttered around the hardware store

long enough to catch the attention of the proprietor. "Can I help you?" a skinny man with a really bad comb-over asked.

"We are just borrowing," Steven said.

"Browsing," I said quickly. "He meant to say browsing."

"Uh-huh," the skinny man said, not believing us for a second. "Let me know if I can help you," he finished, and sidled back to his seat at the counter, where he watched us like a hawk.

"Now what time is it?" Steven asked me.

"Five after five," I told him. "And anytime you want to fill me in on what you're up to would be okay by me."

"We'll wait another ten minutes; then we'll leave. Help me look for something to buy. That man at the counter is looking angry."

We bought some washers, a few screws, and a wrench for a whopping five ninety-five and exited the store. I followed close behind Steven as we made our way back across the street. I was really curious about what he was up to, but something told me I wasn't going to like it.

Steven paused in front of the now darkened attorney's office and peeked through the window. I was beginning to wonder about him, as he seemed far too comfortable peeping in on people. Turning to me, he said, "Around back." Then he moved off from the door and motioned for me to follow him. When we got around to the other side I stopped in my tracks when I saw what he intended to do. "No way!" I said as I watched him tug on a window about shoulder high.

"Yes way," he said sternly. "Now come. I need you to go through here and open the back door. The window is too small for me, so you will have to go."

"Are you outta your friggin' mind?" I asked him without budging. "That's breaking and entering! What if there's an alarm? What if a cop rolls up? What if Roger is still in there?"

Steven gave me a level look. "I am in my mind, M.J. There is no alarm, and there is only one sheriff here, who is most likely on the highway giving out tickets. Roger has left for the evening. He told me he was having dinner tonight with an old friend and he won't be back until tomorrow. We can get in and get out without causing notice. Now come on."

I noted that he failed to comment on the breaking-and-entering thing, and it irritated me that he was ignoring my pleas for common sense. Instead he had his hands cupped and his legs braced, ready to toss me through the window without any regard for my squeaky-clean record.

"I can't believe I'm doing this," I grumbled as I walked over and put my foot in his hands. "Just in case you were wondering, this is going to cost you extra."

"Send me the bill," he said, and hoisted me up. I wasn't prepared for how quickly I'd be shoved through, and landed hard on the other side.

"Owwww!" I said from the inside of the bathroom, noticing only now that my head had barely missed the toilet. "This is so gross," I said, getting up to brush off my hands.

"The back door is out the bathroom and to the left," Steven said as he poked his head through the window.

I grumbled as I exited the bathroom, rubbing my hands together and thinking about how many germs I'd just had a close encounter with, when I bumped into something very large and very furry. I stumbled and inhaled sharply as I felt claws dig into my back. "Yikes!" I squealed, and whirled away, pressing my back against a wall and taking great big gulps of air.

"M.J.?" I heard Steven call from outside the back door. "Are you all right?"

"Fine," I called. "Just bumped into Pete

the polar bear." I looked up and up and up at the mounted thing, which had to be twelve feet tall. I gave a shudder and continued around to the back door. I let Steven in and then went back outside, where I turned and stared at him, folding my arms and giving him a look that meant business.

"What are you doing?" he asked me.

"I'm staying out here," I said. "I want no part of this, so whatever you're going to do in there, go do it and I will be out here, safe, sound, and minding my own business."

Steven gave me a scowl. "But I need your help," he said. "It will go much quicker if you are along."

"And if we get caught we go to jail. I don't know about you, but I hear that prison can be a real drag."

"You're not going to prison," Steven said, blowing out a sigh. "I have money, M.J. People with money don't go to jail."

"Really?" I said, putting my hands on my hips. "Tell that to Martha Stewart and Leona Helmsley."

"Please?"

"No."

"I'll pay you extra."

"How much extra?"

"I'll double your fee."

"Triple."

"Two and a half times."

"Two point seven five, and you let me drive your car."

Steven's eyes narrowed. "Sorry, can't do the car. She's special."

"So am I," I said, not backing down.

We stared at each other for a few seconds before Steven finally gave in. "Fine. Come on then; let's get moving."

I moseyed past him and thought I must be just as crazy as he was. We moved into Roger's office and Steven pointed to the file cabinets. "See if you can find my grandfather's records."

"What are you going to do?"

Steven moved over to the desk and pulled out the chair. "I'm going to see what's on Roger's computer."

"This is so insane," I said, and pulled open the filing cabinet.

Neither of us spoke again for several long minutes. I could hear Steven tapping behind me as I looked through all the Ss in Roger's drawers, coming up empty on the name Andrew Sable.

I wondered if perhaps his folder had been misfiled, so I started with the As in the top drawer and began to work my way down. It was when I got to the Es that I found something interesting. "Well, would you look at that," I said, and pulled up a file.

Steven grunted behind me, and I heard the printer click on. "Make a photocopy of whatever you find. The copier is down the hall behind the counter in the lobby."

I rolled my eyes at how he'd become so familiar with the layout of Roger's office. I certainly hadn't noticed the copier, but then again, I figured I hadn't been the one with this giant master plan for breaking and entering in the first place.

I scooted down the hall to the copier and switched it on, waiting while it hummed to life, making noises that served only to make me even more nervous than I already was. "Come on, come on," I coaxed as I watched the digital readout, waiting for it to turn from WARMING UP to COPY. After what felt like an eternity the screen finally gave me the okay, and I wasted no time laying the papers on the glass and hitting the START button. When I was through I made sure the originals were in order, gathered up the copies, and switched the button to OFF.

Just as I was about to breathe easier I heard a click behind me that froze me in place. This was followed by more clicking, and all kinds of alarm bells went off in my head as I searched the area for a hiding place. Someone was unlocking the front door. As the door started to open and the little bell above it dinged, I shrank down low behind the counter and crept over to the copier, wedging myself between it and the wall while praying that my feet didn't stick out far enough to spot from the other side of the counter.

I waited anxiously as I heard someone come in the door, then close it behind them. Belatedly I realized I hadn't had a chance to warn Steven, and as my heart pounded in my chest loud enough for me to worry about it being overheard, I thought for sure our goose was collectively burned once Steven was discovered.

I peeked carefully around the edge of the copier and saw someone walk by the counter and down the corridor. I couldn't tell if it was Roger, but that was who I assumed it was. Pulling my head back, I racked my brain for a way out of this mess as my ears strained to hear the moment of surprise when he met Steven in his office. The seconds ticked by, however, without a peep, and I began to wonder if somehow my partner had managed to sneak out the back before being seen.

If that were the case, then that would leave me here holding the bag. I squeezed my eyes shut as I fought to think of a way out. Steadying my resolve, I eased out of the small space I'd been hiding in. Hearing nothing, I crawled over to the counter, where I quickly tucked the originals back into the file, hurrying to hide the copies in my jacket, then shoved the folder under some other files lying on the counter and hurried to the door.

There, I hesitated a split second, listening carefully for any hint of footsteps, then slowly opened the door a crack. Just as I was about to pull it open and dash out I remembered the bell at the top. Reaching up, I clutched the bell to keep it from dinging and eased through, closing the door slowly to keep the bell silent. With relief I heard the door click shut, and I quickly walked away from it.

Once I had moved down the street, I checked up and down the block to see if anyone had noticed. There was no one on the sidewalk, and no one came running out of the surrounding businesses pointing at me and yelling, "Thief!" so I figured I was in the clear.

I looked around for any sign of Steven. When I didn't see him, I walked back to his car and waited what seemed like hours before he finally reappeared. "Where have you been?" I demanded when he was within earshot.

"Hugging a polar bear's butt for half an hour. Where have you been?"

"You hid behind the polar bear?"

"You didn't answer my question," Steven said.

"I sneaked out the front door when Roger went down the hallway into his office. I was sure he'd see you."

"I was coming down the hallway to check on you when I saw the handle on the door turn. I had no choice but to go back and hide behind the bear until he left. And that wasn't Roger in the office."

"It wasn't?" I asked. "Then who was it?"

Steven's brows lowered and he said, "My father. Come. Let's go see Gilley. There's a little hacking job I've got for him."

We got to Helen's B and B a few minutes later and made our way inside. By this time it was dark and getting a little chilly, so I was glad to see a fire burning in the fireplace when we entered. Gilley was on the couch sitting on an enormous pillow with an afghan over his legs, typing away furiously on his laptop.

"Hey, Gil," I said when we entered.

"Oh! Hey, you two," he said with surprise

as he saw us. "I didn't expect you guys tonight, but I'm glad you're here. M.J., I've got dirt!"

"Tell us," Steven said as he took a seat in a wing chair.

Gilley squirmed with excitement as he began. "Okay, so you know how you asked me to dig into Maureen and Mirabelle's past? Well, this Maureen character was really a wild one, let me tell you! According to my research, she had a criminal record in Philadelphia that included bootlegging and loan-sharking before she cleaned up her act and moved to Uphamshire.

"She got a job working at your grandfather's house, Steven, and by all accounts he favored her above his other paid help, because there came a point when a parcel of his land was actually deeded over to her."

Steven and I smiled at each other as Gilley told us things we already knew. Neither one of us wanted to point that out to him just yet, so we let him continue. "And Andrew Sable did that for only one other employee in all the years that people worked for him."

"He gave a parcel away to another employee?" Steven asked. "Who?"

"Last year one square acre and the domicile on it were deeded over to a Mr. Willis

348

Brown."

Steven nodded, then signaled for Gilley to continue. "So, the deeds were both held in life estates, but when Maureen died, Andrew recorded an extension of the first life estate to include Mirabelle as well."

"Life estate?" I said. "What's that?"

"It means that when they die the land would revert back to my grandfather and his heirs," Steven said. I looked at him quizzically and he explained, "My grandfather liked the legal parts of real estate. He taught me some things about it when I was growing up."

Gilley bobbed his head up and down in agreement. "Yes, and now here's where it gets tricky. According to county records there is currently an issue before the probate court regarding the life estate held by Mirabelle, claiming it is not valid."

"Why would it not be valid?" Steven asked.

"The plaintiff is arguing that Mirabelle was not of legal age when the life estate was deeded over. In other words, you have to be eighteen to hold title to property, and when the property was signed over to Mirabelle, the suit argues that she was only seventeen."

Steven's brows furrowed. "How could anyone but me be challenging that?"

"Anyone can bring a suit; they don't necessarily have to be considered an interested party," Gilley said.

"Your date with that real estate agent is really paying off for you, isn't it, Gil?" I kidded him.

"Bradley is a fountain of information," Gilley said smugly.

"So who is this plaintiff?" Steven wanted to know.

Gilley's eyes danced, and I knew he had something really good. "Your father," he said dramatically.

"That's ridiculous," Steven snapped. "Why would my father care if Mirabelle had a parcel of land that belonged to me?"

Again I saw Gilley's eyes shine brightly, and I didn't think I was going to like this answer one bit. "I think it's because he's getting ready to lay some kind of claim to it. Steven, did you know that all of your grandfather's land in Uphamshire is being held in life estate by you and your surviving heirs, assuming you have some?"

My eyes darted over to Steven, who opened his mouth to say something, but seemed to stop midthought. After a moment in which we waited for him to speak, I asked, "So who does it fall to if something happens to Steven and he has no heirs?"

"His father, but only on the condition that Steven Senior name a blood-related heir," Gilley announced just as dramatically as he had the first time.

"So Andrew had the last laugh," I said, looking pointedly at Steven. "He resented the fact that your father never claimed you as his son so much that he forced the issue by adding that condition."

Gilley was nodding. "In order to lay permanent claim to the property, one or both of you has to name an heir. This would put a damper on your father's efforts to challenge the will unless he's got another child, and even then he'd have to prove you weren't a direct relation."

"What if there is no heir?" I asked Gilley.

"Then the property would remain in life estate to the grandson until his death, then pass on to the father, if he were still alive, or his named heir. If there is no heir on the father's side then the property would revert to the state, with the condition that the lodge be maintained as a historical land-mark."

"While the property is in life estate, can anyone sell off parts of it?"

"No, according to Bradley. The property would have to remain intact; however, if Steven Senior had a legitimate claim to the property and named an heir, the property would come out of life estate and be his to do anything he wanted with."

"In other words, our friend right here and his heirs can live on the property only until their deaths, but his father can lay full claim to it if Steven Junior is out of the picture and his father claims an heir?"

"Correct," Gilley said.

"Is the land that valuable?" I asked, turning to Steven.

"No," he said, shaking his head. "Except for the lodge and Willis's house and Mirabelle's property, it's undeveloped forest. This is the only town for about fifty miles, and the nearest highway is forty miles to the east. I can't understand why my father would be interested in it — assuming he even is."

"Oh, I think he's interested, all right," Gilley said. "Think about it, Steven. He's been up here a lot, according to the locals, always with some other guy in a suit. And he brings a claim against Mirabelle for something that doesn't even belong to him. There's more to this story, and if I were you I'd watch my back."

Given the little swim we'd taken that morning, I didn't really like the way these little facts were adding up. "So, Steven

Senior may have a vested interest in Steven Junior being out of the picture," I said, giving a knowing look to the doctor in the corner.

"If he's responsible for this morning," Steven growled, as our eyes locked, "I'll kill him myself."

Gilley swiveled his head back and forth between me and Steven as if he were watching a tennis match. "Am I missing something?"

I took that opportunity to reach into my jacket and pull out the copies I'd made of the file from Roger's office. "Given all of this new information," I said as I unfolded the paper, "I think you should have a look at this."

I put the papers on the coffee table in front of me and spread them out so that we could all see them. "Uh-oh," I said as I looked closely at them.

"What?" Gilley asked as he peered over my shoulder.

"Uh . . . it looks like I put the copies back in the folder, and these are the originals."

"Hopefully no one will notice," Steven said as he got out of his chair to come over.

Gilley reached forward and picked through the papers, studying them for a moment. "There are three separate deeds here.

Look," he said, pointing to the second sheet. "The chain goes like this. This is the life estate to Maureen, which then reverts the property back to Andrew in nineteen seventy-four, when she died. This one, recorded in nineteen seventy-four, right after Maureen died, deeds the property to Mirabelle, which clearly lists her age as eighteen."

"Andrew must have wanted to make sure the property went to Mirabelle, maybe as consolation for her mother's death."

"That's plausible," said Gilley.

"Then why is there another one there?" I asked, pointing to the third.

Gilley picked it up and glanced at it before saying, "This date marks it a week before Andrew died. It's signed but not recorded, and it's a mirror of the other, only it lists Mirabelle's birth date of December second, nineteen fifty-seven —" Gilley paused as he looked back to the original deed. "And this deed lists her birth date as nineteen fifty-six."

"So Andrew knew he had to correct the original deed. This one," I said, tapping the unrecorded document, "is the deed that shows her true birth date and would ensure she gets to live in her house for the rest of her life."

Gilley sighed. "Yes. Because the first deed was recorded with a false birth date, it isn't legal. All that needs to happen now is to record it with the county clerk and be done with it."

"Then why hasn't Roger recorded it by now? My grandfather's been dead for three months. What's taking him so long?" Steven said, pointing out the obvious.

"And do you think your father was snooping around Roger's office looking for this, or something else?" I asked.

Gilley's head did the tennis-match thing again. "Wait a second," he said. "*Where* exactly did you get this from, M.J.?"

I gathered up the papers with a nonchalant shrug of my shoulders. "Never mind about that, Gil. I need you to keep doing what you're good at, which is to root out the info. This time I want you to concentrate on Steven Senior. We need to know why he's so interested in this parcel of land."

"Wait a minute," Gilley demanded as I got up and stretched with a yawn. "You two are holding out on me!"

Steven got to his feet as well and mimicked my stretch. "I am . . . so . . . like a shrub," he said.

Gilley and I both looked at him before I broke into a smile. "You're bushed, dear, not shrubbed."

"Yes, that too," Steven said with a flip of his hand. "If you need me, I'll be in my room."

"Me too," I said, following him toward the stairs.

"Hey!" Gilley squawked. "Come back! You're not playing fair!"

"Night, Gil," I said with a wave of my hand.

"It's against the law to be mean to the handicapped!" he squawked.

Later, after I'd put Doc to bed, I heard a soft knock on my door. I hurried to answer it, afraid the noise would wake my sleeping bird. I opened the door to find Steven in a pair of black boxer briefs and a matching T-shirt. In his hand he held two snifters with some sort of amber-colored liquid. "Nightgown?" he asked.

I leaned against the doorjamb and folded my arms together. "I thought you were shrubbed and headed to bed?"

Steven raised one of the snifters to his lips and, looking at me over the rim, he sniffed the contents. "Do you like scotch, M.J.?"

I smiled, liking the mix of his foreign accent with the deep, masculine timbre of his voice. "I've been known to knock back a few shots in my day."

Steven held out the other snifter to me, his eyes lingering on mine until I took it. When I did, he pushed into my room. "Come on in," I said sarcastically.

He ignored the comment. "I like this room. It has . . . how do you say . . . luck?"

"Luck?" I asked, closing the door.

"Yes, I think that is the way you say it when something is warm and inviting."

"Do you mean charm?"

"Yes, yes, that's it," he said, swiveling around to face me.

I cocked an eyebrow at him and asked, "So, what are you really doing here?"

"Having a nightgown."

I rolled my eyes. "It's a nightcap, not nightgown."

"Even better," Steven said as he eased over to my bed and sat down. When I shook my head at him, he patted the bedspread and said, "Come, sit with me and drink your scotch. I promise not to nibble you."

"Bite me," I corrected.

"That is not very nice," he said, sounding slightly offended.

"What?"

"Bite me. That is what the kids are saying when they are not so nice, correct?"

I giggled and moved over to the bed, sitting next to him. "The expression is not, 'I promise not to *nibble* you,' it's, 'I promise not to *bite* you.' "

"Ah, well, that makes no sense. Why would I promise not to bite you when you taste so good?" he purred.

I put my hand on his chest as I gave him a stern, "Buddy, let's just drink our drink and talk our talk, okay?"

"My way is more fun," he replied, giving his eyebrows a wiggle.

"So you tell me," I answered. "Now, about this little land deal that your father seems to be so interested in. Do you have any idea why he would care about the property you own up here?"

"None. Of all the property my grandfather owned, this seems to be the least valuable. Yes, it is a lot of land, but it's not nearly as valuable as some of the other holdings he had."

"Did you know your grandfather put the property in life estate?"

Steven nodded. "Preferably."

I gave him a quizzical look and cocked my head to the side. "Come again?"

"Preferably. You know, on the edge, or the outside."

"Peripherally?"

"Yes, what did I say?"

"Never mind. Anyway, you were saying?"

"I knew, but it didn't click in my head. His attorneys called me in Germany, and I was still so stunned to hear of his death. I remember them filling me with details, but my brain was not keeping with it. I didn't even realize the importance of it until Gilley was talking about it downstairs."

"I see. So let me ask the million-dollar question: Do you think your father is trying to kill you?" I had finally said the thing that was really bothering me. And even though I knew that Steven and his father had no real love for each other, I still couldn't fathom a father killing his own son.

Steven swirled the amber liquid for a long moment. He then took a sip and, without looking at me, said, "He's always been the kind of man who would stop at nothing to get what he wanted."

My chest tightened. "In other words, now that we know he has a motive, you and I need to be especially careful about what tunnels and paths we follow in the dark, huh?"

"I would say yes, that is correct."

"So let me ask the other question that's been bothering me —"

"The answer is the same, M.J.," Steven said, cutting me off. "He is the type of man who would stop at nothing to get what he wanted. Even shoving his own father off a roof."

The room fell quiet as we both thought about that. I tried to think of something comforting to say, but nothing came to mind, and just as I was about to try to change the subject by mentioning the weather, Steven said, "I think it's time for both of us to hit the straw."

"Hay," I corrected, but Steven didn't seem to notice, because he was already up and walking toward the door.

"I shall see you in the morning?" he said, more question than statement.

"Yes," I said, giving him a sympathetic smile. "Get some rest, Steven, and thanks again for the nightgown."

CHAPTER 12

The next morning I woke early, anxious to be up and moving. I crept downstairs and poked my head into the kitchen to say hi to Helen, who was busy preparing blueberry pancakes. "You going out for a run?" she asked me.

"Yeah, should be back in time to gobble up some of those, though," I said, pointing to the batter she was preparing.

"Good to know." She smiled. "Does Doc like blueberries?"

"Does Polly want a cracker?" I laughed. "That bird will devour any kind of fruit except pineapple. For some reason he's got an aversion to it."

"I'll put some in a bowl for him and you can feed him when you get back," she said.

"Thanks, Helen. If the boys wake up before I return, just tell 'em I'm out for a run."

I went outside and did a few stretches,

more just to say I did than to really stretch. Once I'd gone through the motions, I crossed the street and began to jog.

For me, there is nothing better than a nice run, especially on a clear spring morning, when the air is still crisp and the dew is heavy. I felt the usual aches and pains associated with that first half mile, but as the rest of my joints and muscles woke up, I really got into it and began to push myself.

I headed in pretty much the same direction I had the other day, wondering if it was a good idea to run down the street where I'd seen Steven's car parked in front of a certain waitress's cute little ranch.

I hadn't remembered to check the driveway for his car this morning — my mind had been on other things. Now I was faced with the moral dilemma of sticking my nose into business that wasn't mine. After a little back-and-forth I decided, *The hell with it,* and pointed my toes down that street, concentrating on appearing disinterested and aloof.

As I passed Annalise's house I allowed my eyes to roam over the driveway, and what I saw there nearly brought me to a halt. Parked neatly in front of her garage was a shiny silver Rolls-Royce, indicating Steven Senior was in residence.

"Son of a bitch," I panted as I made a U-turn and jogged over to get a better look. I paused along her fence and pretended to stretch out a charley horse, keeping one eye on the house, hoping someone would come out and I might catch a bit of conversation. Nothing happened, and I began to worry that all my massaging of my leg might be overdoing it a little, so I turned and began to run again.

When I'd gone about a half mile I doubled back as an excuse to get another look, and to my surprise the car was gone. "Shit," I said as I passed the house. If I'd hung out a little longer, I might have seen something.

I picked up the pace on the way back to the B and B so I could fill Gilley and Steven in. Once I reached the inn I stood outside for a minute, holding the stitch in my side and waiting to catch my breath before going inside.

"I've been looking for you," Steven said from the doorway as I walked up the stairs. "Did you have a good run?"

I nodded. "Yep. And a good thing I did, because I saw something mighty interesting a few blocks that way," I said, pointing.

"What?"

"Your father's car parked in front of that cute waitress's house."

Steven's face went purple in less than two seconds. "You are pulling on my leg," he said in a voice that sounded dangerous.

"Nope," I said, just a wee bit smugly.

"That bastard," Steven spit as he stormed down the steps.

I watched with surprise as he passed me and headed to his car, fishing around in his jeans pocket for his keys. When he hauled them out he looked back up at me and asked, "Coming?"

I nodded dumbly and moved back down the stairs, belatedly realizing that I must look — and smell — like hell. "I don't suppose I have time for a quick shower?" I asked as I approached.

"This won't take long, and you look good. I like you hot and drippy," Steven said with a small grin.

"Gee, stop with the love talk," I said sarcastically as I got into his car. "It's gonna go to my head."

We arrived at Annalise's house in short order, and Steven wasted no time marching right up to the house and pounding on the door. It was opened a moment later by the very pretty woman I'd seen but never met. "Steven!" she said with warmth. "I didn't expect you. Are you here to check on Shanah?"

"Annalise, we need to talk," Steven said. "Can we come in?"

Annalise looked a bit taken aback by Steven's tone, but she opened the door wide and we trooped on in. As we entered I felt a familiar knocking sensation on my energy that caught me off guard. It was coming from the end of a hallway located off her living room, and while Steven made the introductions I allowed myself to open up to the energy from the hallway.

I sensed a little boy, full of mischief, with the name Samuel. His energy was so noisy and intrusive that I had no choice but to acknowledge him. "It's nice to meet you, M.J.," Annalise was saying to me.

"Likewise. Uh, I'm sorry to throw this at you, but who is Samuel?"

Annalise blinked at me as her perky mouth turned into an O. "Excuse me?"

"Samuel. He says he plays with your daughter."

Annalise gave Steven a look that questioned my sanity. "She's a medium," Steven explained. "She talks to dead people."

Annalise gasped as she turned back to me. "Oh, my goodness!" she said. "Shanah has been talking about this little boy named Sam who plays with her! I thought it was some child from her school, but every once in a while I'll catch her talking to someone who's not in the room, and she's been claiming it's this little boy."

I nodded. "He says that he used to live down the street. He says that he knew you before, when you were with John?"

Annalise gave another little gasp. "That was my high school boyfriend! And there was a little boy about a block away who was hit by a car, and I think his name was Sam!"

I nodded. "He says his mother is still close by, and she won't let go. He says she blames herself, and it wasn't her fault."

Annalise nodded. "Mrs. Trenton. She lives alone in that house and hardly ever comes outside. I heard that she'd gone inside to answer the phone while Sam was in the front yard, and a moment later he was hit by a car."

"Sam says it's really important that you let her know he was here today and told her to let go of her guilt. He says that he's been staying with Bill or Billy . . . and Liz or Elizabeth. He says they are taking good care of him, and she shouldn't worry."

"I'll tell her," Annalise said.

"Has this little boy crossed over?" Steven asked.

I smiled that he was becoming so familiar with my lingo. "Yes, he's safely on the other side, but he's worried about his mother, and that keeps him coming back here to check on her. He also likes playing with your daughter, Annalise."

"I have goose bumps," Annalise said, her big blue eyes wide and unblinking as they stared at me. "Is there anything else, M.J.?"

Sam was fading fast from my energy now that I'd gotten the message out. "No. That's all he had to say. He'll be back later to play with Shanah."

At that moment a petite little girl with large eyes behind giant round glasses came down the hallway on tiptoe. "Come out, come out, wherever you are!" she said. I watched her as she peeked into a room off the hallway and came forward. I smiled at her, knowing she had a very special play-mate.

Seeing us, Shanah stopped for a moment, then moved over to hide behind her mother's legs. "Shanah," Annalise said. "You remember Steven."

Shanah looked up at Steven, then hid her face again behind her mother. "And this is his friend M.J. She just talked to Sam."

Shanah peeked up curiously at me and said, "We're playing hide-and-seek."

I squatted down to be at eye level with her. "I know. He said he had to go home for a bit, but he'd be back later to finish the game."

Shanah nodded and then bolted away from her mother, skipping back down the hallway to her room. We all watched her until she'd disappeared; then Steven asked, "How's her breathing been?"

"Better since the other night. And thank you again for coming over. I know I should have just taken her to the emergency room, but it's twenty-five miles away, and knowing you were close by was a hard thing to pass up."

"Think nothing of it, Anna," Steven said gently. "Now, what was my father doing here this morning?"

Annalise looked taken aback, but recovered quickly. "Honestly, where are my manners?" she said as a diversion. "Come, come. Into the kitchen. I've got fresh coffee." With that she darted past us.

We followed her through an archway and into a tiny kitchen with a small table and three chairs set up against one wall. Annalise busied herself pulling down three cups from the cupboard as she said over her shoulder, "Please have a seat while I pour you a fresh cup."

Steven and I sat and waited while she served us the warm brew. I took a sip; it was delicious. "You make a good cup of coffee," I said.

Annalise took her seat, fully composed again as she replied, "Thank you. I pay a little bit extra for it, but everyone needs an indulgence, right?"

"Are you going to answer my question?" Steven cut in.

Annalise fiddled with the hem of her blouse. "He showed up last night, Steven. What was I supposed to do?"

"Tell him to go to hell," he said bluntly.

Annalise gave him a dark look. "He said he wanted to see Shanah. He said he'd heard she'd been having some health issues lately. Which he probably heard through Andy at the pharmacy running his mouth again, but he wanted to make sure she was okay."

"Why would he care, Annalise?" Steven said meanly.

I watched the two of them in silence, wondering about the history here. It was obvious that there was more to the Annalise and Steven Senior story than I was privy to. "He's changed, Steven."

"Bullshit."

"He says that he wants to be a part of her life. He's willing to step up to the plate and take care of us."

Steven studied her for a long, tense moment, his mouth a thin line of anger mixed with frustration. Then, very quietly, he said, "Annalise, please. Be wise about this man. He will say these things, and then he will leave — just the way he left me and my mother. You will be hurting yourself and Shanah by trusting him."

It was Annalise's turn to get angry. "That's enough," she snapped. "This is none of your business, anyway. I appreciate all you've done for us, Steven, but you're letting your own feelings of resentment for your father color your opinion. I'll decide what's best for Shanah and me."

Steven held her gaze until she was finished. "I just have one question for you," he said quietly. "How can you be sure he's really changed? That this time will be different?"

"I looked into his eyes, Steven; he wasn't lying. He told me it was time he stepped up and took responsibility for Shanah. He's even willing to take a paternity test."

Steven's face darkened, and I found myself a little frightened by the look he was giving the tabletop. After an awkward silence he said, "Come, M.J. It's time to go."

I gave Annalise an apologetic shrug of my

shoulders and got up as well. "Thank you for the coffee," I said as I followed him through the kitchen.

"Don't mention it," she said, not turning around.

We made it back to the B and B without further comment. Steven's mood seemed dangerous, and I didn't want to poke the bear, so I let it go. When we got inside I hurried up the stairs to shower, then came down with Doc on my shoulder.

Gilley was seated at the dining room table, sipping coffee, the big pillow he'd used on the couch firmly tucked under him on the chair at the table. "Hey, girlfriend," he said happily.

"Doc wants a berry!" my bird squawked.

"Hey, Gil," I said as I took my seat, and set Doc on the table to nibble at the bowl of blueberries that Helen had set out.

"Where's Dr. Delicious?" Gil asked.

"I don't know," I said, looking around. "Probably upstairs being gloomy."

"Did you shut him out last night?" Gil asked with a grin.

My cheeks flushed as I reached for the plate of pancakes in the middle of the table. "Noooo," I said, stretching the word out. "I saw his father's car parked in front of that waitress's house this morning on my jog, and when I told him about it he insisted on going over there."

"He confronted his father?"

I forked a bit of pancake into my mouth before answering. "No, his father had gone by then. But he did confront the waitress."

"What's the connection?" Gil wanted to know.

"It appears that Steven Senior may have fathered another child."

"The *waitress*?"

"The waitress's daughter. The poor little girl is mentally handicapped and suffering from a few other health issues."

"Does she look like Steven Senior?"

I shrugged my shoulders. "Mostly she looks like her mom, but there might be a resemblance. You'd have to do a blood test to be sure, but it was pretty clear to me from the conversation that Senior is headed in that direction."

Gilley thought about that for a bit before saying, "So, this would be an heir he could control, someone who would never challenge him. Someone he could lock away in some institution if he wanted to . . ."

Gilley's voice trailed off, and I paused with the fork halfway to my mouth as I realized Steven Senior could — and probably would — do just that. "Awww, man," I said as I set the fork down. "I hadn't thought of that. You're right. He's got enough money that he could probably get custody of her from her mother. Then he could lock her away for the rest of her life and not worry about her growing up and becoming a pain in the ass."

"Which leaves one little sticking point left," Gilley said.

"Steven Junior."

"Bingo."

I sighed and pushed my plate away. "Which still begs the question of why is this neck of the woods so important to Senior? It's undeveloped forest. What's the attraction?"

"Not sure, M.J.," Gilley said. "But I plan to find out."

"You ready?" we heard from the hallway.

I looked up, and Gilley swiveled in his seat to see Steven standing there. "Where're we off to?" I asked.

"Back to the lodge. I want you to try to make contact with my grandfather again. I need to prove that my father killed him so I can keep him from hurting Annalise and Shanah."

Just then Helen rushed in from the kitchen holding the phone. "Steven!" she said, her voice sharp. "It's your house sitter. He says there's been a break-in at your house!"

Steven took the phone, and Gilley and I listened as he talked for a few minutes in short, clipped sentences like, "When?" and, "Where were you at the time?" and finally, "What was taken?" He ended the call shortly after that, and we looked at him expectantly. "Someone broke into my home last night and made a mess of my bathroom."

"What would they want in your bathroom?" I asked.

"Probably drugs. The thief may have known I'm a doctor."

"How come you're just hearing about it?" I asked, wondering why the intern staying at his house hadn't called him earlier.

"My house sitter worked the midnight shift last night, and when he got home he called my cell phone." I cocked my head sideways, wondering where he was going with this. Steven added, "The one I left in the pool."

I looked at Gilley, who was also struggling to follow along. "Why would you go swimming with your cell phone?"

"It's a long story," I said quickly. "Come on, Steven; we need to get a move on." And I got up, giving Doc a kiss on the top of his head. "Call me if you come up with something, Gil," I said as Steven and I headed to the door.

"Gotcha," he said with a grin. "Good luck, you two."

As we headed out to the Aston I saw that elusive gray sedan cruise slowly by the B and B. I tried to glance in the window to see who was behind the wheel, but the windows were tinted and I couldn't get a good look. "What?" I heard Steven ask.

I glanced back at Steven. "Nothing," I said with a shrug, but inside I didn't like the ugly feeling I got when I thought about that car.

Steven and I drove back to the Manse in stony silence. His dark mood of earlier hadn't changed, and I was pretty sure hearing that his house had been broken into for a second time wasn't helping to lighten his frame of mind. Rather than try to talk to him, I allowed him to simmer for a bit.

We arrived at the lodge and Steven coasted his car into a slot near the front door. Once he'd put the car into park he turned to me and offered, "I'm sorry I've been irritated. I'm worried about how things are unwrapping."

"Do you want to call the Cambridge police and follow up with them?" I asked.

"Not right now. I don't think I can keep my temper from going kaboom."

I smiled a little as I opened the car door. "Got it, but just remember I'm one of the good guys, okay?"

"I am noting this," he said, following me up the front stairs to the door. We got inside and listened for any noise that might indicate that Andrew or Maureen was afoot. We heard nothing, and Steven looked to me for the next move.

I nodded and closed my eyes, centering my energy, and then opened that conduit in my brain that could hear what others couldn't. *Andrew?* I called out in my mind. *Maureen?* I waited a few heartbeats, then opened my eyes and motioned to Steven. I had felt the smallest of tugs from the third floor.

Steven and I climbed the staircase in silence, pausing every few steps to listen. As we mounted the second-floor landing we both heard a thump from overhead. "What was that?" Steven whispered.

"I think it's Maureen," I said, and continued to climb. "Come on; she might be willing to talk to me."

We made our way to the third floor and quietly walked down the hallway, ears straining for the slightest sound that might indicate a ghost was afoot. As we approached the bedroom where we'd seen Maureen we heard a much louder thump, followed by a dragging noise. Steven jumped and grabbed my shoulder. "I think there's someone in there," he whispered in my ear.

I nodded and whispered back, "It's Maureen. Come on. She won't hurt you."

We moved slowly into the doorway of the bedroom and looked around. Nothing seemed out of place, but the hair on my arms was standing on end. "It's cold in here," Steven said as he rubbed his arms.

He was right; the temperature felt frigid. We moved farther into the room, waiting and watching. Nothing happened. Finally, I decided to call out to Maureen to try to provoke a reaction. "Maureen?" I said. "We need to talk to you. Please let us know if you're here."

Immediately after I said that there was a crack behind us, and Steven and I jumped as we turned around. I pointed to the nightstand, where the framed picture of Maureen was now facedown. "Thank you, Maureen," I said. "I know you can hear me, and I need your help. Andrew is in trouble. He's stuck and he can't move forward until we understand what happened to him. Can you help us? Can you guide us to help Andrew?"

There was a moment when nothing happened, and then, without warning, a huge chest of drawers on the opposite wall rattled and moved forward several inches. Steven again gripped my arm. "Goddamn!" he hissed. "I don't like when she does that."

I smiled and patted his hand. "She's trying to show us something," I said as I watched the bureau. I decided to reach out again to her. "Thank you, Maureen. I see you're over by the bureau now. But we still need your help with Andrew. I think you know what happened to him. I can hear you if you're willing to talk. Please try to communicate with me."

Without warning I felt a shriek in my mind so loud I dropped to my knees. "Unnh!" I said, holding my head in my hands.

"M.J.?" Steven said, his voice alarmed. "What's happened?"

With effort I got to my feet. "She screamed," I said.

"She did?" he asked me, like he'd missed something.

"Yes, in my head. She screamed. I keep getting this wave of anger with her. She's definitely very upset about something."

"Well, this is ridiculous," he groused. "I mean, we can't keep going around chasing

378

the geese with this woman. Maybe she is intending to lead us in the wrong direction? Remember the last time? She said follow the damn bees, and look at what happened . . ."

Suddenly the giant bureau seemed to jiggle; then we both jumped as it came crashing toward us. "Holy Mother of God!" Steven yelled as he pulled me out of the way. "She's trying to kill us!"

Again I heard a loud shriek in my head, which caused me to wince, but then there was a word that followed that I was able to catch. *Letters* . . . it said.

My eye went to the bureau, and cautiously I moved over to it. "What are you doing?" Steven asked. "M.J., keep away from there and let's get out of here! This was a bad idea."

I held up a finger to my lips and gave him a pointed look. I didn't want him to upset Maureen any more than she already was. He gave me a scowl in reply, and I felt another tug toward the bottom of the bureau. I walked carefully around the side over near the wall, and that was when I saw a small pack of letters taped to the underbelly of the bureau.

I looked up at Steven and shot him a smile. "She's not trying to kill us after all," I said to him as I reached down and tugged the letters free. "She's trying to show us something."

Steven gave me a puzzled look and came over to inspect the bundle. "What are these?" he asked.

I sifted through them, trying to determine that myself. There were about twenty letters, old and worn and written in a lovely fluid style. Though they were in envelopes, nothing but the word *Andrew* was on the front. I opened the first one and began to read.

My darling, Andrew,

Thank you for a lovely evening last night. I had such a wonderful time. I never would have guessed you knew so much about the stars. How special it was to walk in the moonlight, holding your hand and feeling like the luckiest woman alive. . . .

"They're love letters," I said as I flipped through the pages.

"To my grandfather," Steven said as I opened one and began to read. "And they're signed by Maureen."

"Really?" I asked. "This one is signed M. Did she spell it out in yours?"

"No, but it's clear to me who M is."

"I don't know," I said as I felt Maureen come into my energy and give a shake of her head. "I don't think Maureen agrees with you."

"Who else could it be? I mean, we already know they had an affair."

"Mirabelle?" I asked.

"Ewwww," Steven said. "I can't imagine my grandfather bonking a mother and daughter."

"Bonking?"

"Yes, you know. Like what we almost did the other night."

I narrowed my eyes at him. "The term is *boinking,* and if that's what you're calling what nearly happened with us the other night, then don't ever plan on it actually happening."

"Hey," he said, sweeping my hair behind my ear. "That was rude of me. I would not bonk you."

"Boink," I said adamantly.

Steven grinned at me. "Come, let's take these letters downstairs and read them. I can't find a date. Can you?"

"No," I answered, shuffling through the envelopes I had. "There's no postmark, so these weren't mailed. Whoever wrote them must have given them to Andrew directly, which means she would have been local."

"Let's go to the kitchen to read them. I want to get out of this room before more furniture attacks us."

Steven and I headed back downstairs to the kitchen, and we each pulled up a bar stool. While I read through a stack, Steven made some tea for both of us, then joined me at the counter, and we read in silence until we'd made it through our pile of letters.

"What do you think?" he asked me as I put down the last letter.

"This chick really loved your grandfather," I said.

"Kind of . . . how you say . . . consumed with him?"

"Obsessed."

"Yes. She seems to be obsessed with him."

"Yep. And completely jealous of your grandmother. She keeps referring to her as the Evil Queen. So, at least we know these were written while your grandmother was still alive."

Steven nodded. "Which would put it about nineteen eighty-eight or earlier."

"And Maureen died in the seventies."

"See?" Steven said to me. "So it could have been Maureen."

"Yes," I conceded. "But my gut says it's not."

"Another mystery to solve then."

I shuffled all the letters together into one pile on the counter. "None of this makes any sense. Why were these letters hidden in Maureen's bedroom if Maureen didn't write them? Who was this mystery woman, and what the hell does it have to do with your grandfather's death?"

Steven rubbed his chin thoughtfully. "Maybe none of it's connected," he said. "Maybe Maureen is upset that someone else had an affair with my grandfather, and that's the reason for her anger."

I nodded as I thought about that. "Still," I said, "I think there's more to this story than we realize."

"Where do we go from here?" Steven asked.

I hopped off the bar stool. "There's a lead or two left that we haven't tracked down yet. Come on; we need to go back into town."

CHAPTER 13

We arrived in town a little while later, and I told Steven where I wanted to go. Pulling up alongside a spiffy-looking Victorian, we got out and checked the nameplate on the front entrance: CURT BANCROFT, REAL-TOR.

As we were about to head inside, I felt a small tug to my right and happened to turn my head. Just down the street from where we'd parked sat a shiny silver Rolls-Royce. I tapped Steven on the shoulder and pointed to his father's car. "The guy always seems to have the same interests we do," I said.

I watched as Steven's brow darkened. "Come," he said. "It's time to find out what that bastard is up to."

When we opened the door we heard the sound of a doorbell, announcing our presence. A woman about my age, with long red hair and glasses, looked up as we entered. "Good afternoon," she said warmly. "Did you have an appointment with Mr. Bancroft?"

"No," I said quickly, taking the lead. "But we were interested in purchasing some land, and we heard you guys were the best Realtor in town."

The woman giggled. "That might have a little something to do with the fact that we're the *only* Realtor in town. Mr. Bancroft is busy with another client at the moment; then he has a luncheon appointment. Can I pencil you in for one o'clock this afternoon?"

Steven opened his mouth, but I gave him a small slap on the back and said, "That would be great. Pencil us in; the last name is Holliday. We'll go get some lunch ourselves and be back then." With that I turned and walked out, hoping Steven would follow.

He did, but not before grabbing my arm on the front steps and asking, "Hey, what was that about?"

"It's called playing it smart," I said. "If you go in there with guns blazing and half-cocked, your father isn't going to tell you anything. He's obviously doing business with people in real estate, so let's poke around a bit before we start pointing fingers and alerting the media that your dad is a rat bastard, okay?"

Steven surprised me by breaking into a grin. "You are cute when serious, you know?"

I rolled my eyes and headed down the steps. Looking back I said, "Come on. Let's get some lunch and come up with a good story so that we don't make Bancroft clam up like Roger did."

An hour and a half later we were seated comfortably in Curt Bancroft's office, waiting for him to get back from his lunch date. Steven's knee bounced up and down, and he cracked his knuckles enough times for me to want to get up and swat him, so I tried to distract myself by taking in the decor of Bancroft's office.

The room was a honey yellow with rich white molding. There were two watercolors mounted on the wall: one of a sailboat and the other of a harbor. Bancroft's desk was neatly organized, no files or pads of paper for me to snoop around in while we waited.

Finally, ten minutes late and full of apologies, Bancroft breezed into the room, his tie askew and a lipstick smudge on his collar. "So sorry I'm late," he said trying to catch his breath.

"No problem," Steven said easily. "We

have all day."

Bancroft moved around to his side of the desk and sat down. He was about an inch or two taller than Steven. His face had probably once been handsome, but had grown soft like his belly with middle age and too many carbs. His hair was brown and looked freshly mussed, and he must have caught me staring at it, because he was quick to try to smooth it out. "Windy out there," he said quickly.

"Really?" I said with a smirk. "I hadn't even noticed a breeze today."

"Just started up, then," Bancroft said as he scooted his chair forward. "Now, what can I do for you folks?"

"We're from Boston," I began. "And we were up this way about a month ago, visiting my parents, who live in New York, when we got lost and ended up in Uphamshire. Well, I fell in love with it immediately, and I've been just nonstop about how smitten I am with this neck of the woods. I've been going on and on about it to Peter here," I said, pausing to squeeze Steven's arm. On cue, he flashed a smile at Bancroft. "And even though both our jobs would keep us in Boston, someday I'd like to retire someplace between there and my family."

"You'd like to see about buying a little

land, then?" Bancroft said.

Clapping my hands enthusiastically, I said, "Yes!"

Bancroft leaned in over his desk, resting on his elbows and placing his hands together in a steeple. "You definitely came at the right time," he said. "I have the inside scoop that Uphamshire's real estate is about to shoot through the roof."

"You don't say?" I asked, suddenly intrigued. "Big business moving in?"

Bancroft smiled knowingly. "Better. There's a highway set to connect the Mass. Pike with Route Eighty-five through to New York. That means we'll be on the fast track, and land around here will be worth a mint!"

"Really?" Steven said. "When is this highway being finished?"

"Within the next three years," Bancroft said. Then he motioned for us to come closer. When we leaned in, he said in a low, excited tone, "And I met with a gentleman earlier who informs me that a major pharmaceutical company is looking at property just north of here to build a huge facility!"

"A pharmaceutical company?" I asked.

"Yes. You know how Massachusetts laws are so friendly toward all that stem-cell research stuff? Well, apparently, New York isn't nearly as open to the idea, and a major player in that market is looking to relocate without having to uproot all of their employees. This new highway would bring them here without too much fuss."

"And you said that this facility will be just north of here?" Steven asked.

"Yes. There's a large chunk of land that would be a prime location," Bancroft said, pointing north. "It's mostly undeveloped forest up that way. Perfect to build on, especially since the highway will run so close by it."

I watched Steven's face begin to darken. He was getting angry, and I needed to distract him — pronto. I gave a pointed glance at my watch and cried, "Oh, my goodness! Honey, I completely forgot to tell Mom we weren't going to make it for lunch! She's probably got the food laid out for us and is wondering where we are."

Steven turned to me and gave me a confused look. "Really?"

"Yes, oh, this is terrible! Mr. Bancroft, I'm so sorry, but I'm afraid we've got to run. Mom's going to be so disappointed if we don't show up. We'll be sure to come back soon, especially now that we know that land around here is going to appreciate so quickly." I got up and hurried toward the door. "Honey? Are you coming?"

Steven hesitated in his chair, and I knew he was debating whether to follow me or continue pumping Bancroft for info. To my immense relief my cell phone went off at that exact moment and, hauling it out of my pocket, I saw that it was Gilley. "Hey, Mom!" I announced with a flourish as I answered the call.

"M.J.?" Gilley asked.

"Yeah, I know, we're totally late, but we are on our way, I promise. We should be there in half an hour. Come on, Peter, Mom's waiting!"

Steven had little choice but to get up and follow me out of the office. I kept rambling nonsensically into Gilley's ear until we cleared the building and I could explain to him that we hadn't been in an area where we could talk freely. "I thought it might be something like that," Gilley said. "So, here's the scoop. I know why Steven Senior wants that property."

"There's a highway coming through town and a major pharmaceutical company is looking for land to build a plant on," I said.

There was a pause on the line before Gil said, "You *always* beat me to the punch!"

I smiled. "Yeah, but it's nice to know we've both got the same story."

"Well, I may have one eensy little tidbit

more than you. Did you know who is on the board of directors for that pharmaceutical company?"

"I'll take Dr. Steven Sable Senior for two hundred."

"Bingo!"

"What's that?" Steven asked me as we paused by the car.

Quickly I explained to him that Gilley had come up with the same scoop we had, but with the added tidbit about the board of directors. Next I told Gilley to hold on, and I hit the speaker button so we could all talk with ease. "What I don't understand," I said, "is why your father thinks he can so easily get his hands on this property. I mean, if something happens to you, Steven, wouldn't people naturally assume he had a hand in it?"

"Maybe something doesn't have to happen to me," Steven said.

"What do you mean?" Gilley asked.

Steven kicked at some dirt and seemed to struggle with something before spitting out, "He may not be my biological father."

"What?" Gilley and I said together.

Again Steven kicked at the dirt and avoided eye contact. Taking a big breath, he finally said, "When my mother was very sick with her cancer, she told me that before I was born she wanted to make Steven jealous and leave his wife. She said she took another man, a foreigner from Hungary, as her lover. When Steven found out the truth of this, he chased the other man out of town and my mother never saw him again.

"Soon after that my mother said she became pregnant, but I have always wondered which was my real father. That is why I have researched the paternity case against my father. It is true that my grandfather supplied his own blood sample, but he put a . . . what is the word when one thing depends on another?"

"Stipulation?" Gilley said.

"Yes, that's the word. He put a stipulation on the settlement that the results were sealed for a hundred years. It's puzzling, do you not think?"

"In other words," Gilley said, "your father — or who you think is your father — has always suspected your mother became pregnant by the other guy."

"Yes. And this is why I think he continues to reject me. I think it is only a matter of time before he fights me on the rights of the estate."

"He'd have to supply a DNA sample," I said. "But at least you'd all know for sure."

"I believe he's made up his mind that I'm

not his son," Steven said, looking at me for the first time since he began telling the story. His eyes seemed so vulnerable and sad that I reached out and squeezed his hand. "And I believe he's just waiting to get the other life estate holders out of the way before coming after me."

"Which brings us back to Willis and Mirabelle," I said. "Gilley, you seem to know a lot about this life estate thing. We know that Senior is attempting to challenge Mirabelle's right to the property in court, but we've heard from Willis that Senior is taking a different tack. He's been checking in on him, and trying to offer some medical assistance. What's that angle?"

"He could be trying to buy the land from him," Gilley said.

"But I thought that if you held the property in life estate you couldn't sell it?" I asked.

"You can't to anyone other than whom the life estate would revert back to upon your death. In other words, for a price, Willis could give up his life estate rights to the property only to Steven or Steven Senior."

I turned to Steven. "Remember Willis said that he was thinking about moving back to Jamaica Plain to be closer to his daughter?"

Steven was nodding his head. "Makes

sense," he said as he dwelled on it. "He buys off Willis and puts pressure on Mirabelle in court because she won't sell."

Thinking about that, I added, "You know, I really think we need to go have another chat with Roger. The fact that he's had her deed in his hot little hands and hasn't recorded it yet bothers me."

Steven nodded. "Do you still have the original?"

"Yes."

"Good. We'll record it ourselves later, but I agree with you that we need to confront him. Then we will need to warn Mirabelle."

"Anything you want me to research?" Gilley asked.

I hit on a good idea. "Gil, Steven hasn't contacted the Cambridge police yet because he's too pissed off. Can you hack into their system and find out what the police report says? There's something really bothering me about this whole thing."

"I'm on it, M.J. I'll call you when I find out something."

We got into Steven's car and drove over to Roger's office. As we parked at the curb, I'll admit I was a bit nervous returning to the scene of the crime. I shook it off as we approached and walked through the office door, trying my best to adopt an air of total nonchalance. As we entered the office, however, I felt my heart skip a beat.

The place was a shambles. There was paper everywhere, and manila folders littered the floor. Steven and I gave each other a look, and I whispered to him, "Did *you* do this?"

He scowled at me and replied, "No. I left it like it was when we broke in." From the back of the office we heard someone swear loudly, followed by a small crash. "Hello?" Steven called as he put a hand on my shoulder, preparing me to bolt if necessary.

The cursing paused as Steven called out. Then we heard Roger's voice ask, "Who's there?"

"It's Dr. Sable," he said.

"I have it!" Roger said. "It has to be here. Just give me a little more time!"

Steven and I both looked at each other, and I shrugged my shoulders. "How much more time?" he asked, playing along.

Roger appeared from the office and started to say, "I'll have it by the end —" when he noticed us, and that was when he seemed to catch himself from saying anything more. "Oh, it's you," he finally managed. "I thought it was your father."

I narrowed my eyes. I had just realized what he must be looking for. "We know what you're up to," I said.

Roger narrowed his own eyes back. "Up to?" he snarled. "What would I be up to?"

I felt the familiar knocking I get when someone who's crossed over wants to send a message. I opened up and immediately felt an older female's energy with a name that began with an L. In my mind I invited her to speak her name slowly to me, and I got Lily. "Lily has a message for you," I said to him.

Roger's face blanched, and his mouth dropped open a bit. "What did you say?"

"Lily wants you to know she's very disappointed with how you're behaving. She says that she didn't raise a cheat or a liar, and that someone named Max would never approve."

Roger staggered forward a few steps, his eyes big as saucers and his hand propped against the wall like he needed the support. "How could you *know* that?"

"Lily also says that she thinks the car you're driving is fine and there's no need to buy a new one." Roger stood with his mouth agape. "She also says that if you sell the family home, you'll live to regret it, because Miami Beach is not all it's cracked up to be."

Roger's knees seemed to buckle as, without further ado, he sat down with a hard thump on the floor. "Mom?" he said. "Is that really you?"

"Who's George?" I asked, getting the feeling of an older male figure now.

Roger shook his head dumbly before he seemed to make the connection, and he offered, "My grandfather."

"George says that even though he had more trophies than you, there's no need to continue killing these animals, especially when they're already endangered."

Roger blinked at me a few times and moved his mouth up and down, but no words came out.

"This is awesome," Steven whispered. "M.J., keep going."

I didn't really need the encouragement, but gave him a quick smile all the same. "George also says that he's glad you still have one of his guns, the one with a pearl handle, right?"

Roger nodded. "Yes, it's in my desk at home."

"He's very proud of you, but he agrees with Lily about this paper that you're keeping secret. He doesn't want you to do that. He says show it to the public."

Roger's lower lip trembled. "I can't find it," he whispered.

"What?" Steven asked him.

"I can't find it!" he said, and scrambled to his feet, then quickly headed over to the counter and dug around in a pile of folders. Pulling out one of them he announced, "The copies are here, but the original is gone!"

I shot a quick glance at Steven and pulled my jacket a little tighter. The folder was the one I'd made copies of, and the originals that belonged in it were securely tucked into my jean jacket pocket. "What specifically are you looking for?"

"It's a deed," Roger said as he set the folder down and buried his face in his hands. "Your father was going to pay me a bundle to deliver a deed to him, and I can't find it anywhere."

"I see," Steven said. "How much is this bundle?"

"Two hundred thousand dollars," Roger blubbered.

"And when did you make this deal with him?" Steven probed.

"A few days before your grandfather died. He'd done some research on the land around here and come up with the detail that Mirabelle wasn't of rightful age when the property her mother held in life estate was deeded over to her. Andrew knew it at the time, but figured no one would ever find out. Your father started nosing around, and word got back to Andrew. He called me to prepare another deed, which I did, and he signed it, but instead of recording it right away, I held on to it."

"And how did Steven Senior find out about the second deed?" I asked.

Roger glanced up at me, his face contorted in guilt. "I called him and told him about it. I offered to sell it to him, but we couldn't agree on a price. A few days went by and Andrew called me to ask if I'd recorded it yet. I panicked and called Steven Senior to tell him the deal was off — I had no choice but to record the deed — and the next thing I knew, Andrew was dead."

Steven's hands curled into fists. "So, let us help you look for it," I offered quickly. "When . . . I mean, if we find it, we can make sure it gets recorded and make amends, okay?"

Roger nodded dumbly. "It's got to be here somewhere," he said as he shuffled more papers around.

"You go look in the back," I offered. "Maybe I can ask Lily and George for some help."

Roger sighed heavily, then headed back down the hallway muttering, "I'm sorry,

Mom and Granddad."

"Is the deed on you?" Steven whispered.

I patted my jean jacket and said, "Got it right here. Let's wait a minute or two, announce that we've found it, and get to the county clerk."

"No," Steven said. "We have to warn Mirabelle first. The more I think about this, the more I am sure that my grandfather was killed by his own son. If my father learns we're on our way to record the deed, it could put Mirabelle in danger. Remember, she only holds the property in life estate. If she dies, it reverts back to me."

"Good point," I said, and moved to the counter. I looked at the pile of paper and folders cluttering the area, wondering how I could pretend to locate the deed without Roger suspecting I'd had it all along. Thinking of something, I moved over to the copier and pushed on one end of it, moving it away from the wall. I pulled out the deed from my jacket and announced, "Found it!"

Roger came running back down the hallway. "You did?" he said, his face now hopeful.

"Yep. It was behind the copier. Must've slipped back there when you were making the copies."

"Here," he said, holding out his hand.

"Give it to me and I promise I'll record it right away."

Steven stepped in front of him and stood tall and imposing as he said, "I don't think so."

Roger seemed to shrink to an even smaller size. He looked so disappointed I couldn't help but offer, "Lily thinks it's best if Steven and I take care of this. You understand, don't you, Roger?"

"Of course," he said as his cheeks grew flushed. "I'll need to clean up this mess now anyway."

I smiled at him and tucked the deed back into my pocket. "Come on, Steven. Let's hit the road."

Wasting no time, we drove back in the direction of the house. As we got close, Steven began to scan the terrain for the little dirt road that would lead us to Mirabelle's. We arrived at the driveway leading to the lodge and Steven grumbled, "Damn. How did we miss that?"

We doubled back and tried again but couldn't find the entrance. "Guess we're just going to have to go through the woods," I said as we headed in the direction of the Manse.

Steven nodded and we drove to the lodge, then walked around to the back and looked for the pathway that would lead us to Mirabelle's. The day had turned overcast and windy, and I glanced up right before the first droplets of rain began to fall. "Great," Steven said as he too looked up. "Looks like we're going to get wet again."

I smiled at him as I pulled my jacket tighter around me. "At least we know who the better swimmer is."

Steven chuckled and moved over to me. "Yeah, but we also know who's a better kisser," he said, and winked.

I gave him a broad grin and replied, "Yep. I win again. Ah, well, at least you have a nice car."

Steven let out a deep laugh and wrapped an arm around my shoulder. "Come on, funny lady, I think the path is over there."

We found it and began walking in the rain through the woods, which offered a little bit of protection, though by the time we reached the tree that marked the opening to the tunnel I was definitely feeling damp. Steven turned to the left, toward Mirabelle's, when something caught the corner of my eye. "Hold on," I said, looking up. I could have sworn I had seen movement off to my right.

"What's up?" he asked, coming back to stand next to me as I scanned the woods.

"There," I said as I saw what had caused me to pause. "See that?"

On the path leading to Willis's was a cluster of little orbs, bouncing and dancing and looking just like a horde of bees. "Hanging on to you is definitely strange," Steven said as I walked in the direction of the orbs.

"It's hanging *out* with me," I corrected.

"Yes, that is strange too," he said.

"Come on," I said, swatting his shoulder. "I get the strong sense that we need to follow them." The swirling orbs waited until we got within a few feet of them before they moved on down the path, dancing and bouncing with frenetic energy. There seemed to be an urgency to their movements, and the little knot of dread in the pit of my stomach grew as we neared Willis's.

When the small log cabin was in sight, the orbs stopped their jumbled dance and formed a straight line as they zoomed straight for the cabin and through the wall without pause. "Something's wrong," I said as I broke into a run.

"I'm right on your behind," Steven said, and I could feel him at my heels.

We got to the door of the cabin, and I paused only long enough to knock twice, then without waiting, opened the door. "Willis?" I called as I pushed the door wide.

"Willis, it's M.J. and Steve —" I stopped midsentence as my eyes caught Willis slouched in his wheelchair, his face ashen and a small bit of foam at his mouth.

Steven rushed past me, crouching down by Willis as he lifted his wrist to check for a pulse. "Is he alive?" I asked, my voice hushed and shaky.

"His pulse is thready," Steven said as he lifted one of Willis's lids to check his pupils. Next he wheeled Willis over to the couch and began to gently move him from the chair. I walked forward to help him, but Steven stopped me with, "M.J., go to my car. In the backseat is a black duffel bag. Bring it here as fast as you can!"

I turned on my heel and bolted from the cabin, dashing through the woods as fast as my legs could carry me. I reached Steven's car, panting hard. I may be a runner, but I'm a long-distance girl, and I'd taken the trip back to the house in a sprint. I was so worried about Willis that I didn't stop to catch my breath, but just grabbed the bag and bolted back toward the woods. I was about to leap onto the path when I heard someone shout my name. I paused and turned my head. There I saw Willis standing in the woods waving at me. He looked completely well, not at all like the figure I'd left back at the cabin. "There's no need to rush," he said to me. "You don't want to fall again and hurt yourself, after all."

My chest heaved as I realized why I was seeing him. "No," I panted as I stared at him. "Willis, *no!*" I shouted, and that was when he disappeared. "Goddamn it!" I screamed, and ran as fast as I'd ever run in my life through the trees, mindless of the branches that tore at my face and hands and the pounding of my heart as it begged me to slow down. I reached the cabin and bolted inside, wet and so deprived of oxygen that I felt dizzy. Steven had Willis on the floor and was performing CPR. He too was out of breath, and sweat poured off of him as he tried to pump Willis's heart.

I dropped to the floor next to him, my lungs expanding and contracting at such a rapid pace that I didn't know how much more they could take. "M.J.," he puffed, his brow wet with exertion. "Call nine-one-one!"

I nodded and reached into my coat pocket. Finding my cell phone I punched the numbers into the keypad and waited for the dispatcher, knowing in my heart that all of our efforts were just too little, too late.

Two hours later the county coroner had

carted away Willis's body. Steven and I sat at his kitchen table with the sheriff, going over the details of finding Willis in a state of unconsciousness. Steven had found a needle and vial of insulin near where we'd first discovered Willis, and in his best estimation he said that Willis had most likely gone into diabetic distress, followed quickly by coma as his body began to shut down.

I listened while Steven told the sheriff that we'd reached him about an hour too late. "How long had you known Willis?" the sheriff asked.

"As long as I've known my grandfather," Steven said, his voice quavering a bit. He cleared his throat, and it was a moment before he continued. "Willis was a part of my childhood here at the house. He would take me for rides on his tractor, and teach me about the plants and flowers. He was a good man."

"How long has he had diabetes?" the sheriff asked.

"Also as long as I've known him."

"Do you know who his doctor was?"

"No idea," Steven said, then thought of something and got up from the table. From the kitchen counter he picked up one of three prescription bottles, scanned the label, and said, "You can try Dr. Harris. He's in

Twin Lakes."

"That's quite a hike from here," the sheriff noted.

"It's known to be the best hospital in northern Massachusetts," Steven said as he continued to sift through the prescription bottles. I saw him pause, studying one of the bottles more closely, and his stance shifted ever so subtly. He looked up at us and noted that the sheriff was busy writing. Putting his finger to his lips he quickly slipped the bottle into his pocket.

I gave him a questioning look but didn't say anything as he rejoined us at the table. "Do you know if he has any family we can contact?"

I got up and walked over to the framed picture of Janelle. I handed it to the sheriff and said, "That's his daughter, Janelle. She lives in Jamaica Plain, and I think she works at Mass. General."

The sheriff nodded. "I think that's all I need, Dr. Sable and Miss Holliday. Thank you for your efforts with Mr. Brown. I'm sure his family will appreciate that you did everything you could."

Steven and I got up from the table and walked to the door. In the doorway Steven paused, reached behind him, and grabbed my hand. I leaned into him as I squeezed back, and together we walked back through the rain to the lodge.

When we got inside I asked, "You okay?"

Steven walked into the laundry room, returning with a towel for each of us before answering. "No," he said, his shoulders slumped. "It's always been hard for me to lose a patient. And Willis was an old friend."

"I saw him, you know."

"Saw who?"

"Willis," I said. Steven cocked his head at me and I explained. "On the path. When I went to get your bag I was running back to the cabin and he called my name. When I turned around he was there."

"I don't understand."

"It was his spirit. He'd already left. There was nothing you could have done, Steven. He was already gone."

Steven stared at me for a long, long time before setting his towel down and walking over to me. Ever so gently he swept my wet hair back off my face, then leaned in and kissed me deeply. When he pulled his lips away I gave him a small smile. "What was that for?"

"Do you always need a reason?"

"No. Not especially."

"Good. Come. I think there's some rain gear around here somewhere."

That caught me off guard. "I'm sorry, what?"

Steven had already turned to walk into the hallway. "Rain gear," he said. "We have to get to Mirabelle before it's too late."

"Too late for what?"

Steven paused, dug into his pocket, and pulled something out, tossing it to me. I looked at it after I'd caught it. It was the prescription bottle from Willis's counter. "What's the relevance?" I asked as I looked at the pink pills in the container.

"Read the label. The doctor's name is in the upper righthand corner."

I searched the label and my eyes stuck on the name: Dr. S. Sable. "Holy shit!" I said.

"Exactly," Steven said as he came back into the kitchen with two rain slickers.

"Do you think these had anything to do with Willis's death?"

"I don't know. I've never heard of that drug, and I'll have to look it up, but if it contributed in any way, I'll make sure my old man ends up paying for it."

I tucked the pills into my jeans pocket and looked up as Steven said, "Here," and he tossed a rain slicker over my shoulders. "This was my grandfather's. It might be a little big, but at least it will keep you dry."

I donned the slicker and the two of us trotted back out into the rain. It was slow going through the woods this time, as the rain had made the path slippery. Eventually we reached Mirabelle's and made our way to her big blue door. Steven knocked and was rewarded a moment later when the door opened. "Steven and M.J.," she said with surprise.

"Hello, Mirabelle," he said. "Can we come in? It's important."

"Of course," she said, opening the door wider.

We shuffled out of our wet slickers and wet shoes and I gave a shudder, damp to the bone. "Oh, you poor thing," she said to me. "Here, you come over here and sit by the fire. I just got it going a few minutes before you arrived, but it should help warm your bones."

"Thanks," I said as I followed her into the cozy living room. "We would have come by car, but we couldn't find the turnoff for your little road out there."

Mirabelle smiled as she took a seat on the couch, and Steven sat next to her. "That's because it's hidden. It's about a quarter mile away from your driveway. But you can't see it because it dips down from the road, then takes a sharp left. It blends into the woods so easily that not many people can find it."

"I'm afraid we have some sad news," Steven said, getting to the point. He then explained what had happened to Willis. Mirabelle's eyes misted over, and she reached out to squeeze Steven's hand. "I didn't know him well," she said. "But what I knew of him was that he was a lovely man."

Steven went on then to tell her about the deed that Roger had tried to sell to Steven Senior that guaranteed her the right to the property for as long as she lived.

"That rat bastard," Mirabelle said, her face pinched with fury. "The next time I see that weaselly son of a gun I'm going to kick him straight in his gonads."

Steven gave the smallest of smiles. "Do you mean Roger, or my father?"

"Little of both," she said, getting up to poke angrily at the fire.

"We have the deed," I offered as I reached into my jean jacket and pulled it out. "We're willing to get it recorded for you, if you like."

Mirabelle held out her hand and I gave her the paper. She studied it for a moment, tracing her fingers along Andrew's signature at the bottom, and said, "Thank you, but this is my responsibility. The county clerk's should be open for another hour. Would you two mind if I went right over there to take care of this?"

"Of course not," Steven said, getting up. "But there's one more thing you should know," he said. "I think you should be very careful around here."

"Careful?" Mirabelle asked, giving Steven a quizzical look.

"We've learned that my father has a financial interest in this property. If something should happen to either one or both of us, he will benefit. And with Willis now dead, and his parcel of land going back to the estate, it would be a good idea to watch behind you."

Mirabelle's mouth opened a fraction, then closed with determination. "Don't you worry about me, Steven. I can smell a rat bastard a mile away, and I'm a very good shot, just so you know."

Mirabelle offered to drive us back to the lodge, but I noticed she sneaked a glance at her watch as she asked. "That's okay, Mirabelle. You need to get that deed recorded, and it's getting late. We've got slickers; we'll be fine."

"Thanks for understanding," she said as we hurried to the door.

Just then something struck me, and I turned back to her to ask, "One last thing,

412

though. Do you remember hearing any rumors of Andrew having an affair with someone other than your mother?"

Mirabelle gave me an odd look, then said, "Yes. And trust me, that is a story. I don't have time to tell you about it now, but how about after I get this recorded I stop by and give you the down and dirty?"

"Awesome," I said. "But, just out of curiosity, did the woman's name begin with an M?"

I was rewarded with a bright smile. "Yes, it did. Is that intuition of yours on over-drive?"

I laughed. "I'd love to take credit for it, but we found some love letters to Andrew back at the house, and I just had this feeling that they weren't from your mother."

Mirabelle glanced again at her watch as we reached her driveway. "I'd love to take a look at them when I get back. I'll be as quick as I can," she called as she jogged to her car.

Steven and I trudged back up the hill, grateful at least that the wind seemed to be letting up. About midway to the lodge my cell phone chirped, and I pulled it out of my back pocket. Noting that the caller ID said GILLEY, I quickly answered the call. "Hey, buddy," I said. "What's the word?"

"I have so much to tell you!" he began. "First, the police report on the break-in at Steven's is very odd. Until the good doctor returns, they can't determine whether anything was stolen, but the digital pictures taken at the scene are so weird."

"Why are they weird?"

"The bathroom was ransacked. The police think that the thief was looking for drugs, but I don't think that's it. And I'll tell you why in a minute."

"I'm listening," I said, ducking low under a branch.

"After I checked out the police report I moved on to do a little more research on that pharmaceutical company and came across something *very* interesting."

"Do tell."

"There is a recently published white paper from one of the staff members at the company that reports that some of their stem-cell research indicates that one of the drugs used to treat mice in the laboratory actually affected their DNA."

There was a pause on my end as I digested that and tried to find the relevance. "I don't get the connection," I finally said.

"Isn't it obvious?" Gilley asked. "If you were Steven Senior, and you knew that the one way to convince a court of law that you were not the father of an illegitimate son was to submit a DNA sample which was *guaranteed* not to match said son . . ." Gilley's voice trailed off with his implication.

"Oh. My. God," I said, finally understanding how Senior planned on getting around a possible match in DNA to Steven. "That's why Steven's bathroom was the only room ransacked! The thief was after his DNA so that Sable Senior could test it against his first to make sure it didn't match, and if it did, then he'd take the drug and alter it so that it wouldn't!"

"Bingo. He could then successfully challenge the will and lay claim to the property. The only other fly in his ointment would be that deed, M.J. You two have got to get that thing recorded before it's too late!"

"Mirabelle's on her way to get it recorded right now," I said.

"Good. In the meantime, you two be very careful."

"Planning on it," I said. "Great work, Gil, and we'll see you soon."

Steven waited for me to tuck my cell back into my pocket before coming up beside me. "Was that Gilley?"

"Yeah," I said. "I'll explain everything when we get out of this rain."

A while later we broke through the woods

and hurried to the kitchen door, but it was locked. "Damn," Steven said as he tried the handle. "I must have locked it when we came out to go to Mirabelle's. Come on; I have the key to the front door."

We circled our way around to the front and came up short. There, parked in the driveway with its windshield wipers going, was a silver Rolls-Royce, and next to that was that gray sedan I'd seen all over town. "No way," Steven said as he walked with purpose to the front door. Unlocking it, he pushed the door open and said, "Go inside. This won't take long."

If I hadn't been shivering so hard that my teeth were chattering I would have stayed and watched the fireworks, but the cold won out and I moved inside. Taking off my rain slicker, I moved into the kitchen to heat some water and make tea when I stopped cold. There at the counter was Maria, and in front of her were the love letters to Andrew.

My breath caught in my throat as everything clicked into place, and, like a movie, I saw it all unfold in my head. She must have heard me behind her, because she turned her head and her tearstained cheeks confirmed everything I believed. "It was you," I said to her. "You pushed Andrew off that roof."

She gasped and shook her head vehemently back and forth. "No! No, I would never do that!" she said, then buried her face in her hands. I knew she was telling the truth, and as I stood there the movie in my head changed and I felt a knowing confirmation that I was absolutely right on target this time.

"It was your suicide note, not Andrew's," I said.

Maria sobbed but nodded her head.

"You were going to kill yourself by diving off the roof, but Andrew found you and tried to save you, and he slipped."

Again, a vigorous nod yes.

"And you were the one who pushed Maureen down the stairs."

Maria stopped sobbing abruptly and looked up at me, her eyes large and frightened. "Yes," she said at last. "It was me. I loved him from the moment I began working for him. All those years of caring for him like he was my husband. She did not love him like I did, but always, he wanted her. The night of the ball she was so full of herself, so sure that she and Andrew were going to be together. I was young and foolish, and when she sniped at me to keep away from him, I reacted, but I never meant for her to die!" she said, her eyes pleading with me to believe her. "I was angry, and I wanted to teach her a lesson, but I never meant to do any real harm."

"Did Andrew know?"

Maria hung her head. "Yes, he knew. The moment he saw her at the bottom of the stairs he knew I'd done it. I had a temper, you see. He never said as much, though, at least, not until right before he died, so I fooled myself into believing that he didn't suspect me. But then, a few weeks before his death he called me into his study, and he told me the way of it. He said that he would make sure that Willis was taken care of, and Mirabella, but for my sin I could never be rewarded for what I'd done. He said that he would make good on the retirement account he'd set up for me, but that when he died I would never be a part of this house. He was holding me accountable."

"And you couldn't live with the guilt of knowing that he understood what had really happened on that staircase."

"I couldn't bear it. That morning he ordered his oatmeal and began to speak of hiring someone else to care for him. He was even kind about it. He said that I had worked for him long enough, and that perhaps someone younger should come in to take my place."

"That was the last straw, then," I said. "And you headed to the roof."

"Yes," she said, her voice a whisper.

Thinking of something else I said, "The morning we found you here. You were looking for your old love letters, weren't you?"

Maria's eyes became large again. "Yes. But you three arrived before I could get them on the third floor. I figured they were safe up there, but you managed to find them."

"That's why Maureen pushed Gilley. She was confused, and she thought it was you!" I said.

"Your friend was pushed down the stairs?" Maria said, worry in her voice.

"Yes, but luckily he's all right. You were pushed that time when Steven first came here, weren't you, Maria? The ghost of Maureen shoved you down the stairs."

She nodded. "Yes, that time and two others, but by then I had learned to hold tight to the banister. I always knew it was her, coming back to claim her revenge."

"I'm amazed you continued to work here," I said.

"I understood her need to hurt me. I deserved it, after all, and I wanted to be near my Andrew. I was careful."

"So you came back today to retrieve the letters," I said, putting all the pieces together.

"Yes. I spotted you and Steven going into the woods. I wanted to get the letters before you two got back."

"And is that your gray sedan out front? The one that's been flanking us?"

"No," Maria said with a puzzled look on her face. "My car is at Willis's. I brought him some food, but he must be out, because when I knocked he didn't answer."

I winced. I considered telling her about Willis, but decided to wait and see if I could get a little more info out of her first.

"Was it you in the woods that night, Maria? And in the tunnel?" I asked carefully.

Maria's expression seemed to go blank. "The woods? A tunnel? What are you talking about?"

At that moment angry voices erupted from the front hallway, and I realized that Stevens Junior and Senior had just burst into the house. Maria and I left our conversation and hurried to the front foyer. Steven Junior was yelling something at his father, and he was so angry that the sentences held both Spanish and German words. His father simply looked at him with a sneer on his face, and it was then that I caught the two in profile and realized something with a jolt: The family resemblance was unmistakable. Both had identical ears, matching jawlines, and the same small bump on the ridge of the nose. Even their hairlines were similar from the side.

"I will ask you only one more time," Senior said with menace when Junior had finished. "Where is the deed?"

"Get out of my house!" Steven roared. Senior didn't budge, but there was movement to his side, and that was when I saw another man partially hidden beside Senior and felt goose bumps line my arms.

"It's not your house!" Senior roared back. "It belongs to the Sable bloodline, of which you are not a part."

"Prove it," Steven sneered. "Come on, old man. Offer me some DNA to give a sleep to this matter."

"Oh, I plan on it," Senior snarled back. "In the next few weeks, you little Argentinean bastard, expect to be served!"

The man to Senior's side bent down to tie his shoe, and suddenly something clicked in my head. "You!" I said as I pointed to him.

Senior and Junior stopped yelling at each other long enough to look in my direction. The man by Senior's side looked up at me, and I knew I wasn't wrong. I'd never had a close look at him, but there was something familiar about his movements and build. "You were the one who followed us up here," I began, my voice angry as I walked over to Steven, my finger still pointing in the man's direction.

"Who the hell are you?" Senior asked me.

"Never mind that," I spit at him. "Your goon was the one who followed us that night into the woods. He was the one who was in the tunnel and the one who tried to kill us and, if I'm not mistaken, also the one who broke into your house, Steven!"

Sable Senior rolled his eyes and crossed his arms. "Great theatrics, sweetheart. Now why don't you let the men here deal with business and you run along somewhere else."

"Do not speak to her like that!" Junior roared.

"I've seen him before," Maria said, sidling up from the corridor leading to the kitchen. "You were that surveyor that Andrew hired last year to parcel off Willis's house."

I looked from Maria back to the man standing next to Sable Senior. "*That's* how you knew about the secret door! You *did* try to blow us up in the tunnel!"

The man seemed to shrink back slightly at the accusation. Senior turned to him and said, "Bill? What the hell are they talking about?"

The man named Bill smiled crookedly at Senior before he said, "Just doing my job, sir."

"So you hired him?" Steven asked his father. "You bastard!"

Sable Senior seemed to waffle for a moment as he thought through what Bill had just revealed. "Hold on there," he said, putting up his hands. "I never told you to blow anyone up!"

"Sometimes things get messy," Bill sneered, and I could feel the malice oozing from him. "Sometimes they get extra messy, and you have to take care of things your own way. Sometimes — like now, that is." And with that he reached into his coat pocket and pulled out a gun, pointing it at us.

"Put that thing away!" Senior said. Bill pointed the gun at him, and that shut him up. I heard a yelp from behind me and looked up to see Maria fleeing into the kitchen.

"Hey!" Bill yelled, turning to aim the gun at her. Thinking fast, I picked up a small bronze statue from a table to my right and chucked it at him. It hit him square in the kneecap, and he buckled and sprawled on the floor.

Steven pulled me down low and hauled me quickly around a corner. As we scanned the area, trying to find the safest possible place, I could hear Bill swearing about his knee, while Sable Senior screamed at Bill that he was fired. Suddenly, there was an explosion, then a loud thump that sounded an awful lot like a body hitting the marble floor.

Steven ran hunched over to the left, holding tight to my shirt as he guided me along the maze of rooms that made up the ground floor. We ducked behind a couch in the sitting room, my heart pounding in my chest. I looked behind us and through the window saw Maria hurrying across the lawn over to the path in the woods. I prayed that she'd be able to reach help in time.

Footfalls echoed from the hallway off the sitting room where we were hidden, growing closer, by the sound. I felt Steven squeeze me tightly as the footsteps stopped just outside the room.

"I'm going to find you, ya know," Bill said, sounding decidedly unhinged. "Can't leave any witnesses behind." I wanted to remind him that one witness had already escaped, but given the fact that he held a gun and I held nothing, I thought I'd better pick my battles.

After a bit we heard the footsteps fade again, and Steven whispered, "Come with me." Crouching low, we hurried as quietly as possible out of the sitting room and into the hallway. I held my breath as we saw Bill's back when he turned left and went into the study. Steven motioned me forward frantically and we darted into the kitchen. I followed him around to the island, and we ducked down low as we listened again for the footfalls. They sounded very faintly from the other side of the house. "When I give the signal," Steven said, "we run out the back door. You must get to the woods and take the path to Mirabelle's."

"Where are you going?"

"I'm going to get Bill's attention and lead him away from you. I'll take the other fork and head for Willis's. That should give you enough time to get to safety and call for help."

"But —" I protested.

"No," Steven said adamantly. "Do as I say, M.J. Go to Mirabelle's and wait for me there."

I wavered as I looked at him. I thought the plan was dumb. We both needed to head to Mirabelle's. She had a gun there, and I was fairly certain it packed a bigger punch

425

than that handgun Bill held. Steven's eyes, however, held a stern look, and I finally nodded. "Fine," I mumbled. "On your signal then . . ." and as if on cue we heard a great groaning and creaking noise just to our left.

"Aw, crap! The damn elevator's waking up!" I hissed as Bill's footsteps pounded through the house, heading right toward us. Steven scrambled up to a bent-over position and grabbed my shirt as he took me with him. We could see the elevator doors begin to open five feet to our left, and the door to the outside seemed much farther away. Bill was coming too quickly for us to make it, I realized with a sinking sensation, and Steven must have felt that too as, with a grunt, he pushed me forward, away from the back door, and half threw, half helped me through the opening of the elevator. He joined me a split second later, crashing against the side of the boxcar.

"Hit the button!" he shouted, and I reached for the CLOSE DOOR button. To my relief, the doors stopped separating and began to close. Just then a powerful sound like a firecracker filled my ears, and something hot whizzed past me just to my side. "Down!" Steven said as he crouched low.

I ducked, but another gunshot echoed all

around us as I saw Steven's hand snap back and he crumpled to the floor. I slammed my hand on the button panel of the boxcar, and the doors finally closed. Another slam on a button and the old elevator gave a jolt upward and we began to move. There was another explosion, followed quickly by a dent in the door, and immediately after a great howl of pain from outside.

Steven held his hand as it oozed a fountain of red. "Ohmigod!" I said as I sat next to him. "You've been hit!"

Steven's breathing was labored and his face was contorted in pain. "I need to stop the bleeding," he said. "M.J., take off my shirt and see if you can rip a strip from it."

I looked at his white face and thought there was no way I was going to try to lift his shirt off and risk hurting his hand even more. I reached under my sweater and tugged my tank top up. Wriggling, I got it over my head, and quickly put my arms back through the sleeves of my sweater.

I pulled hard at the tank top's seams and it split open. Using my teeth I ripped again and had a good long strip. "What floor did you press?" Steven asked through gritted teeth.

"The third. We still have a little way to go," I said, looking up as the dial on the top of the boxcar indicated we were just approaching the second floor. "Thank God this thing takes forever," I added as I wadded up the rest of the shirt and gently took Steven's hand away from covering his other one. He hissed through his teeth, and what was revealed made me woozy, but I swallowed hard and placed the shirt over the gaping hole in the top of his hand, wrapping it tightly with the strip I'd torn off.

"He'll be waiting for us," Steven said as I worked, his face chalky and his brow sweaty.

"I'm not sure about that," I said, tying the strip. "That boy doesn't seem to be very bright. That last bullet ricocheted. He may be down for the count."

"I will distract him," Steven said. "When I do, you run like hell and get away."

"Don't be an idiot," I said as I sat back and listened to the wheels and gears groan. "First he has to find where this thing lets out. Remember the hard time we had?"

"Do as I say," Steven said to me as he pulled his hand close to his chest.

"Or what?" I asked as I stood up and helped him to his feet. "You'll box me for it?"

Just then we heard the gears slow down, and with a jolt of panic I saw the dial at the top creep up to the number three. "It's go time," I said as I moved Steven and me over to the side of the boxcar, which would offer us only the briefest protection as the doors opened. The dial and the boxcar stopped at the same time, but the doors did not open. A sudden chill filled the elevator.

"Andrew," I whispered as I felt a knock on my energy.

Willis said to help you, he said in my mind.

"Where is the man with the gun?" I said aloud. "Can you see him, Andrew? Can you see the intruder with the gun?"

I felt him nod. *He's coming up the stairs,* he said.

Steven sagged beside me, and I knew that we had very little time before he lost consciousness. In my mind I called out to Andrew, *Please! Find Maureen for me, Andrew! Bring her here now!*

Instantly I felt Maureen's presence enter the boxcar. I called out to both of them with a plea, hoping against hope that they would assist me. "Maureen," I said aloud. "There's someone on the staircase who wants to hurt your daughter." The fact that he wanted to hurt us first was a small sticking point at this moment. "He needs to be stopped, Maureen, or he'll hurt Mirabelle. Can you stop him? Can you go to the staircase and stop him from reaching the top?"

The energy around me seemed to swirl for a moment, and I could feel Andrew and Maureen having a heated discussion. I knew this was not the best way to use my medium skills, but figured I'd deal with that karmic lesson later. I could feel Maureen's energy shift angrily as she talked with Andrew, and a second later she left the boxcar, though Andrew's energy remained. As we waited and my heart beat frantically against my chest, we suddenly heard a shriek, followed by another gunshot.

My first reaction was to duck, even though we were tucked away in the elevator. Steven's breathing quickened, and I knew he was fading into shock. Then we heard an oddly familiar sound. It was the tumbling of a body down the staircase and ended with a thud that shook the house. Just then I heard Andrew say, *You're safe now, and Willis says I need to go with him. Take care of them, won't you?* And with that, his energy left the boxcar and the doors of the elevator opened up.

I helped Steven to the bed and laid him down. With a shaking hand I reached for the phone, but in the distance I heard the sound of approaching sirens, so I pulled my hand back. Help would be here in a few moments, and as I sat on the bed with Steven and watched the tank top around his hand turn crimson, I could only pray that it got here in time.

CHAPTER 14

I stayed with Steven until the police and ambulance arrived. They found the senior Sable in the front foyer, a nasty bullet wound to the shoulder and a very large bump on his head, but otherwise no worse for the wear.

Bill was sprawled at the bottom of the staircase, still alive, with a bullet in his thigh from the ricochet off the elevator and a broken back that left him paralyzed from the hips down. The police said that when they found him, they could have sworn they saw a cluster of funny-looking lights hovering over him like a swarm of bees.

Steven was rushed to the emergency room and treated for shock and blood loss. They flew in a colleague of his, one of the best hand surgeons in the world. The doctor attempted to repair Steven's hand, but we learned later that there was just too much damage done. He would most likely never hold a scalpel again.

Gilley and I returned to Boston, and Gil recovered in no time from his broken tailbone. Of course, Bradley — completely undaunted by Gilley's fire drill — had a lot to do with the tender loving care Gil received in the weeks that followed.

We also found an unexpected surge in business following our return. Many of our clients were personally referred by a certain doctor with a funny take on English, and I was busy busting houses in the some of the wealthier suburbs of Boston.

And even though I was content with work, and Gil was on the mend, I found that when I was left alone with my thoughts, they often drifted to Steven. I hadn't heard from him since Gil and I had visited with him briefly at the hospital, and I suspected he needed to go through a period where he could be left to deal with the fact that he would never operate again. I couldn't imagine how that must feel, and a part of me really wanted to lend him some support, but another side felt that he needed to process it on his own for now.

I was rationalizing this to Teeko one afternoon at Mama Dell's about six weeks after we closed the Sable case. "So I think it's important to wait before I call him. I mean, he's probably not even in town. I'll bet he's gone back to Germany, even."

Teeko's face never registered anything other than a patient smile as I rambled on. "Uh-huh," she said as she sipped her coffee.

"Yeah, so the fact that I'm still thinking about him and wondering how he's doing is a waste of time. I need to freaking move on already."

"So what's stopping you?" she asked demurely.

I paused and stared into my own coffee for a minute. "In a small, completely insignificant way, I think I might miss him."

"Insignificant, you say?"

I leveled a look at her. "Whatever. The point is moot, because Steven's out of the country."

"Really? What country might I be in?" I heard a baritone voice thick with an accent say from behind me.

I felt my jaw drop, and the smirk on Teeko's face opened into a big, fat grin as she said, "Dr. Sable, so nice to see you again. M.J. was just telling me how much she misses you. Won't you have a seat?"

"Thank you, Karen," Steven said as he sat down next to me and edged his chair very close.

I felt my cheeks grow hot, and I made sure to glare at Teeko before swiveling around to Steven. "Hey," I said.

"Oh, my goodness!" Teeko cried as she looked at her watchless wrist. "I have an appointment I have to get to. Would you two please excuse me?" And with that she gathered up her things and hurried away from the table.

"Is this true?" Steven said when she'd gone.

"What?" I asked.

"That you are missing me?"

I forced a laugh and hurried to explain. "Oh, that! No, I'm afraid what Karen meant by that was that I missed you after you left the hospital. I called, but you had already been released."

"I see," he said, the smile on his face telling me that he wasn't buying it for a minute.

I fiddled with my swizzle stick and tried to think of a way to change the topic quickly. I noticed his hand was still wrapped in a huge bandage and my heart went out to him. "How's it doing?" I asked, pointing to it.

Steven glanced down. "It will heal, and with some physical therapy I'll manage quite well."

"Do you think there's a chance you'll be able to operate again?"

Steven's eyes held mine quietly for a long moment, and I could see that he'd come to terms with his reality. "No," he said. "But I have been offered the opportunity stay on as a lecturer at the university, so all is not lost."

"That's fantastic!" I said brightly, then cleared my throat and added in a more subdued tone, "So you'll be staying here, then?"

"Yes. I think I will stay in the United States for a time. There are other things I want to do. Which brings me to this," he said, and reached down to lift a large shopping bag onto the tabletop.

"What's that?"

"A gift," he said, and pushed the bag toward me.

I smiled and peeked over the rim. There was a box wrapped in pink paper and a colorful bow. "For me?"

"Yes. Open it," he encouraged.

Inside the box was a brand-new night-vision camera. "Oh, wow!" I said, as I turned the camera over. "It's so light," I said.

"State-of-the-artist stuff," he said to me. "I gave Gilley the same model a few minutes ago."

"You went to see Gil?" I asked.

"No. I went to see you, but Gilley was there, so I gave him his gift and he said you were here."

"Ah," I said, and busied myself by putting the camera away. "This is really kind of you. We're very grateful."

"The least I could do after your old camera went for a swim." I nodded, and he continued. "So, the real reason I'm here is that I have made some decisions, and I wanted to talk to you about them."

"Shoot," I said, then glanced at his hand and instantly regretted it.

Steven chuckled. "First, I have moved Maria into Willis's cabin. I learned that she and her sister weren't getting along as well as she first suggested, and I think she has suffered enough for her sins, don't you?"

I smiled at him. "I think that's a great idea."

"Next, I need you to come back with me to Uphamshire. I remember that you told me my grandfather had gone with Willis, that he had crossed over, but we need to take care of Maureen as well."

My smile widened. "Gil and I already took care of that while you were recovering after surgery. Actually, we even got Mirabelle involved. Maureen was far more willing to listen to me with Mirabelle on hand, and she went to the other side without too much trouble."

Steven looked slightly disappointed. "I see," he said, and sat back in his chair. "Well, then that leaves only one more thing to discuss."

"Which is . . . ?"

"I want to offer you funding."

I cocked my head. "What do you mean, funding?"

"I want to invest in your business. I have seen your work and believe that you offer a great service, but that with the right equipment, like the proper monitors and cameras and measuring equipment, you and Gilley won't have to struggle so much to close your cases."

"That's awfully generous of you," I said incredulously, thinking that Gilley would foam at the mouth if he heard Steven make this offer. "But what would you want in return?"

Steven sat back in his chair as his finger swirled small circles on the tabletop. He took a moment before answering, and finally said, "I would want to join your team."

"As our financial backer?"

"No. I would want to join you on the hunt."

I grinned at him. Was he really asking me what I thought he was? "You want to be a ghostbuster," I said, more statement than fact.

"Yes," Steven said. "When we were on our bust at the lodge, I felt . . . how do you say . . . like with energy and adrenaline?"

I giggled. "You felt jazzed, and yes, I know what you mean."

"So what do you think?" he asked me.

I looked at him for another long moment as I weighed it out. In my heart I already knew the answer, but I wanted to go about this rationally. Finally I leaned in and said, "Fine. You're in. But here are the ground rules. . . ."

ABOUT THE AUTHOR

Real-life psychic **Victoria Laurie** has used her unique understanding of intuition and the business of being a professional psychic to create her series characters M. J. Holliday and Abby Cooper. She lives in Austin, Texas, with her two miniature dachshunds, Lilly and Toby. Find out more about her psychic abilities at www.VictoriaLaurie.com.